You first met Conn
(Special Edition #401
love—all his own.

Sparkles of light glanced off a woman's dress.

She was standing at the edge of a rocky point above the water, one hand clutched tightly around a sheaf of papers. Con's breath caught. She was so still she could have been a statue.

Distantly he heard the lapping waves of the lake. The woman was staring fixedly down at the water.

His stomach twisted. "My God," he whispered in disbelief. She was going to jump! "Hey! Hey, you!" He was running toward her before he realized he was moving.

Hearing him, she stiffened, savagely tearing up the papers she held, then tossing them into the water. Before Con could reach her, she'd melted back into the shadows.

"Wait!" Con stopped short, searching the grounds for her. But all he saw were the glittering spangles on her dress as she fled....

Dear Reader,

If you're looking for an extra-special reading experience—something rich and memorable, something deeply emotional, something totally romantic—your search is over! For in your hands you hold one of Silhouette's extremely **Special Editions**.

Dedicated to the proposition that *not* all romances are created equal, Silhouette **Special Edition** aims to deliver the best and the brightest in women's fiction—six books each month by such stellar authors as Nora Roberts, Lynda Trent, Tracy Sinclair and Ginna Gray, along with some dazzling new writers destined to become tomorrow's romance stars.

Pick and choose among titles if you must—we hope you'll soon equate all Silhouette **Special Editions** with consistently gratifying romance reading.

And don't forget the two Silhouette *Classics* at your bookseller's each month—reissues of the most beloved Silhouette **Special Editions** and Silhouette *Intimate Moments* of yesteryear.

Today's bestsellers, tomorrow's *Classics*—that's Silhouette **Special Edition**. We hope you'll stay with us in the months to come, because month after month, we intend to become more special than ever.

From all the authors and editors of Silhouette **Special Edition**,
Warmest wishes,

Leslie Kazanjian
Senior Editor

NATALIE BISHOP
Imaginary Lover

Silhouette Special Edition

Published by Silhouette Books New York

America's Publisher of Contemporary Romance

SILHOUETTE BOOKS
300 East 42nd St., New York, N.Y. 10017

ISBN: 0-373-09472-8

First Silhouette Books printing August 1988

Printed in the U.S.A.

Books by Natalie Bishop

Silhouette Special Edition

NATALIE BISHOP

lives within a stone's throw of her sister, Lisa Jackson, who is also a Silhouette author. Natalie and Lisa spend many afternoons together developing new plots and reading their best lines to each other.

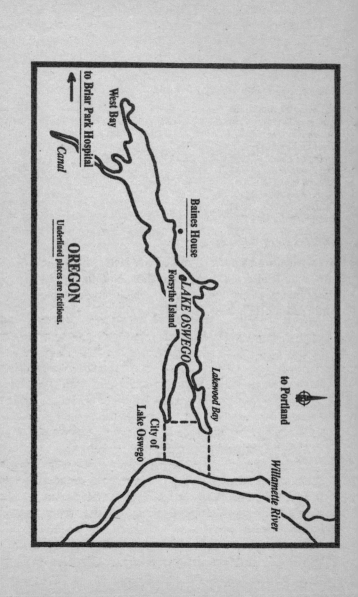

Chapter One

Lake Oswego's water rippled green and black beneath the rocky ledge. Candace McCall stared down at it and drew a long breath. What she wouldn't give to dive into its murky depths and forget about her father's party.

But that was wishful thinking. She glanced behind her at the island mansion, at the mullioned windows glowing mistily in the hot summer night. Music swelled around her, echoing across the lake, but all Candace could think was that she wanted to break down and cry.

Sighing, she glanced at the paper held tightly in her right fist. Moonlight made it glow a ghostly white. What bitter irony that she should receive both dreaded letters in the mail today. Closing her eyes, she tried to forget the words of this particular missive, but they were burned into her brain.

She moved sharply, her silver dress sparkling, her teardrop diamond earrings quivering. Glancing again at the paper in her hand, she was overwhelmed with sorrow.

I can't go back, she thought unhappily, then looked again at the restless water.

Connor Holt stopped short at the edge of the narrow torchlit bridge and exhaled on a sound of disgust. Disgust at himself. He felt as if he'd stepped back fifteen years to a time in his life he'd rather forget. Chest tight, he jerked impatiently on his tie. Why did it seem he was always standing on one side, staring at the other?

And what in God's name was he doing at Forsythe Island?

Suddenly he laughed aloud. He was out of his mind to even think about coming here tonight. The last thing he wanted to do was hobnob with lake people.

With a grimace he stepped onto the bridge, walking across in half a dozen ground-devouring strides. The island itself was no more than three acres—a jagged rock thrusting through jade-colored water, capped by pruned hedges and riotous flowers. Toward the west end stood the Forsythe home, a bluestone mansion that sprawled over the rocky hillside. He could see Christmas lights blinking on and off behind the arched windowpanes.

Christmas lights. Only this wasn't Christmas. It was the twenty-third of July, and the outside temperature was hovering in the eighties.

Shedding his jacket, Con tossed it over his shoulder. He wasn't comfortable with lake people. He never had been. Yet he'd had to compete with them all his life.

His jaw hardened as he thought back. He'd grown up in a cottage on the outskirts of Lake Oswego. Run-down, with a sagging porch and a backyard that had gone to seed long before he'd been born, his home had been a far cry from the immaculate mansions that graced the lake. As a kid he'd wondered what it would be like to live in one of those homes, to have servants and status and loads of money. Those fantasies had nearly become reality, and it had taken him a fast-lane career as a Los Angeles lawyer and a failed marriage to make him realize he wanted nothing to do with that kind of life. He was happy being plain old Connor Holt.

Hot and sweating, he stopped halfway up the hill. From an open window he could hear the strains of "Silver Bells" hanging in the night air. Baffled, he shook his head. Christmas in July. Whose idea was that? Weren't there enough holidays already without tacking on another one?

Determined to make the best of it, Con gritted his teeth. He didn't want to go to this party, nor did he want to meet the man who was such an icon of the Portland social scene. Yet an invitation to one of Forsythe's parties was not to be taken lightly; the other attorneys in his office had looked as though they would gladly have killed their own mothers to be in his shoes.

Con moved purposely forward. What the hell. It was only for a few hours.

He chose the long way toward the house—up a row of carved stone steps that wrapped around one end of the island. He was on the farthest curve when he saw a flash of something bright and silver.

Con squinted. Sparkles of light glanced off a woman's dress. She was standing at the edge of a rocky point above the water, one hand clutched tightly around a sheaf of papers. His breath caught. She was so still she could have been a statue.

Distantly he heard the lapping waves of the lake. The woman was staring fixedly down at the water.

His stomach twisted. "My God," he whispered in disbelief. She was going to jump! "Hey! Hey, you!" He was running toward her before he realized he was moving.

Hearing him, she stiffened, savagely tearing up the papers she held in her hand, tossing them into the water. Before Con could reach her, she'd melted back into the shadows.

"Wait!" Con stopped short, his gaze searching the grounds for her. All he saw were the glittering spangles on her dress as she disappeared toward the back of the house.

He blinked. He felt off balance. Maybe she hadn't intended to jump, after all.

Feeling foolish, Con shoved his hands in his pockets and continued on his trek to the house, his thoughts on the mysterious woman. There'd been something about her, some desperate quality that had made it seem as if she'd given up. Or was that just his imagination?

When the butler answered his knock, Con was enveloped in a cloud of music and song. He showed the gold-embossed invitation to the dark-suited man, who then nodded silently and beckoned him inside. *Good God,* Con thought, staring after him. *This is too much.*

The air was heavy with exotic perfumes, and the women's dresses floated before him like a moving rainbow, each more elegant than the last. Con felt as awkward as he had when, at seventeen, Tricia Wellesley had made fun of him in front of her spoiled, debutante friends.

Fleetingly he thought about putting on his coat and readjusting his tie, then decided he didn't care enough to try to impress Joshua Forsythe. Instead he lifted a glass of champagne from a passing silver tray, saluted the waiter, tossed his jacket over a rose-colored divan and sauntered into the main room.

The Christmas tree was dazzling. A good twenty feet high, it took up one corner of the room and was even surrounded by lavishly wrapped gifts. He should have been impressed, he supposed, but all he could think about was that he was sweating.

He saw Joshua Forsythe standing at the bar, pouring drinks for the guests. He, too, had shed his coat, but instead of a plain white shirt like the one Con wore, his chest was decorated with red suspenders, one of which said Merry, the other, Christmas.

As if telepathic, Forsythe looked up and saw him at that instant. "Connor!" he boomed, beckoning him over.

Con saw heads swivel his way. They probably wondered what he was doing here as much as he did. Curiosity might have brought him to the Forsythe door, but nothing was going to convince him to stay. He would give his regards to Forsythe, then hightail it to some cool, secluded bistro on the lake.

Joshua Forsythe signaled to the bartender to take over for him, then pushed his way toward Con and extended his hand. The man's handshake was enough to break all the bones in Con's hand, but Forsythe's smile was warm. "Glad you could make it. It's an annual event, y'know."

"The party?"

"You bet. Comes around once a year."

"Like Christmas?"

Forsythe laughed. "Well, Forsythe and Company has gained a reputation for its Christmas-in-July party. I've got an image to maintain." He shrugged. "Need a drink?"

Con lifted his champagne glass to let him know he'd already taken care of that, then looked beyond him to stare disbelievingly at the steaming mugs of hot buttered rum sitting on the bar.

"Not too many takers for those," Forsythe admitted wryly, following his gaze. "Too hot. Come on. Let's go find a quiet place to talk."

"Here?" Con's brows lifted.

"There's always my den."

His white-haired host held the door to the hall open, and Con was led away from the merrymakers. The air was slightly cooler here, and Con gratefully swept in a deep breath. Unlocking the room at the end, Forsythe motioned Con inside.

Floor-to-ceiling windows covered the entire south wall, and a massive desk reigned in the center of an enormous Aubusson carpet.

Only the best.

"You probably wondered why I sent you an invitation," Forsythe began, perching on the edge of the desk and folding his arms over his chest.

"It had crossed my mind."

Forsythe eyed him critically from head to toe. Con could just imagine what the man was thinking about his wrinkled shirt and loose tie. But then the older man waved him toward a chair, and Con gingerly lowered himself into it.

Forsythe cleared his throat. "You work for Pozzer, Strikeberg and Carmen. A fine firm."

"That's right."

"I was wondering if you would like to come work for me."

Con had figured his invitation must have something to do with a job offer. What other interest could the man have in him? But Forsythe's reasoning escaped him. "I'm not much of a corporate lawyer. I tend to go for more personal cases."

"I know that. That's precisely why I want you. Forsythe and Company has gotten too removed from the personal. We need someone with your talents on the staff."

"Well, I'm pretty happy where I am."

He smiled. "Small potatoes for a man like you. Where's your ambition? I don't have to tell you what a move like this could do for your career."

Connor eyed him steadily. He couldn't decide whether he should be insulted or flattered. What Forsythe didn't know was that Con had taken a good hard look at his own ambitions a while back and hadn't liked what he'd seen. He'd made mistakes—too many to count—and he'd be damned if he would make the same ones again. He was fully satisfied being small potatoes.

A knock on the door prevented his answer. With a scowl, Forsythe demanded, "Who is it?"

The door opened a crack, and a man's head appeared. "Dan Morrison, sir. Er . . . I think you should come out here. It's your daughter."

"She can take care of herself."

"She's been, uh, asking for you."

The deference in the younger man's tone made Con uncomfortable. Had he been like that once? Intimidated by the boss? Not in the same manner, he supposed, but there had been a time when he'd made certain the boss liked him. And then, of course, there had been Linda, the boss's daughter, Con's own ex-wife. . . .

"All right, all right." Joshua Forsythe growled under his breath, "Damn it all to hell. What's she done now?"

He waved his hand impatiently. "Tell her I'll be there in a minute."

After the man left, Forsythe turned to Con. "Morrison's a hell of an attorney, but he hasn't got the element we're talking about. You have."

"I'm still not interested."

He chuckled. "I'm not through persuading you yet. Stick around until I get back."

"I'll try."

"No, never mind." He changed his mind with a curt shake of his head. "We'll meet for lunch on Monday. This party's a damn fool place to conduct business. Enjoy yourself, and I'll see you Monday."

With a click, the door shut behind him.

Almost against his will, Con smiled. The old tyrant hadn't even waited for a reply.

Standing, Con stretched and walked to the window. It was a relief to know he didn't feel that pressure anymore—that need to fight his way to the top. As far as he was concerned, the Joshua Forsythes of the world overrated their importance.

But it wasn't always that way, he reminded himself. *There was one senior partner in that L.A. firm whom you wanted to impress pretty badly. Remember him? Your father-in-law?*

The air-conditioning was more effective in the office than in the front room, and Con stood in front of the vent, letting the chilled air rush across his face. He knew he wasn't going to take Forsythe up on his offer. Someone else could be the man's bleeding-heart pigeon. It was a little late for a man like Forsythe to acquire a conscience.

Not that Con had anything against Forsythe's business acumen. He was sharp as a tack. Cleverer than most.

Certainly powerful enough. He was just a little too used to getting what he wanted.

Con didn't know how long he'd been standing there before he heard footsteps in the hallway—a woman's footsteps. He turned, and his gaze fell on the door just as a woman in a silver dress walked in.

"Oh," she said, stopping dead upon seeing him. It was the woman from the ledge.

Her hair was blond and came down straight, curling in under her chin. Beneath a fringe of gold-tipped lashes, a pair of green eyes regarded him uncertainly.

"I was just leaving," Con said.

"No, don't. I was just looking for... somewhere cooler."

He had the impression she'd been about to say something else. His gaze traveled downward; he couldn't help himself. The rest of her was sleek and curved. A pair of beautiful legs peeked from beneath an uneven silk hem. Light glimmered on smooth skin, and Con had to admit she was the most elegant woman he'd seen in a long, long time. He realized she didn't know he was the man who'd called out to her on the ledge.

"There must be three hundred people in the other room," Con said. "It's really hot."

"Sweltering." She smiled, then glanced around, as if she didn't quite know what to do now that he was here.

"Are you a client or an employee?" he asked.

"Of the firm?"

"Of the firm." Con smiled back, but her gaze shifted away, and he sensed she was thinking about something else.

"None of the above."

"Really." His brows lifted. "And here I thought you had to be one or the other to get an invitation."

She gave him a swift, upward glance. "Which are you?"

"Potential employee, I guess."

It was as if he'd said exactly the wrong thing. She stiffened. "Well, I guess I'm cool enough," she said with a faint smile, backing out the door.

"Wait a minute. Where are you going?"

Con followed her. He just caught the gleam of her silver dress as she turned a corner at the end of the hall. Like a schoolboy struck with puppy love, he kept after her, seeing her disappear into the crowd. Between the main room and the foyer. He hoped she wasn't leaving.

The champagne tray came by again, but he shook his head, searching the room. He'd always been a sucker for mystery. And beauty, he thought wryly. The woman from the ledge had both.

He caught glimpses of her through the crowd, but like quicksilver, she never stayed long in one place.

"You'll have to stand in line," said a voice at his ear, startling him.

Glancing around, Con recognized the man who'd come to pull Joshua Forsythe back to the party. "For what?"

"For Candace," he answered with a knowing smile. Thrusting out his hand, he added, "Dan Morrison."

His handshake was smooth and curt, a message in itself. Con gave him a careful once-over. Morrison was the epitome of smooth, from his baby-soft face to his knife-creased suit to his polished black shoes. And he was hungry. Hungry for power. Hungry for success. Con knew those feelings only too well. Some part of himself that still regretted the past took an instant dislike to the other attorney.

Inclining his head in Candace's direction, Morrison said, "Her dance card is filled, pal."

"With your name?"

"Something like that."

The one thing Con could never resist was a challenge. "I imagine the lady probably has a mind of her own. Let's let her make it up."

He strode into the crowd.

Candace was standing by a glossy baby grand, in the process of placing one empty champagne glass on a forgotten tray and lifting another. She still had that distracted air about her, as if her body had come to the party but her mind had strayed somewhere else.

Con leaned against one of the pillars near the front door, watching her. From this vantage point he could see her without being detected.

"More champagne, sir?" a black-coated waiter inquired.

"I don't suppose you have Scotch? Or beer?" Con added hopefully.

"We have imported beer, sir."

"That'll do."

He settled his gaze on the woman again. *Candace,* Morrison had called her.

He became vaguely aware that the group of women huddled nearby were interested in her, as well. They were watching her sympathetically, and Con leaned closer to them, hoping to find out more about her.

"... It's so unfair. I don't know how she can even stand to be here. She's been floating around like that all summer."

"I can't believe Jeff was really seeing Renée Southfield. And Renée—she must be more interested in advancement than any of us guessed."

"Advancement...and other things." This last voice was scornful.

"It's too bad about Candace, though. There's a lady with class...."

A lady with class, Con thought idly. Yes, that was what she was.

The women's conversation petered out, and they moved away, one of them giving him a dark look for eavesdropping. Con winked at her, then laughed as a wave of color rode up her neck.

The imported beer was brought with a frosted glass, but Con just lifted the bottle. His eye on Candace, he wove his way across the room toward her.

She gave him a slight smile of recognition as he approached.

"I hate to see a beautiful woman drink alone," he said, leaning against the piano.

"I don't mind being alone." She took a sip of champagne. "Sometimes I even enjoy it."

"Is that a polite way of saying 'get lost'?" She didn't answer, but Con was undaunted. Her lack of response only fueled his desire to know more about her. "You're really a mystery, you know that? Not an employee or a client..." he added musingly. "That must make you some kind of friend of the family."

"Some kind of friend," she allowed.

Her eyes were shadowed, as if her thoughts weren't particularly pleasant ones. Con was searching his mind for something else to say when she suddenly looked up, regarding him thoughtfully.

"Want some free advice?" she asked.

"Sure." He half smiled.

"You won't get far with Forsythe and Company dressed like that."

Con glanced down at himself in surprise. "Dressed like what?"

"Like you are."

"What makes you such an expert?"

"You don't have to be an expert to know the Forsythe image," she said. Then, apparently hearing how cynical she sounded, she lowered her eyes and murmured, "Excuse me. I'm still too hot." In a swirl of silk and silver spangles, she headed out the French doors to the balcony.

Connor had experienced the brush-off a few times in his long career with the opposite sex, but never with such icy polish. She was a lady who knew her own mind, he decided, wondering why he felt compelled to change it. Grimacing, he followed her outside. She was right about one thing, it was too damn hot.

On the balcony he was greeted by her stony stare. He held up his hands. "Look, I give up. You want to be left alone—fine. But I needed some air, so you'll have to share the balcony for a few minutes."

She digested that in silence. Her eyes glanced down, then at the wrought-iron railing, then across the lake—anywhere but at him. Finally she emitted a soft sigh. "I'm not usually so rude." She made a face. "It's just been a—a terrible day."

He remembered the papers she'd tossed into the lake. "Did you get bad news?"

"What do you mean?"

"It's just that I saw you outside, on the cliff ledge."

Her intake of breath was audible.

"You threw something in the water. Look, it's no big deal. I just couldn't help noticing."

It hadn't been his intention to back her into a corner, he'd only wanted to find out more about her. But she suddenly looked stricken.

"Yes, I got bad news. It's not something I want to talk about."

"Hey, it's none of my business, anyway. Look... Candace... I've gone about this all wrong. Let me start over. The name's Connor Holt, and I just wanted to... I don't know..." In lieu of an explanation he gave a self-deprecating shrug.

She was waiting for him to finish, so Con heaved a sigh. "It's not every day I see a beautiful woman standing on a ledge looking like she's going to throw herself off. It got to me. Then I saw you in Forsythe's den, and, hell—" he raked his hand through his hair in frustration "—I just wanted to talk to you."

The sound of a piano warming up came floating through the open door. A chorus of voices burst into the first verse of "God Rest Ye Merry Gentlemen."

"It's all so ridiculous," she suddenly burst out, and to Con's amazement her eyes were glistening with tears.

She swayed and he reached for her, but he wasn't quite quick enough. She slumped against the railing. Con's hand inadvertently grazed her hip as he tried to pull her into his arms. A moment later he was uncomfortably aware of the pressure of her breasts against his chest.

"Get me out of here," she said, somewhat desperately, "before I make a complete fool of myself."

"Where's your car?"

"Across the bridge."

He could see the golden strands at her crown in the slanting light from the windows. He didn't know what her problems were, but he knew he wanted to help. Gently he helped her toward the back steps that led to the grounds, but the evening's silence was shattered by a voice behind their heads.

"Candace! Where are you rushing off to?"

She tensed, and Con turned to see the newcomer. He groaned inwardly when he recognized Dan Morrison.

"Hello, Dan," she said warily.

There were undercurrents here Con didn't understand.

Morrison came over, the same false smile plastered across his face. "I see you've met Mr. Holt," he said.

Con was a little surprised the man knew his name.

Candace's face flushed, and she pulled herself away from Connor. "Er—yes."

"Did he tell you about Joshua's job offer? He's our new left-winger. Out to save the little people." Envy was written all over the young attorney's face.

"Watch your mouth, Morrison," Con warned, unable to stop himself.

He feigned surprise. "I didn't know I was stepping on toes."

Con's smile was a thin line. "I hope you have more tact in the courtroom, for Forsythe and Company's sake."

As Morrison's lips tightened, Candace turned swiftly to Con. "You took the job?" she asked, her green eyes wide and vulnerable.

For some reason, his answer seemed extremely important to her. Because Morrison was listening avidly, he said ambiguously, "Not yet."

"But you will."

"What? Is that a crime? I haven't actually—"

Con didn't have a chance to explain before Morrison shifted position, sidling closer to Candace. "We haven't had a chance to dance. Don't leave yet. You owe me one."

Con didn't like the man's moves one bit. He was gratified, therefore, when Candace leaned closer to him. "I'm sorry," she said. "Maybe next time."

Morrison's hand was on her forearm. "One dance. That's all."

She was no longer leaning—she was pressed against Con. Cutting through the thick atmosphere, Con squeezed her shoulder and said briskly, "You ready?"

When she nodded jerkily, Con practically muscled Morrison out of the way as he guided her down the stairs. They were halfway across the bridge before she let out a shaky breath. "Thanks for the rescue."

"Any time."

"Dan's kind of—" She sought the right word.

"Overbearing? Insufferable? Pompous?" Con felt a little twinge of conscience. There was something about Dan that cut close to the bone—he seemed a reflection of Con's worst faults minus his good points.

She almost laughed. "Good breeding prevents me from any comment."

Con warmed to her. He found himself dying to get inside her head and find out all about her.

"How did you know my name?" she asked. "You said it before Dan showed up."

"He told me your name was Candace."

Her brows pulled together. "That's all he told you about me?"

Con grinned. "This is getting better and better. I mean, how much more is there to know?"

"Why do you want to work for Forsythe and Company?" she asked abruptly. "You seem—"

"What?"

She lifted one shoulder. "To have a mind of your own."

"Does working for Forsythe and Company mean you can't have a mind of your own?"

"Have you met Joshua Forsythe?"

"Briefly."

"He likes total control."

The breeze came up to tease her hair, blowing it across her lips. "That's pretty cynical," he observed.

"It's the truth."

"How do you know Forsythe so well?"

Her eyes searched his. "Do you really not know?"

"You're not an employee or a client. You're a friend."

"I may have misled you there a little. I have worked for Forsythe and Company."

"Ahhh . . . you're an ex-employee."

"Who's sort of helping out this summer," she admitted. "I'm a secretary of sorts."

"Then the mystery's solved." Con's tone was light. "And I don't care who you are, anyway. All I know is that I'd like to see you again."

She looked off across the water. He waited for her to reply, but as silence lengthened between them, he realized she wasn't going to.

"I get the feeling I've missed something important," he prodded gently.

"Oh, I don't know how important it is." She leaned her forearms on the bridge railing and sighed. "My name is Candace Forsythe McCall. Joshua Forsythe is my father."

Chapter Two

Candace had seen many reactions to the fact that Joshua was her father, but Connor Holt's was unexpected. He looked totally dumbfounded, and surprisingly the connection didn't seem to be one he particularly liked. He stared at her, a handsome man with gloriously thick dark hair and long-lashed blue eyes—eyes now filled with disbelief.

"Good God," he muttered.

Candace took a deep breath. He was wondering if he'd stepped out of bounds, she realized with disappointment. For a moment she'd thought he might actually be different from the Dan Morrisons and Jeff McCalls of the world.

Her interest in him died a quick death. She had other things to think about—important things. "I've got to be going," she said, and was unnerved when his hand suddenly clasped her arm.

"Wait."

The command was soft, but one Candace instinctively obeyed. She gave him another look, seeing his determined mouth and tanned throat. Was he more dangerous than he seemed? She couldn't trust herself to tell anymore.

"You're Joshua Forsythe's daughter?" At her brief nod, he swore softly. "Why in the hell do I always fall for the wrong ones?"

Candace felt perilously close to tears. The events of the day swirled before her and, as on the balcony, she felt suddenly weak and lost. "Somehow I don't think you've really fallen," she managed to choke out.

"Try me."

She didn't believe him for an instant. It was just his way of relating. She bet it worked on most of the women he encountered, too. Another time it might even have worked on her.

But not tonight.

"I've got to go," she murmured.

"Can I see you again?"

She shook her head. "Are you really taking the job with Forsythe and Company?"

"Will you go out with me if I do?"

"No."

"Will you go out with me if I don't?"

"No. Please—" She pulled away from him. Away from his persuasive touch. Heat settled over her like a cloak as soon as she stepped off the bridge. The night was much too warm. She thought fleetingly of her silver fox stole. She could get it later. It was too hot to think about tonight.

He was right on her heels. "You look like you're about to collapse."

"I'm all right."

"Which one's your car?"

They were in the parking area on the shore side of the bridge. Cars were lined up in uneven rows. "That one," Candace said, pointing to the black Jaguar. "My husband bought it for me."

She always overexplained. Why was that? she wondered. Why couldn't she gracefully accept the fact that she had more money than she knew what to do with?

"You're married," Con said stiffly.

She opened her mouth to explain that she was divorced, but stopped when she saw a way to end this relationship before it could begin. No one knew her divorce was final. She'd tried to tell her father this evening, but he'd had no time to hear about her personal life.

"Yes," she lied. "I'm married."

"Your husband wasn't with you tonight."

"He's rarely with me, Mr. Holt, as I'm sure you'll learn if you take the job with Forsythe and Company."

"Actually, I don't want the job."

His lack of respect threw her. Every lawyer in town wanted a job with Forsythe and Company. For the first time since the medical report had arrived, Candace found herself really thinking about something else. "Why not?"

"I've got a good job already."

"Joshua will make you an offer you can't refuse."

"Why do you call your father by his first name? What happened to good old *Dad*?"

"You don't call Joshua Forsythe *Dad*. It's not the done thing."

He laughed aloud. "What *is* the done thing?"

"Accept a job with Forsythe and Company and get damn good at licking boots."

She hadn't meant to sound so bitter. In fact, she was appalled at her tone. Connor stared at her and his expression grew hard. "I've never been good at bootlicking," he said grimly.

She turned toward her car. What had seemed a short distance to cross suddenly appeared interminable. She took three steps and stumbled, her vision blurring as in her mind's eye she once again saw those three terrible printed words: Lab Test Positive.

His arm was around her once more. "Candace?"

Tears welled. She wanted to crawl into his arms and cry against his white shirt, but she couldn't. Years of fighting back her feelings came to her rescue now. She held herself in control—until he twisted her around and pressed her face against his chest.

"I don't care what's wrong," he said softly. "Just let it out." His arms were tight and comforting.

Kindness was her enemy. She trembled with emotion, squeezing her eyes shut. She could feel his strong chest, the steady beat of his heart. Distantly she was aware of an unexpected need unfurling deep inside her.

His hand was stroking her hair, and Candace tore herself away, breathing hard. She swiped the backs of her hands against her damp cheeks. "I'm sorry."

"For what?" He smiled.

"You don't understand anything about me."

"I understand a few things."

She couldn't stay here. Couldn't have this conversation.

"Are you really working at Forsythe and Company?" he asked.

"Yes." She took two steps away. "Are you taking the job?"

"You don't want me to, do you?"

She thought of Jeff, of how he'd used her to ingratiate himself with her father. "I don't really like lawyers," she admitted. "I don't trust them."

"Really," Connor murmured. "What does your husband do for a living?"

Candace broke free. She practically ran the last few yards to the Jaguar. Her fingers fumbling with her keys, she unlocked the door and slid behind the wheel, shaking. She wondered what Con must think of her. What had he made of Dan's advances toward her? A married woman?

Only she wasn't married.

The engine purred to life. Releasing the emergency brake, she drove through the quiet evening, seeing Connor standing by the bridge, a dark figure on a hot summer night. She lifted a hand in recognition, and he gave her a quick salute.

The breeze through her open window whipped her blond hair against her face, and she squinted to keep it from stinging her eyes. She kept sight of Con in her rearview mirror until his image disappeared as she rounded the first curve of the lake road.

Almost instantly her thoughts turned back to the medical papers she'd destroyed. Lab test positive. She shuddered. She wasn't going to be able to have children.

"The cells of your cervix may be sloughing off. We'll know as soon as we get the report," Dr. Evinrud had explained several days before. "If so, you'll need an operation to remove your cervix."

"How soon?" Candace had asked, frightened.

"It depends. The condition will progress. You'll need to be carefully monitored. I would say a year, maybe longer. It's just a matter of time until your cervix deteriorates completely."

Candace had been numb. She'd known even before the results had come through that the test would prove positive. And the operation would end her childbearing days.

No child. No baby. No one.

What a terrible irony it was that her divorce should just now be finalized. She didn't even have a husband to father a child. Not that she could really see Jeff as a parent. He was still too much a child himself.

But where did that leave her now?

Stamping on the accelerator, Candace gritted her teeth. The Jaguar screamed around the tricky corners above the lake. Poor little rich girl. That was what she'd always been. Her mother had died when she'd been young, and her father... well, her father had loved her as best he could, considering that he had no idea what to do with a quiet, introverted girl. Candace had been raised by a succession of governesses who had only left her yearning for something more.

A part of her had always expected to lavish the love and attention she'd missed on her own child. Now that chance would be gone forever.

The drive was short to her small house at the north end of the lake. She'd grown up at the Forsythe home, and though she considered it a drafty, ostentatious monstrosity, she had always enjoyed living on the water. When she'd married Jeff they'd bought the cottage. Jeff had wanted a place on the lake for the prestige; Candace had chosen it for its peacefulness.

She parked beneath the carport and ducked under a clematis that was heavy with deep purple blossoms. Walking down the steps to the back patio, she skirted the lights and made her way directly to the water. Moonlight dappled the restless surface. Candace breathed deeply and closed her eyes. Tomorrow, she thought wryly, was another day.

The heat wave hadn't abated by Monday, and Candace appeared at work in a pale pink sleeveless blouse and a white skirt. Her hair was plaited down her back. She looked, she decided, catching sight of herself in the mirrored hallway, about ten years younger than she felt. Making a face at life in general, she walked to the oak double doors at the end of the hall and raised her hand to knock.

"He's got meetings scheduled all morning at the Claremont," a voice said behind her. Marion, her father's personal secretary, looked up from her paper-strewn desk.

"Oh, that's right." Candace frowned. It was so typical of her relationship with her father that they couldn't even properly schedule a time for her tell him she was divorced.

"Is there something I can help you with?" Marion asked hopefully.

Marion was more than a secretary. She was almost a mother figure to Candace, and a friend to boot. But this was something Candace needed to discuss with her father.

"No, I'll just check with him later. What would you like me to do first? Some filing?"

At one time Candace had been a full-time legal secretary, but when her problems with Jeff had arisen she'd chosen to become more of an aide. She'd always thought she would quit to have a baby.

Marion clapped her hands together. "Hallelujah! My prayers have been heard." She dragged Candace toward the filing room. "It's a disaster in here. Do you mind? If you could get started on this it would be the biggest help."

"This'll be fine," Candace laughed. One of the things she liked best about her father's secretary was that she wasn't impressed by the fact that Candace was a Forsythe. Glancing around at the stacked files, she added lightly, "It's a good way to keep busy."

Marion's expression changed. "If you need a willing listener, I'm here."

"Thanks. But really, I'm okay." Candace gave her a crooked smile.

I'm okay. How many times had she said that in the past few months? Ever since Jeff's affair with Renée had become hot office gossip, Candace had been defending herself. She'd had to quit work for a while until Jeff had taken another job. But even when she'd returned to Forsythe and Company, everyone had tried to become her confidant. All Candace had wanted to do was forget.

Filing was an undemanding, mindless job that Candace was actually enjoying today. She'd spent too many hours worrying about her future. Sometimes she wished she had become pregnant before Jeff had left her. Then at least she would have a child.

"Lunchtime," Marion said several hours later, knocking on the open door to the file room.

"I'm not really hungry."

"Then come and keep me company. Terri's on vacation, and you know what a stone-face Pamela is. You couldn't get her to crack a smile if your daddy offered to double her salary."

"Now that's an exaggeration. She's as money-motivated as the rest of us."

Marion hooted with laughter. "You? Money-motivated? Candace, my dear, you've never even learned what to do with the money you've got! One of these days I'm going to have to give you a lesson." She waved for her to follow, and Candace, who had no real reason to refuse, trailed after her.

Marion chose a small restaurant on the ground floor of the Forsythe Building, and she and Candace were seated at a table near the window. "You seem better," Marion observed as she attacked her salad.

"What do you mean, better?"

"Oh, I don't know. Less tense." She gave Candace a sharp look. "You've gotten over him, haven't you?"

"Who, Jeff?" Candace was amazed anyone still thought she cared. "I got over him a long time ago. It was just hard to give up the marriage." She chased a few leaves of lettuce around with her fork, then set the utensil down with a sigh.

"Well, there're scads of men out there, honey. Most of 'em just waiting for someone like you. I know a few in our office alone who wouldn't mind asking you for a date." She smiled slyly.

"I'm not interested in another lawyer," Candace replied. "In fact, I'm not interested in another man."

Marion snorted. "Jeff McCall is a first-class fool. Why did he ever let you get away?"

"Because he'd used me as much as he could to climb the corporate ladder," Candace said lightly. "He didn't need me for anything else."

Marion tried to protest, but Candace deftly changed the subject. In her heart she knew just why Jeff had asked her to marry him. She also knew she'd accepted because he'd seemed like the perfect husband: handsome, successful, determined. What she hadn't counted on was his being a clever actor, too. He'd made her believe he loved her. She'd learned much later about the string of affairs that had finally culminated with Renée Southfield. By then it had ceased to hurt... almost.

The subject of Candace's faithless husband wasn't brought up again until they were in the elevator.

"Jeff will come crawling back one of these days, mark my words," Marion said as they sped upward.

"But I don't want him back."

"Nevertheless, he'll come back." The iron-haired secretary nodded positively. "Maybe you'd better start thinking about how you're going to handle that. He can be very charming when he wants to be."

"Tell me about it." Candace actually smiled. Marion had nothing to fear about Candace losing her heart again. Once burned, twice shy.

As they stepped into the pearl-gray outer offices of Forsythe and Company, Candace nearly collided with a man punching the elevator button. Her heart leaped as she recognized Connor Holt.

In the light of day he looked less determined. His blue eyes, when they fell on Candace, simmered with humor, as if he were remembering a private joke. Mouth twisting crookedly, he drawled, "Well, hello, Mrs. McCall."

"Mr. Holt," she answered reservedly. She was flustered, and it embarrassed her. For some reason she had to fight to hold on to her composure—a task she generally managed without thinking. "I thought you weren't interested in a position with us."

"With *us*?" He looked amused. "I didn't know you had such company spirit. I got the impression you thought a position with Forsythe and Company was a fate worse than death."

She flushed, belatedly sensing that Marion was watching this exchange with interest. "Uh, you go on ahead. I'll be there in a minute," she said to the secretary. Reluctantly Marion took her cue and left.

Turning back to Connor, Candace said, "I'm assuming they told you my father's been out all morning."

"They didn't have to. I was with him."

"You were?" Candace felt cheated. She hadn't realized how much she'd expected from this man until he'd suddenly proved her wrong. "So all that talk about not taking the job was just lip service for my benefit?"

He shook his head. "Boy, you're touchy. What's the problem with my working here, anyway?"

"Nothing." Candace was too rattled to try to explain about Jeff and her phobia concerning lawyers. Connor Holt wouldn't understand, anyway.

"Well, forgive me for misinterpreting." His tone was sardonic. "Should I check with you before I make my decision?"

He was teasing her, but it hurt—hurt deeply, in a way she only half understood. She couldn't answer; her mind was a blank. Connor Holt, though, was a master of the fast comeback, and he lifted his brows, silently laughing at her discomfiture.

She realized suddenly that she liked him, truly liked him, and that she wanted to impress him. Good grief, hadn't she learned anything from Jeff?

Appalled by her unexpected feelings, Candace reacted with instinctive self-protection. "Maybe you ought to," she said icily. "I'll see if I can put in a good word for you with the boss."

He simply stared at her. As soon as the words were out she regretted them, but there was nothing to do but suffer the consequences. She half expected him to blast her, but when he spoke it was in a soft, dangerous tone. "I'd appreciate that, Mrs. McCall. Now, if you'll excuse me, I've got to go practice my bootlicking."

She'd wounded his ego. It was precisely what she'd meant to do, but why, oh why, had she really done it?

The elevator doors slid shut behind him, and Candace watched the lights flash on and off as he descended. She was horrified at herself. With a groan of humiliation she hurried back to the filing room.

Con counted to a hundred as the elevator sped to the bottom floor. It came to a halt with a shudder and he stepped out, his face a dark glower. *Damn, damn, damn.*

That better-than-thou attitude stung. Deep. He wanted to slam his fist through the nearest wall.

He controlled himself with a conscious effort, yet he still felt a deep-seated anger toward all Forsythes. He'd thought Joshua a master at manipulation, but Candace— Con took a deep breath. She was worse.

Pushing open the revolving door, Con stepped into the afternoon heat. The sun beat down on concrete and cement, hot air swelling around him. Where was the mild Oregon climate now? he wondered irritably. The whole damn summer had been a furnace.

There was a small bar around the corner from the Forsythe Building, the Front Street Café & Bar, a trendy neon-lighted rectangle that catered to the after-work crowd. Con stepped inside and made his way to the bar.

"What'll you have?" the bartender asked over his shoulder as he poured several foaming drafts.

"I don't care. Just give me two of it, whatever it is."

"That bad, huh, pal?"

"Worse."

"Beer okay?"

"Yeah, fine." Con let out his breath. Why had she gotten to him so much? He'd learned to deflect that kind of criticism a long time ago.

His thoughts turned to Linda, his ex-wife. She'd called again last week, and though they'd been divorced more than a year, she still was able to make him feel guilty, as if their failed marriage had been all his fault. Rationally he knew she was wrong, but his own regrets over the mistakes he'd made couldn't be forgotten.

The bartender handed him one of the beers, and Con's thoughts moved to his meeting with Joshua Forsythe. The man was disarming, he had to give him that. Forsythe knew exactly what buttons to push and just how hard to push them.

"One of our customers is involved in a custody battle," Forsythe had explained as soon as they'd sat down. "The mother wants the child back. The father says she's unfit. He wants the child, and he wants us to represent him."

"So where do I fit in?" Con had asked cautiously.

"It's what you do best," Forsythe had answered simply. "You've got a reputation for defending the person who needs it most—in this case, the child. You don't take a case if you don't believe it's in the best interests of the injured party."

Con had felt the net tightening around him. "You seem to think you have me pegged. What if I disappoint you?"

"You won't." His smile had been almost patronizing. "You're an idealist. You put families back together. You fend off corporations seeking to turn apartments into condominiums. You fight against might and for right. You're for the underdog. And you're successful.

"I'll be straight with you—you're simply the kind of man my company needs right now."

Con's laughter had been half disbelief, half genuine amusement. "Let's say you're right about me. You think you can buy me?"

"Forget about me. The little girl I'm talking about needs to be with the right parent. You won't be able to turn your back on her."

It was Joshua Forsythe's assurance that had infuriated Con the most. "Watch me," Con had said, and he'd ended their meeting abruptly.

The man's unmitigated gall was more than Con could stand. That, and the fact that he'd somehow managed to make Con feel guilty over this one child, as if her future rested in his hands alone. Good grief! There were thousands of cases like hers. She was just a statistic.

Con had spent a couple of hours trying to work off his anger at his club, but even after a shower and change of clothes he'd still felt frustrated and sensitive. He'd felt like telling Forsythe where to get off. If the man couldn't treat him with respect, fine. He didn't deserve any, either.

He'd gone back to Forsythe and Company with that intention, but along the way something had happened. He'd realized that for all Forsythe's misplaced motivation, the idea was right: Forsythe and Company could use a little of the human element.

When he'd found out Joshua Forsythe hadn't returned yet, Con had decided to come back later. Then he'd run into Candace.

And she'd let him know what she thought of him.

It burned that she didn't know the least thing about his ethics. Her father obviously did. Good Lord, that was why the man wanted him.

Con put down the empty mug from his first beer, wiped his mouth with the back of his hand and, still glowering, picked up his second. A part of him wanted to take the job just to prove her wrong. Who cared what Forsythe's reasons were? Con would handle cases to benefit the parties involved. It didn't much matter that Forsythe and Company would bask in the glow of good works as a by-product of his work. What mattered was that he could practice the kind of law he wanted and help the people who truly needed help.

Con blinked. Was he really considering taking the job?

He was mulling that surprising thought over in his mind when the door opened and Dan Morrison walked into the bar. Con stifled an epithet, and he thought once again of Candace. She was married, she'd said. So what was Morri-

son's interest in her? Or did the bonds of matrimony hold
no meaning for his kind? And why the hell was she so dead
set against Con coming to work for Forsythe and Company?

Morrison spotted Con and raised his glass in a salute.
Reluctantly Con lifted his in recognition. Then he sighed
when the young lawyer came his way.

"You're settling right in, aren't you?" Morrison observed, ordering straight Scotch.

"My tastes are just a little less refined." Con's gaze moved
from Morrison's drink to his gold cuff links.

"Oh, I wouldn't say that. I think Candace McCall might
even take offense."

Con said nothing. Half of him wanted to renounce Candace McCall as the snob she was; the other half didn't want
Morrison to know the lady already thought him one of
earth's lowest life-forms.

"What did you say to the old man that got him so riled?"
Morrison asked. "I met him at the Claremont after you left.
He was pretty unhappy."

"I turned down his job offer."

Morrison looked unimpressed. "So he didn't get your
weakness right, huh? Well, don't worry, he'll find it."

Con felt his temper smoldering. Actually, it was a case of
Forsythe and Company's weakness. They needed a new
image. "What weakness of yours did he exploit?" Con
asked, setting down his empty glass.

"I suppose I should say money. But that's not quite it."

It was clear Morrison liked to talk about himself as if he
were a third party. It was just the kind of pseudo-
sophisticated chatter Con detested most.

"I'd say it's power, then," Con remarked idly. "That's
where Candace comes in, right?"

The man's neck turned brick red. Con watched detachedly. *I know you, buddy,* he thought. *Better than you think.*

"He said you were brash," Morrison bit out. "I'd call it foolhardy."

"I think you're worried the old man might like me better than you."

"Foolhardy and reckless," Morrison said through his teeth. Then he slammed down his drink and left.

Con watched him leave. If Joshua Forsythe wanted to change his law firm's image, he was going to have to get rid of lawyers like Dan Morrison.

"Another draft?" the bartender asked.

Con looked around. Suddenly he knew what he was going to do. "Maybe later," he said, tossing a few bills onto the counter. "I've got something to do first."

Candace looked down at the message the receptionist had handed her: Dr. Evinrud called. Please call back as soon as possible.

She felt cold all over. Before she could pick up the phone, the elevator doors whispered open and Joshua Forsythe strode into the reception room.

"What are you doing standing out here?" he asked Candace brusquely. "Hold all my calls, Terri. I've got a lot of work to do."

Terri's face took on a long-suffering expression, but she nodded.

"I want to talk to you," Candace said distractedly, her mind on the message. What did it mean? She was afraid to find out.

"Well, it'll have to be now. I'm busy."

Glad to put off the phone call, Candace preceded her father to his office. Joshua Forsythe threw himself into his cushiony desk chair and heaved a sigh of frustration, his mouth taut. Only after several moments had passed did he notice Candace's preoccupation. "Well?" he demanded.

"My divorce is final. I got the papers."

"I...see..." He shifted with discomfort. Candace knew fatherhood had never come easily to Joshua Forsythe. "Jeff has—had—his good points. But he wasn't for you, I suppose."

The faint tone of regret in his voice wasn't lost on Candace. He'd breathed so much easier when she'd been someone else's responsibility. "I'm a grown woman," she found herself saying. "I know when a man isn't good for me."

"Of course. Of course." He waved at her in a friendly manner, embarrassed. "So what're your plans now?"

"I don't know. I'd like to work for a while and try to figure out what I want to do with the rest of my life."

"You don't have to work, y'know."

"I've got to do something."

He grunted his acknowledgment. The one thing Joshua Forsythe understood was hard work. "What about law school? I know you gave up the idea when you married Jeff, but—"

"I'm not cut out to be a lawyer," she said swiftly.

He almost smiled. "Well, then, what are you cut out to be?"

Candace was saved from answering by the intercom buzzing imperatively. With a growl of exasperation, her father snatched up the phone. "Terri, I don't want to be disturbed!"

"I know that, sir." The receptionist's voice was hesitant. "But there's a Mr. Connor Holt here to see you and he's already halfway down the hall."

Joshua chuckled, but Candace looked around desperately for some escape. Her cheeks reddened as she recalled her last remark to him. "Never mind, Terri," her father said. "I'll take care of Mr. Holt."

He strode across the room just as a determined rap sounded. Candace waited, frozen. With a "Well, it's about time you reconsidered," Joshua threw open the door.

Connor looked much the same as he had when he'd left a few hours earlier. He shook Joshua's hand amid the older man's greetings, but his eyes met Candace's. There was a coldness in their blue depths that she knew she deserved. Still, it bothered her.

"It's just as well you're here," he said to her in a friendly tone. "Seeing as I was supposed to let you know my decision first."

Candace's lips parted in pain, and Joshua Forsythe asked gruffly, "What do you mean?"

"Nothing." He turned back to Joshua and didn't waste any more time. "I've given your offer a lot of thought. I've decided I want the job after all."

Chapter Three

Well, that's wonderful news," Joshua crowed, clapping Connor on the shoulder. He turned to Candace. "Isn't it?"

"Wonderful," she murmured, unable to meet Connor's eyes.

"I take it you've met my daughter, then," he went on without missing a beat. "Candace works here part of the time."

"So she said." Con's voice was cool.

"I, uh, have some things to do," she said, anxious to escape. Trying to circumvent Con and her father, she found there was no easy way to get to the door and ended up brushing the sleeve of Con's jacket in her effort to leave. She glanced upward, saw his forbidding expression and managed a weak "Excuse me."

He didn't answer, only watched her with assessing blue eyes.

Feeling compelled to say something else, she murmured, "And congratulations," as her hand twisted the knob.

"Thanks."

His mocking tone rang in her ears all the way down the hall, and when she reached the tiny filing room she found she was trembling. She hated herself for letting it matter so much, yet she couldn't seem to help it.

Connor Holt was a lawyer. Period. There was nothing wrong in that.

But does he have to work for Joshua?

Candace was still standing in front of the open filing cabinet nearest the window when she felt someone enter the room behind her. Her blood chilled when she heard Connor drawl, "You didn't even wait for us to break out the champagne and caviar."

"Sorry." She turned and gave him a tight smile. This was the time to try to put things back on track between them. She'd been unforgivably rude, and she owed him an apology. But right now she just wanted to melt into the carpet and put Connor Holt, Forsythe and Company and her own worries about the future on permanent hold.

"What? No comment? No advice? And here I expected a full-blown lecture about the evils of being a lawyer."

"You don't understand..." she began unhappily, then let the words trail off when she realized there was absolutely no way to explain.

"Oh, but I do understand. Perfectly." He flashed her a white smile that held no warmth at all. "You're Candace Forsythe McCall and I'm Connor Holt. That sort of says it all, doesn't it?"

"What do you mean?" she asked, truly puzzled.

He shook his head as if she'd somehow disappointed him. "Never mind. It doesn't matter." With a shrug he turned on his heel, then hesitated at the door, asking brusquely, as if he didn't really want to know, "Look, are you all right? You're white as a sheet."

"Am I?" she repeated distractedly, touching her cheek. She wasn't really surprised. She felt totally wrung out, and it didn't help to know that Dr. Evinrud was waiting for her call.

"Actually, you look like you've seen a ghost."

She made a choked sound and turned back toward the window. Perhaps she had seen a ghost— Connor Holt was the haunting image of Jeff McCall before greed and lust for power had turned him into someone she didn't know, someone she didn't even like.

Sensing Con was still in the room, she said, "You can leave. I don't need a baby-sitter."

"For God's sake," he muttered, circling around to peer into her face. She set her jaw and tried to avoid his eyes, but it was impossible. His gaze was too assessing, too clear. It probed the very depths of her, sending an unwelcome jolt of awareness along her nerves.

"What is it?" he asked.

"Nothing." She uttered a short laugh that sounded strangled even to her own ears. This was not the time to be honest. She couldn't afford to let him see that much of herself.

He made a sound of frustration. "You are one of the hardest women to understand I've ever met—and that's saying a lot."

"There's not that much to understand."

"It's lines like that, Candace—bald-faced *lies* like that— that drive a man crazy." At her continued silence he said impatiently, "Okay, fine. Your secrets are your own. I'll see you tomorrow." He headed for the door.

A hot flush crept up her neck. What was the matter with her? Glancing back, she said anxiously, "Mr. Holt—Connor—I really do wish you the best of success. I'm not trying to be difficult. I just hope you've...made the right choice."

His lips twisted. "Back to that 'it's a fate worse than death' tone, hmm?" Cynicism gleamed in his narrowed eyes. "Don't worry, Mrs. McCall, I can hold my own."

"I'm sure you can."

He gave her a long look, seemed to want to say something more. His jaw tightened and relaxed, and Candace held her breath expectantly. But he just shook his head and pushed through the door, shutting it behind him with a soft click.

The room closed in on Candace. She released a deep sigh and realized she felt terrible. A headache was beginning to form behind her eyes. That's what you get, she thought wryly, slamming shut the file drawer. Connor Holt probably thinks you're a coldhearted bitch.

Remembering the call from Dr. Evinrud, she gathered up her courage and went in search of a telephone. The spare office next to Marion's was empty, so she perched on a corner of the desk and lifted the receiver. Pausing, she stared vaguely out the window. Was she really up to talking about her condition? Her headache was dissolving into a dull lassitude that affected her whole body, yet she knew she wasn't sick. She was depressed. It was the same depression that had dogged her since she'd found out about Jeff's affairs.

Not that her marriage had been rock-solid. On the contrary, she'd sensed she was heading for divorce long before she'd learned about Jeff's infidelities; she'd just been too stubborn and frightened to face life alone. Still, Jeff's affair with Renée Southfield had been a tremendous blow—in part because she'd liked and trusted Renée. The woman's flamboyance and zest for life had filled Candace with mild envy. It was as if Renée had epitomized everything she had always wanted to be. Jeff apparently had felt the same way.

"But that's the past," Candace reminded herself aloud. She dialed Dr. Evinrud's number from memory.

"This is Candace McCall returning Dr. Evinrud's call," she said to the receptionist on the other line.

"One moment, please."

The line clicked and Candace was put on hold. Good. Anything to keep from facing her decision.

"Hello, Candace? This is Kathleen Evinrud," the doctor answered briefly. "I'm glad I caught up with you. How are you doing?"

Candace made a face. "As compared to what?" She managed to inject some humor into the remark, but even so, her voice was thready with distress.

"I know how difficult the last few days have been for you, and I imagine you still have a lot of questions. I've got about an hour this afternoon, if you would like to come in and just talk."

Surprised by the offer, Candace murmured, "Well, I don't know...."

"I'm free after five if you could meet me at my office. I would really like to talk some more about your cervical condition."

Cervical condition. Candace shuddered. She wasn't up to it. Yet could talking to Dr. Evinrud be much worse than returning to the empty loneliness of her house? "Actually," she said slowly, "I would like to come in."

"Fine." The doctor sounded pleased. "I'll be waiting for you."

Glancing at the clock, Candace realized she had just enough time to drive from downtown Portland to the Briar Park Medical offices by five o'clock. "I'll see you in thirty minutes," she said, and as she hung up she felt better.

* * *

Dr. Evinrud's reception area was empty when Candace walked in. She glanced around, her gaze falling on several of the magazines scattered across the chairs. The first two titles leaped out at her: *New Parenthood* and *Your Baby's Special*. Candace's heart squeezed, and she glanced away.

Muffled footsteps sounded on the carpet beyond the reception desk. "Candace?" Dr. Evinrud called, peering around the corner. "Hi. Come on in."

The tall, middle-aged doctor opened the inner door, her smile warm and friendly. Kathleen Evinrud was one of those doctors who inspired confidence, yet Candace had never been able to fully open up to her. Every time she felt like pouring out her heart, something prevented her.

"Take a chair. Could I get you something? Coffee? Tea? Believe it or not, I even have some iced."

"You're kidding." Candace sat down carefully in one of the lemon-colored chairs placed around Dr. Evinrud's desk. "Iced tea would be great."

The doctor disappeared for a moment and returned with two glasses of iced tea and a small sugar bowl. Candace shook her head when offered the sugar and sipped the iced tea gratefully, wishing she could hold the glass to her hot forehead.

"When I asked you how you were doing on the telephone, it wasn't just small talk," said Dr. Evinrud.

Candace nodded.

"You've had some pretty hard choices to make this last week. I'd like to know if you've made them."

Candace regarded her blankly. "Choices? I thought you said I had time. You said maybe a year...."

"You do have time, but my experience is that as soon as people are faced with a serious medical dilemma they make a decision right away no matter how much time they have."

Candace carefully set her iced tea down on the corner of Dr. Evinrud's desk. "I'm going to wait as long as I can. I don't want to panic."

"I understand." Dr. Evinrud unfolded a file on her desk and glanced at it, a line deepening between her eyebrows. "Have you talked this over with your husband at all?"

Candace drew a breath. Here was an issue she'd adroitly skirted. "Jeff is—we're not married anymore."

"Oh." It took a lot to shake Dr. Evinrud's aplomb, but Candace's belated confession did. "I understood you were separated."

"No, we're divorced."

The silence in the room was telling. Candace knew Dr. Evinrud was rethinking the whole situation.

"Do you have anyone you can talk to?" the doctor said at length. "Anyone at all?"

Candace thought of her father and felt an inward shrinking. "I guess not," she said on a short laugh.

"Then let me be blunt. We haven't really discussed what you plan to do concerning having a family of your own. Are you interested in having children?" Dr. Evinrud's face was sober.

"Yes, I'm interested," Candace answered unevenly.

"You only have a few months left, a year or two at the outside, to bear your own. It won't be much longer than that."

Candace said nothing. What was there to say?

"This is a delicate subject," the doctor went on. "Some women object to even discussing bearing children when there's no husband involved. How do you feel about it?"

"I—hadn't given it much thought," Candace murmured, mentally crossing her fingers at the lie. "It would be hard. I guess if I want children I'll have to adopt."

"Candace." Dr. Evinrud's voice grew softer. "The reason I asked you to come here this evening was so I could get a better handle on how you felt about your diagnosis. The surgery is, of course, foremost, and that's what we've concentrated on. But having your cervix removed is going to cause other problems."

"Do I really have to have it removed? I mean, is there any chance I might just get better? Without surgery?"

Dr. Evinrud regarded her squarely. "I'd like to say yes, but I'd be a liar. You have a precursor to cervical cancer. It's not going to get any better. But after surgery there's no reason you can't lead a normal, healthy life."

"Except I can't have children."

Dr. Evinrud closed the file and searched Candace's tense face. "If you want a child, you're going to have to have it now."

The thought had been bubbling around in Candace's subconscious, something she couldn't quite face but couldn't abandon completely, either. "As you said, I don't have a husband," she pointed out tonelessly.

"You don't need a husband to make a baby."

Candace almost flinched. "But if I don't have a husband, the baby doesn't have a father."

Dr. Evinrud conceded the point with an inclination of her head. "I'm not telling you what to do, Candace. That's up to you. You have to ask yourself how badly you want to have your own child. The morality issue is something I can't address. The fact is simply that your time is running out."

"I know. I do know." She offered a weak smile, unable to reconcile herself to this cold way of bringing a new life into the world. Yet rationally she knew it was the only way she could look at it.

Sensing her patient's confusion, Kathleen Evinrud said, "I've treated other patients with this problem."

Candace surfaced, blinking. "You have?"

"They've all dealt with it in various ways."

"Did any of them decide to have a baby?"

"All of them. But two couldn't conceive, and therefore they adopted."

The words hit her like a dash of cold water. Candace hadn't even considered the possibility that she might not be able to get pregnant. Swallowing, she asked, "Were they married?"

The doctor nodded. "Yes, they all were."

Rising from the chair, Candace walked to the window, rubbing her bare elbows. "So my situation doesn't even apply," she said with a trace of bitterness.

"No, but there is one woman who was forced to make a hard choice. She'd had her family, you see. When her condition was discovered, her son and daughter were already halfway through high school. But in the meantime she'd been divorced and remarried, and her new husband really wanted a child of his own. They'd wrestled the idea around for several years, but then she found she was going to have to have her cervix removed. They decided to go ahead and have another baby."

Candace's palms were wet. She glanced down at them, rubbing them together. "And everything went well?"

"The best. They're very happy now, and Scott's a year old."

"This woman—she had the surgery?"

"Right after Scott was born."

"No problems."

"No problems," Dr. Evinrud assured her.

Outside the window a young couple were sitting on a park bench, heads together, tossing crumbs of bread to a swirling pack of finches. Candace could barely see them.

She felt short of breath and scared, as if she were being forced into a monumental decision right this instant.

"If I were married...no matter how unhappy that marriage might be...I would probably try to get pregnant," Candace admitted. "But I can't go back to Jeff now. I won't. It's impossible. And I'm sorry, any artificial way is just too cold for me."

"That's understandable."

"So I guess what I'm saying is that I won't be having my own child." She tried to keep her tone light, but it came out filled with despair.

"You have some time, Candace. You may meet another man and start a relationship. The future's never what we expect it to be."

Candace's spurt of laughter was so full of pain that she cut herself off, afraid of disintegrating into tears. "Another man," she repeated hollowly. "I wouldn't know what to do with another man if he walked into my life this very moment."

"What you could use is a friend, Candace. Here—" she scratched out a note, ripped it off the pad and extended it in Candace's direction "—this is the phone number of Susan Woodwin, the woman I was just telling you about. I've already called her and explained your situation. I thought you might like to get in touch with her."

Candace accepted the note. She couldn't imagine discussing her problem with a total stranger. On the other hand, Susan Woodwin was more likely to understand than anyone else she knew. "Thank you. I might."

"Was there anything else you would like to ask? Something you would like clarified?"

"How often—how often should I come see you?"

"I'd say once a month is fine, and if there's no change for a while we can lengthen that."

"But in the end I'll have to have surgery."

Dr. Evinrud didn't raise false hopes. "Yes."

"Okay." Candace offered her a watery smile.

Walking her to the door, Dr. Evinrud said, "Call in tomorrow and make an appointment."

"I will."

"What are you doing these days to keep busy?"

It was a friendly question, meant more as small talk than as a serious inquiry about her mental health. But for some reason Candace thought about the quality of her life and was depressed. Work was all she had, and it wasn't a very rewarding job. Maybe she should have gone after that law career. Yet could she really be a lawyer?

A lawyer like Jeff. A lawyer like Connor Holt.

She shook herself. "I'm filling in at my father's law firm. It's been really busy."

"Good."

Candace walked through the door into the early-evening air. Heat radiated up from the tarmac in waves, shimmering in front of her eyes. She thought about the way she'd treated Connor and felt embarrassed. It wasn't his fault he was a lawyer. Most women would consider his choice of profession laudable, for crying out loud. He had a right to be angry with her.

Sliding into the Jaguar, Candace wiped the sweat from her brow and considered the weeks ahead. Connor would be joining her father's firm, and she would be working with him.

She grimaced. She was going to have to start making amends in a big hurry.

The Forsythe Building rose like a splendid gray steeple from the banks of the Willamette River. Though it was narrower at the top, its base covered nearly a city block, and as Candace pushed through the revolving doors, smiling at Harry Pendergrass, the security guard, she wondered why she always felt guilty about her family's wealth. It ran on both sides. Her mother's family had been notorious for making money hand over fist, and when she'd married Joshua Forsythe the blending of their two families had received nods of approval from everyone. Financially, they'd been one of the soundest couples around, but emotionally—that had been a whole other story.

Candace's mother had been awed by her dynamic husband, or so Candace had learned from the few tidbits of knowledge she'd gleaned about Elizabeth Forsythe. Elizabeth had died in an automobile accident when Candace had been two, and Candace's memories of her were hazy and more fantasy than reality. Elizabeth had loved her husband, and Joshua, though more reserved in his feelings, had apparently loved her, too. Certainly there had been no other woman in his life since.

But the driving force of the Forsythes was making money, and Elizabeth's death, though devastating to him, hadn't altered Joshua's thrust for success and power. If anything, it had honed it. He hadn't had time to deal with a bewildered daughter. He hadn't known how.

Now, as the elevator bore Candace skyward with a whispered whoosh and a soft purr of machinery, she wondered where she fit in her powerful family. She was it. The end of the line. And she wasn't even going to have a child on whom to bestow the fabulous Forsythe heritage and wealth.

Which didn't matter one bit. All she wanted was a baby. For her. No one else.

Gloomily Candace watched the numbered lights flicker until, at the thirty-second floor, a bell softly dinged, the elevator slowed and the doors silently parted.

A male voice greeted her. "Hello, Candace."

For a moment she thought it was Con. Somehow she'd avoided him for nearly a week, but now her heart pounded erratically and she glanced up with a start. But it was Dan Morrison. The smile on his face was both friendly and hopeful.

"Hi, Dan," she said, disappointed. "How's the Tempe case going?" She edged toward the inner office door, waving to Terri, whom she could see through the glass wall, seated at the reception hub.

"So far there's no settlement in sight. We go to court tomorrow."

"Think you'll win?"

"We'd better. Bart Tempe's a mean-tempered bastard. If his son's company goes down the tubes, he'll blame Forsythe and Company rather than admit sonny's a financial moron."

Candace thought of Bart Tempe's son, Lance, who might be better off if his father didn't bail him out of every dismal business venture he jumped into. "I think Bart Tempe knows the facts."

She pushed through the doors and met Terri at the desk, hoping to end her conversation with Dan. "Is Marion in yet?" she asked, slightly disconcerted to find Dan right behind her.

"Not yet. But if you're looking for work, I've got all kinds of letters to type, and Pamela called in sick today. Can you believe it?"

"Yes. She looked terrible yesterday. What kind of letters?"

"These." Terri shoved a stack of folders her way. "I swear, every partner and junior partner has something that has to go out today. Think you can help?" she asked hopefully.

Candace was already moving toward Pamela's desk. "I'll give it my best shot."

"Looks like you need your own secretary," Dan said as Candace pulled out the office chair, seating herself in front of Pamela's computer screen.

"I can manage." Candace smiled to take the edge out of her voice. She wished Dan would just leave her to work in the privacy of Pamela's partitioned office space.

"Is there some way I can help?" Dan asked.

From the corner of her eye she saw Terri's eyebrows raise. "No, really, I'm fine." To her consternation she felt a blush begin climbing up her neck. It was this kind of extra attention she received as the boss's daughter that she detested the most.

"Why don't I check back later? You might need a little R and R. Maybe even a real live date."

"Oh, Dan, thanks, but I'm not . . . ready for that."

"Still a wife, huh?" Dan said thoughtfully. "Even though you and Jeff are separated."

"Well, yes." Her blush grew. This was the time to bring up her divorce, but the words stuck in her throat. Somehow she just couldn't.

"If you change your mind . . ." He left the sentence unfinished, gave her a smile and pushed his way out the front doors, giving Terri a wink on his way out.

"Yuk." Terri's voice floated over Candace's head.

Candace smothered a smile. "Oh, Dan's not so bad."

"Give me a break."

"At least he's friendly."

Inserting a piece of paper in her electronic typewriter, Terri said matter-of-factly, "When it suits his purposes."

Secretly Candace agreed, but rather than voice her opinion about the pompous attorney she slipped the word-processing diskette into the computer and flipped the switch.

One of these days you're going to have to figure out what you want to do with the rest of your life. You didn't get a degree in business just to become a pencil pusher.

Candace stared at the flashing cursor on the screen. *I'd like to be a wife and mother.*

It was at that moment that Connor Holt breezed in. Glancing up, Candace froze.

"Hi, Terri," he said, his attention diverted by the receptionist. "Any messages for me?"

"Yeah, several." Terri pulled out a pile of little pink slips and handed them to him. Connor thumbed through them, his expression thoughtful, his dark hair tumbling over his forehead, one hand automatically loosening his tie. In a dark suit showing a snowy white shirt collar and cuffs, a briefcase tucked under his arm, his blue eyes narrowed in concentration, he looked both urbane and tough, as if he somehow managed to fit into the role of a professional but it didn't quite suit him. To Candace he seemed confined, as if he were just waiting for the chance to rip off his suit coat and tie and toss them aside.

"God," he muttered. "Linda."

"Linda?" Terri asked, glancing up at him. Candace, too, pricked up her ears.

"Yes, Linda." With a grimace he began slowly walking toward his office, still leafing through the notes. Candace pulled her gaze back to the computer and began typing a letter. Out of the corner of her eye she saw Connor turn in her direction.

"You," he said softly, "are not Pamela."

Candace kept her eyes trained on her monitor. "Pamela's sick today."

"And you're taking over?"

"Filling in."

His tone wasn't exactly disparaging, but it wasn't friendly, either. *Your own fault,* Candace told herself.

"Tom Brinkwood's called three times," Terri informed Con. "I didn't put that on his message."

He swung around, giving her his complete attention. "When was the last time?"

"About fifteen minutes ago."

He inhaled through his teeth and muttered, "I'll call him right back. Thanks, Terri."

"Any time," she answered, throwing Candace a look that said, "Now there's a man worth thinking about."

He walked past Candace without another word.

For several moments Candace stared at the amber-colored words on her screen. She had a mountain of work beside her, but all she could see were a pair of mocking blue eyes set in a lean, sensual face. A pair of blue eyes that would obviously be just as happy if she evaporated off the face of the earth.

"Damn it all," she said under her breath, and Terri's head swung around in shock.

Candace Forsythe McCall never swore.

Chapter Four

Con pushed open the oak door to his office, crossed the gray-and-black carpet to his desk, picked up the phone in midstride and pulled up his chair with one hand while dialing with the other.

"Tom Brinkwood, please. Connor Holt returning his call."

He counted the seconds as the woman at the other end transferred his call. The Brinkwood custody case wasn't going well. Brinkwood was a foreman at a plant that built microchips; Brinkwood's ex-wife, Michelle, was the daughter of one of the principal owners of the company. The custody battle between them over their seven-year-old daughter Janice had become an all-out war, with Tom Brinkwood and his ex-father-in-law, Edward Faulkner, the main players. Michelle didn't seem to give a hoot about the outcome or, more importantly, her own daughter's welfare, but Faulkner was making damned sure his ex-son-in-law didn't gain custody of Janice. It wouldn't do for a mere foreman to have control of the only Faulkner grandchild.

Connor sighed and tugged on the hair at the back of his neck. Brinkwood's tenacity amazed him. The way the man stayed working for the company though he knew his ex-father-in-law was searching for a way to replace him was beyond belief. But then, Faulkner was having trouble firing Brinkwood. Tom was a model employee, and the other men working in the plant were extremely loyal. If Faulkner got rid of Brinkwood, he'd have innumerable labor problems—and he'd come off like Simon Legree. So instead the battle was being fought over poor Janice.

This was the case Joshua Forsythe had dangled in front of Con's nose. This was the case Con intended to win—for Janice, and no one else.

"Mr. Holt?" Tom Brinkwood sounded anxious.

"Right here. Call me Connor. I hate standing on ceremony. I just learned you've phoned a few times. What's wrong?"

"Michelle's taken Janice out of the state. They're gone."

Con was instantly incensed. For a split second he thought about Linda's calls—the ones he wasn't going to return. Michelle's actions were being orchestrated by her daddy, just as Linda's actions had been orchestrated by hers. "She can't do that. She granted you temporary custody."

"Well, she did it. And I can't leave work to go after her."

"Are you certain she took Janice out of the state? That's against the law, Tom."

There was a telling pause. "I don't have proof, if that's what you mean. But yesterday Michelle and I had a fight, and she as much as told me she wasn't bringing Janice back. I told her she had to, and she just tossed her head and didn't say anything more." Tom heaved a sigh. "She's got a new boyfriend who lives somewhere around San Francisco. I've got a feeling that's where she's taken Janice.''

Connor boiled inside. This was Ed Faulkner's work. He could smell it. ''Never mind, Tom. I'll handle this. Don't worry. Just sit tight and wait for my call.''

He slammed down the phone, flipping through his Rolodex for the direct number to Faulkner's office. He wanted to nail Faulkner to the wall, and he recognized the importance of Michelle's actions. She couldn't ignore the law this way. Janice should be with Tom now, and Con meant Mr. Edward Faulkner to know it.

''I'm sorry,'' Faulkner's secretary said after the line had rung several times with no answer. ''Mr. Faulkner's not taking any calls. Please leave your name and number and he'll get back to you as soon as possible.''

''Tell him Connor Holt called.'' Con's voice was cold and direct. ''From Forsythe and Company. Oh, and tell him I know where Janice is, and if he doesn't want the FBI on his neck he'll return my call soon.''

''Uh, yes, Mr. Holt,'' the woman answered dubiously.

Connor replaced the receiver with deceptive softness. He felt an anger way out of proportion to the circumstances. What it came down to, he supposed, was that he couldn't stand seeing a guy like Faulkner slowly crushing a good man like Tom Brinkwood.

With a harsh laugh, Con assessed his own rampant feelings of injustice. Yes, he was just what Forsythe and Company needed: a man interested in honor above expediency. But it bothered him like hell to know Joshua Forsythe could gauge him so accurately, use him to his own advantage. ''The old fox really does have your number,'' he muttered to himself.

Leaning back in his chair, Con closed his eyes. Michelle Faulkner would be only too glad to give up custody of her daughter; Con had spoken to her twice and had received the same impression both times. But her father was setting a precedent. He hadn't approved of the marriage of his beautiful, empty-headed daughter to the hardworking, responsible foreman; he'd fought loudly and furiously against it. But Michelle, in what must have been the only moment of individual thought she'd had in her entire life, had ultimately opposed her father, eloping with the man she loved. Then Faulkner had cut off her funds and renounced her, and Michelle had eventually come crawling back to Daddy, Janice in tow.

Tom Brinkwood was the fly in the ointment. He hadn't wanted to give up his wife, and he refused to give up his daughter. The war had waxed and waned for two years, and now it had come to a head. The divorce was final, the custody suit the last issue to be resolved.

And Connor wanted to make certain little Janice was taken care of.

Right against might, Joshua Forsythe had said. Well, maybe it was so. Forsythe and Company was really taking a leap into the unknown by backing the underdog.

The pile of pink slips beckoned him and Con sifted through them. Linda's message was a surprise. *Call at your convenience.* What did that mean? She'd never been one to think of his feelings. What she wanted, she demanded, and woe betide anyone who didn't dance to her tune.

And that's what ended your marriage, pal, Con thought ruefully.

He made a few more phone calls, sorted through some work, then stepped out of the office in search of the coffee machine. He'd hit the ground running as soon as he'd signed on with Joshua Forsythe's company, and he'd found there was no time for the small, mundane pleasures of the office—like coffee breaks.

Stepping into the small kitchen area, he found Candace McCall dunking a tea bag in a cup of hot water, the concentration she gave this task suggesting she was miles away.

"Twice in one day," Con remarked lightly, lifting the glass pitcher from the coffee maker and pouring himself a cup. "I must mark this on my calendar."

She jumped, the hot water sloshing over the hand that held the cup. "Oooh," she said, sharply sucking air between her teeth.

Con swept the hot cup from her hand before she could drop it. "Are you all right? Sorry. I didn't mean to startle you. Are you burned?"

She shook the hot water from her hand. "No, no. I'm fine."

"Let me take a look."

"No."

She was so definite that he stopped in the act of putting down the two cups and reaching for her hand. She backed up frantically, her eyes wide. Con set his jaw. She didn't want him bothering her; that was plain. Still, that underlying vulnerability of hers made it impossible to hate her for being the snob she was. "Please let me take a look, Candace," he said soberly. "I feel responsible."

"I'm fine. Really. See?" She held out her hand and turned it over for his inspection. He could see her soft skin turning an angry red color.

Refusing to be put off, he ignored her protests and advanced on her, practically crowding her into a corner before he could clasp the burned hand. Her wrist couldn't have been stiffer if she'd been stricken with rigor mortis.

Turning it back and forth, he looked at the pinkened flesh, then glanced up into her green eyes. "I am sorry," he said.

For Candace, time seemed suspended as she met his direct gaze. She felt breathless and strange. She wanted to snatch her hand away, but she knew she'd already overreacted. "It's—it's okay."

"You should probably run this under cold water." He lifted her hand, examining it more closely, his face so close she could feel the heat of his skin against hers.

Candace's heart began to pound in the most ridiculous way. There was nothing intimate about his perusal. He was as clinical as any doctor. Yet her foolish defenses were running on high, her nerves working overtime, warning lights flashing through her mind.

"Come here," he said, gently pulling her toward the sink. Turning on the taps, he waited until the water was ice-cold, then thrust her hand beneath a soft trickle. "Is that better?" he asked.

In truth, she felt very little pain. She was too unraveled by his touch. "Much better," she managed to say. "You've missed your calling. You should have been a doctor."

"Is that another way to tell me your opinion of lawyers?" Candace shrank back instinctively, but Con held on to her arm. The water cascaded over her skin in a sheet. "Besides, we've already got one doctor in the family," he added conversationally, as if he weren't holding her prisoner. "My brother-in-law. Dr. Tanner Baines."

"Tanner Baines?" Candace asked, surprised.

Con shot her a look she couldn't decipher. "You know him?"

"Well, his family lived on the lake, didn't they? Maybe they still do. His father was a—"

"Dr. Gerrard Baines is not one of my favorite people," he said, cutting her off. Releasing her arm, he returned to his forgotten cup of coffee.

Candace regarded him curiously. Con had always seemed so open, yet here was a part of his life he obviously didn't want to discuss. Seeing that there were pieces of his past he didn't like to recall endeared him to her in a way nothing else could have.

"I don't remember Tanner," Candace said softly. "We didn't go to school together. He was a few years older."

"He graduated the same year I did." Con's mouth twisted ironically. "Although we went to different schools, of course."

"Why do you say of course?"

He concentrated on his coffee, his blue eyes narrowed, his mouth set. Candace wondered what he was thinking about, but waited silently, sensing she'd inadvertently touched on some sensitive issue.

"Tanner's administrative head of surgery at Briar Park Hospital now," said Con after a moment.

Vaguely Candace remembered hearing about the illustrious Dr. Tanner Baines. She'd been too young to care, but now she recalled some of the gossip that had surrounded him. An automobile accident had crushed his hand, ending a brilliant career as a surgeon. His wife had died about a year later. He'd returned from Boston to put his life back together and had apparently married Con's sister. Con's sister. Candace suddenly wanted to meet her. "So they live around here, then? Tanner and your sister?"

"Maggie." He nodded. "They live on the lake in the Baines house."

Candace shut off the water and dried her arm. "Small world," she remarked. "I live on the lake, too."

"With your husband."

It wasn't a question, really. But she could hear the doubts behind it. And no wonder. Her hands—which he had to have noticed—were bare of rings. She never spoke of Jeff.

It was as if she were single, which indeed she was. "Hasn't anyone at the company told you about my relationship with my husband?"

"I haven't asked."

"I'm surprised you haven't heard anyway. It was hot gossip a few months ago."

She hadn't meant it to happen, but her voice suddenly deepened with humiliation. Glancing away, she wished she'd never gotten into this conversation.

"You're not living with him, then," Connor guessed.

"No."

Before the conversation could enter more dangerous waters, the door opened and several of the other young lawyers stepped inside the coffee room, their voices raised in animated conversation about a particular case. Candace used the moment to escape to the hallway, but was detained when a strong hand encircled her upper arm. Catching her breath, she saw her image and Con's reflected in the mirrored hallway; he so dark, and she so fair.

"Wait a minute," he said. "I want to make sure you're okay."

"I'm fine, really." She tried to pull away, but his hand slid to her wrist. "You're making a big deal over nothing."

"Look, I don't want to get sued, all right?"

This time she smiled as he examined her palm. "You lawyers are all so paranoid."

"Lady, your father's one of the most powerful and prestigious attorneys in this city. My paranoia has just cause."

Several people walked past them, staring curiously, but Con just edged closer to her, so close that she could smell the deep, musky scent of his cologne. She noticed the lines of white around his eyes where he'd squinted against the sun, and the thick furl of his black lashes. "I promise not to sue," she said, a trifle breathlessly.

"Can I get that in writing?" he asked teasingly.

He still had hold of her hand, and Candace gently pulled it back. "You won't need to." She ducked past him and headed down the hallway to Pamela's desk.

"That's what they all say," Con called after her, and the deep, rich chuckle that followed made a shiver chase down her spine.

Two hours later, in the midst of legal briefs and notes of letters to be typed, she came across one of Con's missives. It was to Pamela, who he'd assumed would be typing his letters.

Pamela, could you get these back to me ASAP? I know you hear that all the time, but I fouled up on when these were due, and if you can't get them done today I'll be forced to type them myself (which alone could ruin the reputation of Forsythe and Company). Thanks. C.H.

The corners of her mouth twitching, Candace quickly prepared the two letters he'd scratched out on his notepad. She liked it that he was self-effacing. No other member of the firm was—and that included her father.

As soon as she was finished, she walked down the hall to his office and raised her hand to knock. Then she thought back to his last remark and, biting her lip on a smile, headed back to the computer. She tapped out another letter, ran it off on the printer and signed it with a flourish totally unlike her own precise handwriting. Carrying the letters to Con's office, she rapped lightly on the door. At his deep "It's open," she stepped inside and placed the letters on a pile on the side of his desk.

"Thanks," he said without looking up.

"My pleasure."

His head jerked up. "Oh—Candace. I was still expecting Pamela. I forgot it was you."

"I have that effect on people sometimes," she said lightly.

"I'd bet not often." His eyes were assessing. "Am I mistaken, or have we declared a truce?"

"A truce about what?"

"I don't know. About my being a lawyer, I guess. Or whatever else it was that made you so angry with me."

Candace nodded, unable to think of anything to say. With a smile she left his office, closing the door softly behind her.

The rest of the afternoon flew by in a haze of work. Candace didn't even realize she'd missed lunch until Terri unceremoniously dropped a turkey sandwich wrapped in plastic on her desk.

"Sustenance," Terri said succinctly as she pulled out her own swivel chair.

"Thanks. Does this service generally extend to Pamela, too?" Candace asked, unwrapping the sandwich.

Terri gave an undignified snort. "Yeah. Right."

Candace grinned. Though the taciturn Pamela had never rubbed her the wrong way, she certainly hadn't endeared herself to the rest of the office staff. "Careful, Terri. I'm going to think I'm getting preferential treatment."

The young blond woman bit into her own sandwich, rereading the letter she'd just pulled from her printer. "You are getting preferential treatment. Anyone who cracks a smile gets preferential treatment."

Candace laughed. "Oh, Pamela's not that bad."

To this there was no reply whatsoever.

Just before five, the phone on Candace's desk buzzed. She didn't bother to pick it up; all Pamela's calls were answered by Terri.

"It's for you," Terri said, pointing to Candace's phone.

Immediately Candace's stomach plummeted. Who would call her at work but Dr. Evinrud? Had something else turned up? "Hello," she answered unsteadily. "This is Candace McCall."

"Candace, could you come to my office?" Con snapped. "I'd like to discuss something with you."

"With me?" she asked, taken aback.

"Yes." His voice was as cold as a northern gale.

Candace straightened in her chair, her heart beating irregularly. What had she done? "Okay," she said slowly. "I'll be right there."

She took a few moments to straighten the papers on her desk, thinking fast. Her mind flew to the letter she'd written earlier, the one she'd deposited on his desk, the one she'd written in a blithe moment of silliness. Grimacing, she realized he'd taken it the wrong way.

Well, then, I'll just explain, she told herself as she knocked on his door.

His stern "Come in" was enough to make her mouth go dry, and she took a deep breath as she walked into his paneled office.

"Is it about the letter?" she said anxiously before he could speak. "I'm sorry, I was just being silly. We were joking and I just wrote it for fun."

Con didn't reply, the scowl on his face answer enough as his eyes scanned the missive in his hands. It was indeed the letter she'd written, and Candace felt impatient that he couldn't realize when she was teasing.

It didn't help that she felt like a schoolgirl, standing in the center of the room, waiting, not knowing where to put her hands. They hung loose at her sides, and she mentally kicked herself again for taking a chance, no matter how small.

"You mean this letter," he said, extending it toward her.

"It was just a joke." Exasperated, she snatched it from his fingers. Her father's name was scrawled at the bottom in a poor attempt at forgery. On Forsythe and Company stationery, the letter did look official and intimidating, its contents enough to scare even the most stalwart attorney, she supposed.

Con folded his arms across his chest. "Since when is it funny to tell an attorney you're suing him for—let me get this straight—malicious bodily harm?"

"Well, whatever." She was embarrassed. "I was kidding."

He came around his desk, moving closer, reaching for her hands. She was surprised, and the letter slipped from her fingers. "If I'm getting sued for this, I think I need a doctor's opinion."

Candace peered into his blue eyes. With a rush of relief, she realized he was putting her on. Then she was mad at herself. Of course he would know it was a joke. She was so gun-shy these days she could hardly think straight. "That might be a good idea." She sighed hugely, looking down at her hands. "I was thinking a settlement might be in order."

"Really."

"Really. I told my father and he suggested I get a good lawyer."

"Anyone in particular?" Con turned her palms skyward, his fingers wrapped lightly around her wrists. But his gaze was on her face, and there was humor in the slight twist of his lips.

"Well, it couldn't be you, now could it?"

"No, I guess not."

Candace smiled. There was an intimacy in the room that made her warm despite the air-conditioning. She was glad she'd taken a step to show him that she wasn't really like his first impression of her. Yet now that she had, she hardly knew what to say.

"Candace, I'd like to be friends," Con announced, throwing her off guard. "We're going to be working together, and I'd just as soon have you on my side, so to speak."

"The Forsythe and Company motto," she said with attempted lightness. "Unite and Conquer."

"Now there you go again. As soon as I make any overture of friendship, you get all defensive. Why is that?"

His directness threw her. "I don't know," she admitted.

"Candace, when we first met I wouldn't have asked you out if I'd known you were married. Are you holding that against me?"

Startled, her eyes wide, she said, "Oh, no."

"Then what?" Con asked frustratedly. "What is it? Why don't you just tell me what you don't like about me and get it out on the table."

"That's not it! I—like you."

"You just don't like lawyers."

"My father's a lawyer."

His blue eyes stared into hers. "You know what I think? I think you've got a lot of problems. And to be perfectly honest, I don't think any of them have to do with me, or your father, or this law office. It sounds to me like you've got problems closer to home. Maybe you and your husband should have a good old heart-to-heart and clear the air."

Candace swept in an angry breath. "You sure are free with your advice," she said bitterly without thinking. "Especially about things you know nothing about."

"I know when somebody's hurting." Con was sober. "He hurt you and you can't forgive him. Maybe you ought to, to make this marriage work."

Oh, the problem with lies. They fed on one another. She'd created an avalanche out of a tiny snowball. "My husband is not the issue. It has nothing to do with him, it's just I can't—"

"You can't what?" Con prodded when she clenched her teeth together.

She struggled to go on but was defeated by the enormity of her own unhappiness. She should tell him the truth about Jeff right now, but she couldn't bring herself to talk about him. She smiled wanly. "I'm just a neurotic female. Don't even try to understand me. I don't understand myself."

He laughed, and Candace was amazed that he could be amused by her even while she was deliberately sidestepping him. It was a facet of her personality that had driven Jeff crazy.

"This husband of yours is an idiot, Candace," he said with surprising tenderness.

Something inside her broke wide open, a wound that had never fully healed. "Jeff McCall is anything but an idiot," she answered swiftly, bitterly.

He was taken aback by her vehemence. "Jeff McCall?" Con frowned.

He would remember who Jeff was eventually, Candace thought wearily. You couldn't be an attorney in this town without having heard Jeff's name at one time or another.

"Well, he's an idiot to give up on you," said Con. "I wouldn't have."

The phone on Con's desk purred, preventing Candace from an answer. Her face was flushing furiously, and she was glad his attention was diverted. He let her go to snatch up the receiver.

"Connor Holt," he answered, a bit impatiently. Then his gaze darted to the clock on the wall, and with a sudden change of tone he added, "I've been waiting for your call, Mr. Faulkner. We have an important matter to discuss."

Taking this as her cue to leave, Candace moved toward the door. She felt Con's gaze lingering on her and couldn't help glancing back. There was a purposefulness to the set of his mouth that hadn't been there before. Was it owing to this call, or did it have something to do with her?

"My client has temporary custody," Con said in a chilling voice. "If Michelle doesn't produce Janice by eight o'clock tonight, you can expect police involvement. I'll send them to your door if necessary. And I might just tip off the evening news team, too."

Candace's gaze flew to his face. Jeff, even in the turmoil of his toughest cases, had never been so openly challenging. He tended to pour oil on troubled waters until a settlement could be reached. He never antagonized anyone if he could help it.

But Con was heading for all-out war, his expression dark and dangerous. Glad she wasn't on the receiving end, Candace let herself out into the hallway and walked back to her desk, thinking hard. She was going to have to respect Con's business style. Still, there were sides to Connor Holt she knew nothing about.

At five o'clock Candace began closing up Pam's desk, one hand searching through her purse for her keys. Her fingers crackled against a piece of loose paper. Drawing it out, she realized it was the name and address of Susan Woodwin, Dr. Evinrud's patient, the woman who had been in a similar position to Candace's, the woman who'd had the baby anyway.

Candace looked at the phone, her pulse skipping. Before she could lose her nerve, she punched out the number.

"Hello?" a harried female voice answered.

"Hello. This is Candace McCall. I'm a patient of Dr. Evinrud's. She said she would call and—"

"Sure, you're the one she told me about." The voice grew kinder. "You want to talk?"

It was such a simple response, so straightforward and full of understanding, that Candace was overwhelmed. "Yes," she answered in a strained voice.

"Well, why don't you come on over here? You've got the address?" At Candace's affirmative answer, she said, "My husband and two daughters are at a movie, and I'm just here with Scott."

"Scott." Emotion flooded through Candace.

"My baby boy." Susan Woodwin's laughter rang with pride. "Come on over and you can meet him."

"I'll be there," Candace said unevenly. She swept up her purse and headed for the door, realizing only after the elevator had started its descent that she hadn't remembered to turn off her computer.

Con wrote furiously on his notepad, trying to remember his every thought. His mind churned. He wanted Ed Faulkner. He wanted to hang the bastard. He wanted it so bad he could taste it.

Faulkner was playing God, and Con wanted to make him pay. He couldn't stand powerful men who moved people around as if they were pieces on a chessboard. He'd had firsthand experience with those kind of men—and one of them had nearly ruined his sister's life.

His jaw taut, he grabbed his coat and headed for the door. Edward Faulkner was in for a fight.

Con nearly ran into Dan Morrison on his way out, and the other attorney made a big show of stepping out of his way.

"I was just coming to see you," Morrison said.

"Oh?" Con answered without real interest.

"How's the Faulkner case going?"

"It's going."

"Don't want to talk about it, huh? Well, that's all right. Just thought you might like some advice."

"About what?" Con was halfway down the hall.

Morrison pursed his lips, taking his time. "About Edward Faulkner."

Con stopped short. There was nothing he hated worse than this kind of game-playing. It wasted so much time and accomplished so little. But he'd be a fool not to hear what Morrison had to say. "You know Mr. Ed then," Con said with a yawn. "Okay, I'll bite. What's the big news?"

Morrison looked nonplussed by Con's attitude. "Faulkner's got money behind him. A lot of money. Your client's no match."

"Money's not the issue," Con pointed out, a bit testily. "At least it's not for me. And it's not for Joshua Forsythe, either."

"Faulkner's also got Jeff McCall—Candace's Jeff McCall—representing him. How do you like that?"

Con's gut tightened in a peculiar way. "Jeff McCall, the opposing counsel, is *Candace's* husband?"

"One and the same. I imagine Joshua isn't going to like that too much. He always liked Jeff."

Con was blown away. Jeff McCall was *Candace's husband*. The irony was too much. "I knew McCall was Faulkner's attorney, but I hadn't made the connection. So where do you get your information?"

Dan ran his fingers through his hair and emitted a soundless laugh. "I just ran into Jeff at the Front Street Café & Bar. He told me himself."

Con said nothing. He felt as though someone had kicked him in the stomach.

"He was with Renée Southfield."

Anger moved through him, quicksilver-hot. The affair was apparently still going on, and McCall had no qualms about it. "I didn't know Candace's husband was a lawyer," Con said grimly, remembering how Candace had skirted the question when he'd asked her on the bridge outside her father's home.

"There's something else you don't know, too, I bet. I didn't until just a few minutes ago."

Con was still digesting the fact that not only was Candace's husband a lawyer, he was going to be facing him in court, when Morrison added, "McCall isn't Candace's husband any longer. The separation's over and the divorce has begun. Jeff's already moved in with Renée."

Con's head snapped up. *"What?"*

"I knew you didn't know." Morrison smirked. "Jeff got the divorce papers the day of Forsythe's party. I imagine Candace received hers at the same time. Nice of her to tell us, wasn't it? Though I suppose it doesn't matter. She's free now." He took a breath and smoothed his tie. "Just thought I'd let you know I'm swinging my campaign into high gear where she's concerned. And may the best man win," he added mockingly, thrusting out his hand and shaking Con's.

Con stared after him as he pushed his way out the glass doors. But it wasn't Morrison's face that swam before his vision. It was Candace's. Her beautiful, emerald-eyed, lying face. He boiled inside at the incredible gall of the woman. She'd deliberately withheld the news of her divorce from him.

Not good enough.

Once more he'd been tricked into believing he was an equal; once more a wealthy woman had put him in his place. Hard. For no reason at all.

Well, Candace McCall was going to learn a lesson about who was good enough and who wasn't.

He'd had all he was going to take.

The Jaguar hummed smoothly as Candace scanned the road signs for the turnoff to the Woodwin home. Thank God for air-conditioning, she thought. She didn't know how she would have made it otherwise.

By the time she found the narrow gravel drive that curved through a row of fir trees, she felt exhausted. Parking the car in front of the one-story home, she unlatched the door and swung a leg outside. Even in the shade of the trees the heat was unbearable. It must be over ninety, she thought wearily, shrugging out of her taupe linen jacket. Her clothes felt melted to her skin, and her throat was dry and dusty. If she'd been smart she would have gone straight home and dived into the lake.

A dog set up a wild barking from around the side of the house. Hearing it tear madly her way, Candace braced herself for the attack. But as soon as its head appeared, a chain stopped it short. Instead of the ferocious monster she'd imagined, a half-grown, wriggling black Lab howled and whined at her.

"Well, hello there, boy," she said. The dog's tongue lolled out of the side of its mouth, and in his exuberance he jumped up, his claws just reaching the Jaguar's front fender.

"Harold! Get down!"

Candace swung around. A tiny woman clad in an oversize T-shirt and faded jeans, her hair tied back in a ponytail, was clapping her hands fiercely as she shot like a bullet through the front door. She charged up to the dog, dragging him back.

"You must be Candace," she panted. "Sorry about the car. Harold's a monster." Then: "God, it's a Jag!"

"It's all right," Candace assured her. "Really." She checked the black paint, saw a few tiny nicks and felt a perverse sense of satisfaction. Jeff would have apoplexy if he could see it.

"I'm Susan Woodwin," the woman greeted her, dragging Harold toward the back of the house. "Could you move your car back a few feet? My God, look at that. I'm sorry. I'll pay for it. Bad dog," she said, glaring at Harold.

Harold looked totally unrepentant, and Candace had to laugh. "Please, don't worry about the car," she said, climbing into the driver's seat. "I'm getting rid of it anyway."

She backed up, hearing her own words echoing through her mind. Yes, she would get rid of the car. It was part of her old life.

At the front door, Susan's pretty face was anxious. "Just let me know how much it'll cost to fix it. I mean it."

Candace didn't know how to tell this young woman that she couldn't care less. Candace could tell from the way Susan was examining her sleek suit and taupe calfskin pumps that it was a matter of pride.

"You'll have to excuse me," Susan went on, wiping her hands self-consciously on her jeans. "The place is a mess, but I guess that's what happens when you have children."

Candace stepped inside a front room filled with toys. Susan snapped off the television and led Candace into a small kitchen. A clattering air conditioner was going full blast, creating an enormous racket, but the room was cool.

"I like your house," Candace said, and meant it. The Woodwins' home was everything hers was not: cluttered, haphazard and full of signs of family.

Susan was rinsing her hands under the faucet. "Yeah, it's a real palace," she laughed, but there was no envy in her tone. "Have a chair," she said. "Would you like something to drink?"

"I'd love a glass of water."

Candace sat down at the oval kitchen table. Grocery coupons were spread across its top.

"Here you are," Susan said, setting a glass of ice water in front of Candace and sweeping aside the coupons. "Let me go get Scotty."

Taking a long swallow, Candace leaned back in the chair, tiredness rushing over her again. She wasn't certain she had the mental stamina for her talk with Susan. What had possessed her to come today? She'd be better off relaxing at home in the luxury of her tree-shaded back deck.

A moment later Susan returned, a sleeping baby in her arms. He was dressed in a pale blue jumpsuit, chubby limbs sticking out in all directions.

"Would you like to hold him while we talk?" Susan asked.

Candace's heart lurched. Yes, she wanted to hold him, but her arms felt weighted down. She was almost afraid. "Sure," she said in an odd tone.

The baby was transferred to her arms. His lips moved in his sleep, and his fist connected with the material of her sleeveless blouse, the tiny fingers digging in. Candace couldn't help cuddling him close.

"You're thinking about having a baby, then."

Candace looked down at Scott's sweet face, his pudgy nose, his clean little brow. "Not really. Dr. Evinrud told me I would have to have a baby right away if I wanted one, but it's not, er...convenient."

"It wasn't convenient for me, either, but I had him anyway."

Glancing up, Candace murmured, "You have a husband; I don't."

Susan tilted her head. "So that's the problem."

"One of them. The biggest one." Candace's smile felt more like a grimace.

"If you were married, would you try to have a baby?"

"Oh, yes." Susan was quiet as Candace swept her fingertips across Scotty's forehead, touching the fine dark hair. "He's beautiful."

"Don't let him fool you. He's a tyrant. My two daughters want to send him back, I'm sure."

"Oh, no." Candace shook her head at the mere suggestion, and Susan's mouth curved into a grin.

"It's not all roses, you know. Last night he had me awake every hour on the hour. I thought I'd die. If I hadn't been nursing I would have kicked Phil out of bed and made him fix a bottle."

Candace leaned down and touched her lips to Scott's forehead. He smelled of baby powder and ointment, and she drank in the odor as if it were a stimulant. Her heart squeezed. *I want a baby,* she thought fiercely. *I want my own.*

"It's nice holding him," she said softly.

Susan didn't answer, but Candace saw understanding in her eyes. A long moment passed in which the only sounds were those of the air conditioner and Scott's even breathing. Then Susan drew a breath and remarked, "Dr. Evinrud said you had some questions."

"Yes, about the surgery," admitted Candace. "I just wanted to talk to someone who's gone through it."

"Well, I had it done shortly after Scotty was born. It wasn't so bad.... But I was glad when it was over and there were no more decisions to make."

"Decisions. I know what that's like," Candace said shakily.

Susan was matter-of-fact. "You have some time, you know. Dr. Evinrud wouldn't steer you wrong. She'll give you time to make your decision."

"But there really is no decision." Candace swallowed. "I'm not going to have a child. I've—I've faced that, so I might as well have the surgery now."

Susan regarded her sympathetically. "I get the feeling you really want a baby."

Candace couldn't answer. She felt the infant stir in her arms and had to stop herself from squeezing him closer.

"I can't speak for you," Susan said slowly, watching Candace closely, "but I know what I'd do in your situation, husband or no. I'd go out and have that baby."

"That's easy to say when it's not you."

Susan inclined her head. "Maybe."

"There are so many ramifications. I couldn't do it," Candace said, almost to herself. "I just couldn't." She bit her lip.

The baby moved in her arms, turning his head, searching through the material of her blouse for a nipple. Looking down at him, Candace felt a jolt of possessiveness so intense it scared her.

"I think he needs Mom," she said shakily, handing him to Susan as she climbed to her feet.

"You're not going?" Susan was on her feet, too. "I'm sorry if I was too blunt."

"No, you said what you felt. I appreciate it. It's just—too hard to think about." Candace headed blindly for the door. Her blouse was damp where the baby had tried to nurse.

"Phil always tells me I'm too opinionated," Susan said. "You came here to talk about the operation and I got on my soapbox. I feel terrible."

"Don't. Really." Candace pulled herself together with an effort. She didn't want this nice woman to worry about whether she'd done the right thing or not. "It's just hard, you know?"

Susan's eyes were serious. She nodded. "I do know. You've got to ask yourself what you want."

"That's the hard part," Candace admitted.

The evening heat hit her full in the face as she walked toward her car.

"I'd like to pay for the scratched paint," Susan called from the porch. "Really. It's a beautiful car."

"It was—" She cut herself off. She'd been about to say it was a gift from her husband, about to apologize once more for having too much money.

But Susan, she realized, had something she would probably never have, and Candace would willingly have traded every penny she owned for a son like Scott.

"Thank you," Candace said to Susan. "I'll keep in touch."

Candace drove aimlessly for miles. Sticky, hot, lost. When she finally surfaced she found herself downtown, a drifter among the cars jockeying for position. She needed someone. Someone to talk to.

The Jaguar was purring softly, patiently, in her usual parking space in the underground garage, before Candace fully realized what she was doing. She was going to see her father. He was the only one she could possibly talk to. A wave of urgency passed over her, drowning her, as she rode up the elevator to the main floor. She stepped into the building foyer on rubbery legs. Harry was long gone. The building was nearly empty.

The elevator to the upper floors seemed to take forever. She leaned against the wall, eyes closed, choking with emotion. Father, she thought. Joshua. Be there. Please. I need you.

The doors whispered open. The outer hallway to Forsythe and Company's offices was deserted. Candace pushed against the glass door, encouraged to find it wasn't locked.

She walked quickly, her footsteps muffled by the pearl-gray carpet, her heart pounding, deafening, threatening to explode. A sob was fighting its way out of her throat.

She ran the last few feet, twisting the handle. The doors to his office were locked.

Candace stood there for several minutes, trying to bring herself under control. But it was as if everything had bubbled to the surface, hot and hurting, impossible to quench. Her limbs quivered. Her mouth trembled. Like a child she threw herself against the oak panels, twisting and twisting the knob.

"Candace?"

It was Con's voice. She whipped around, her back to the doors, regarding him warily.

The look on his face nearly did her in. It was full of disgust and anger and revulsion. Candace stared at him, hollow-eyed, and he said flatly, "You're such a lovely liar. What's the matter? Daddy not there to run to? Don't worry, there's probably a broad set of shoulders out there just waiting for a woman like you. There always is."

His attack was so unprovoked she couldn't speak. He waited, but when she just stood there he gave her a short mocking bow. "Good evening, *Mrs.* McCall," he said, stressing the title. Then he turned and strode angrily down the hall.

Chapter Five

Candace was too shaken to move. She wanted to cry but couldn't. She needed him to put his arms around her and tell her everything was going to be all right. What had she done to deserve this scorn?

His attack had been uncalled-for, and as she thought about it she grew angry. Who was he to say those things to her? With vague thoughts of ripping off her shoe and throwing it at him, she drew herself up stiffly, marched down the hallway, grabbed his elbow and spun him around.

"I don't need you to attack me," she said in a low, tight voice. "If you don't like me, then stay out of my way. But don't confront me again. Especially not here, at my father's offices."

Con's dark eyebrows rose in surprise. She was a tigress, her eyes chips of green ice, her mouth, though it was quivering, a thin blade of fury. "Your wish is my command," he said mockingly.

"You're a bastard."

His eyes narrowed. "Are we reduced to name-calling now?" He made a clucking sound with his tongue. "I thought you had better manners."

To his shock and Candace's mortification, her eyes filled with sudden tears. She swept past him, stumbling in a numb haze toward the outside doors.

Connor swore under his breath. For all his faults, he was not an insensitive man. With a gesture of entreaty she couldn't see, he followed after her, catching her at the elevator. "Okay, forget it. I made a mistake. I was angry and I let my temper get the best of me. It's nothing to me what you do in your personal life."

Candace set her jaw against more tears. She stared straight ahead.

"I'm not going to say I'm sorry again. You asked for it, you got it. It's unfortunate if your feelings got hurt."

She turned on him. "What did I ask for? To be humiliated? How did I ask for that?"

Glaring at him, she stabbed the elevator call button with a vengeance, and Con wondered just what was going on. "You're not Jeff McCall's wife anymore," he said flatly.

She went rigid. Her lips parted, and for a moment she was suspended, shored up by an anger that was fast disappearing. Then, just as suddenly, her knees caved in. He caught her by the elbow just as she crumpled, all fight gone. "Oh, that," she said, a bit hysterically. "I'd forgotten."

"Forgotten?"

His soft intensity penetrated her fogged brain, and Candace made an attempt to pull herself together. She drew back, but he held on to her, his eyes dueling with hers in a silent battle of wills.

"You look like you're about to drop," Con said.

"I feel worse."

She closed her eyes, expecting him to shake her or scream at her or heaven knew what else. She did deserve it. What point had there been in lying?

"Come back to my office and sit down," he said. "I'll get you a glass of water."

"No thanks. I just want to go home."

"And I want to know why you felt the need to hide your divorce from me."

Candace let him lead her back down the hall, partly because she needed to explain, partly because she was just too weary to resist. She sank into the chair next to his desk and Con stood over her, his hands on his hips, looking for all the world as if he'd like to wring her neck.

How did she get herself into these messes?

"I just hadn't told anyone about my divorce. It had nothing to do with you."

"It doesn't feel that way."

Candace leaned her head back, watching him from beneath her lashes. It had been a long day—too long. She wasn't capable of dealing with him now.

"I'm supposed to be somewhere else," Con said into the silence. "The Brinkwood custody case is coming right up."

"So why are you still here?"

"Because your friend Dan Morrison dropped the bomb on me about you."

Candace looked down at her hands. "I don't see why my divorce should be such a big deal," she murmured.

"Don't you? When your ex-husband is Michelle Faulkner Brinkwood's attorney? When I have to find out via office gossip that the Jeff McCall I'm going to face in court is your ex-husband?"

Candace's stunned gaze swept his dark, furious face. "You don't mean—"

"Get off your high horse, Candace. You may be the boss's daughter, but when you step into my case, I'm the boss."

His logic was totally lost to her. "It's not my fault that Jeff is Michelle Brinkwood's attorney. I didn't even know."

He arched a disbelieving brow. "Oh, really."

"You're mad at me because I didn't tell you I was divorced. It has nothing to do with Jeff," she said. "That's just coincidence."

"I don't like being played for a fool," he said tautly. "And that's what you've been doing."

"You're crazy." Her temper was coming to her rescue again. "No one knew about my divorce but my father. It's personal. It has nothing to do with you. You can be mad all you want, but I didn't ask for your attention!"

"My attention," Con repeated angrily. "What do you mean by that?"

"You've been after me from the moment you laid eyes on me," Candace shot back recklessly, wondering what drove her to say such things. "At the party and here at work. And now I've wounded your male pride by lying about Jeff."

"You have a warped idea of reality, lady," Con said through his teeth.

"Do I?" Candace lifted her chin. "Well, you have an awfully sensitive ego. You can't handle any woman who doesn't grovel at your feet."

"How would you know?" he demanded, a muscle jumping in his jaw. "You're so packed in ice you don't know what it's like to even *feel*."

White-hot fury surged through her veins. Candace leaped to her feet. "I feel," she said, trembling, her eyes shadowed with pain. "I feel more than anyone has a right to. And what I feel right now is pity. For you. For any man who can't handle rejection."

His hand flashed out and grabbed her arm. Lines of outrage grooved beside his mouth, and for a moment she thought she'd gone too far. "You're really a bitch, you know that?"

"Now who's calling names?"

"I am. And the name fits pretty damn well." His fingers dug into her elbow. "I think you're getting me confused with someone else. I can handle rejection just fine. But I don't like someone lying to me."

"Like me?" She glared at him in a way that usually froze men in their tracks.

"Yeah, like you." His nostrils flared.

If she hadn't been so angry it would have been funny. What were they fighting about? She could hardly remember. She stared pointedly at the white-knuckled fingers gripping her arm. "What is your problem with me, Mr. Holt?" she asked icily.

"My problem is you're Candace *Forsythe* McCall."

His admission caught her off guard. "Is that it? Is that what this is all about?"

Even Con looked taken aback. "No," he said, but his expression grew distant, as if he were doing a quick reassessment in his mind.

She suddenly remembered his comment about attending a different school from Tanner Baines's. Out of the blue came a remembered remark her father had made: "He's not Ivy League, but then, what would you expect with his background? The important thing is Connor Holt is a damn good attorney."

"You're sensitive about your background," she said softly. "Well, for pete's sake, I'm sensitive about mine."

His harsh laugh made her realize he wasn't through being angry. "Trying to get down to my level?"

His mouth was in her direct line of vision. She saw the emotion that tightened it. "You hate me," she said on a sad note of discovery.

He made an impatient sound. "No, I don't hate you. I don't know you well enough to hate you. Call it active dislike."

Candace tried to laugh, but nothing came out. Tears filled her eyes, then skimmed down her cheeks. With a sigh of regret, Con drew her into his arms, his hand stroking her hair.

"I'm sorry," he said, shaken.

"You said you weren't going to say that again," she choked out, her tears wetting the front of his shirt.

"I don't dislike you. I was . . . just angry. My sister, Maggie, always tells me I speak before I think."

"No." She shook her head, closing her eyes to the tender pressure of the hand smoothing her blond hair.

"Candace. Oh, God, Candace." He sighed. "You caught me at my worst."

Candace thought about her visit to Susan Woodwin's and about her beeline to her father in search of some modicum of comfort. But it was Con's arms she'd found, and she was glad. "You caught me at my worst, too."

Her fingers clutched his shoulders. She pressed her face into the warmth of his neck, her features twisted with emotion. His arms tightened, and his cheek was against her crown. All she could feel were Con's arms around her, Con's chest beneath her cheek. All she could hear was his heavy heartbeat and her own ragged breathing.

He inhaled slowly, drawing back to peer down at her. "Are you okay?"

She nodded, not trusting her voice, swiping at the remains of her tears. She glanced up and was stunned to read the desire beginning to flame in his eyes. He looked away, frowning.

Candace watched him, realizing an answering spark had started somewhere deep inside her. She was suddenly sensitized to the heat from his hands, the brush of cloth against skin, his warm, masculine odor. Bemused, she did nothing to stop the sensations, neither moving back nor leaning forward. She just waited.

His glance sliced back, focusing on her mouth. His own mouth was grim and taut. His finger moved hesitantly upward, tracing the line of her lips almost against his will. "I don't want to get involved with the boss's daughter."

"Now who's lying?" she whispered breathlessly.

"I don't, Candace. I did that once before."

"I got involved with a lawyer once before," she answered boldly. "It brought me misery and heartache."

Her remark was so unexpected that Con smiled. "Don't, Candace," he added seriously.

"You asked me out once. You wanted to get involved then, even though I was Joshua's daughter."

"I don't want to get involved now."

She grew silent. She knew she would be embarrassed later, but for this moment she wanted him to kiss her. She wanted to feel his lips crush hers. She wanted to believe someone desired her, needed her.

Her eyes met his, soft and green and slumberous. Her mouth trembled uncertainly. Con closed his eyes and groaned, opening them again to tip up her chin with one finger. "Damn everything," he muttered as he lowered his mouth to hers.

The feeling of his lips on hers was glorious, but the force of it took her by surprise. His mouth moved on hers with hungry ardor, and for a stunned moment Candace was passive. She'd expected it, hoped for it, but now that it was here she felt paralyzed. Con seemed to have no such qualms, his lips rubbing insistently, shaping and fitting hers, urging them to part.

Then her mouth relaxed and his tongue plunged inside. Candace could scarcely breathe. Dizzily she groped for support, clinging to him in a way that had them both fighting to retain their balance.

It was Con who broke away first, breathing hard. He gripped her tightly, his body tense, his gaze knifing into hers, searching for her reaction. Candace was weak, her lips slack and swollen, her eyes glazed, her chest heaving. She made a faint sound of protest, but it came out sounding like desire. His gaze moved from her lips to her breasts, their rapid rise and fall seeming to mesmerize him. Almost in slow motion his hand cupped one, and Candace saw her nipple, taut and protruding, outlined against the thin fabric.

"Candace," Con said softly, his voice unsure.

In answer she placed her hand on his, trapping him to her warm flesh. When Con glanced up her eyes were melting emeralds, and seeing them, his control snapped. His hand moved against her breast, his fingers kneading her nipple, his body hardening against hers with a primitive desire.

Candace's head was reeling. She leaned back weakly, and his mouth found the soft white arch of her neck. He groaned, unleashed, pulling her to him with a ferocity that both scared and intoxicated her. She wanted him to want her. She wanted him to take her. But when he bent downward, his mouth closing around her nipple through her blouse, she nearly cried out.

His mouth was hot and moist, and she dug her fingers into his hair. If someone had told her moments before that she would be passionately making love to Connor Holt she wouldn't have believed it. Yet here she was, wanton moans of pleasure issuing from her own throat.

His hands slid convulsively up and down her spine. She could feel how tightly he held her to him, even as she sensed him trying to pull back. He moaned, too, his fingers searching for the hem of her skirt, whispering it upward until his hands were on her thighs, drawing her closer to him, so close that she was wedged intimately against his maleness, her legs quivering, trying to hold her weight as she instinctively sought a closer melding.

"Candace!" Con expelled a strangled breath, tearing himself away from her. He clasped her forearms to keep her from falling, holding her at arm's length, his breathing ragged. "God Almighty. What are we doing?"

She was too undone to be embarrassed. She just stared at him with wide eyes, shocked.

"This is crazy," he muttered under his breath.

"Yes," she agreed with a shaky laugh. "Yes, yes, it is."

"Do you realize we're at the office? What if someone should come back, like you did?"

Candace didn't want to think about that. "It would be embarrassing."

"Downright mortifying," Con corrected, drawing an unsteady hand through his hair. His blue eyes stared at her as if she were someone he'd never seen before. "Would you like to go to—" He drew a sharp breath, cutting himself short.

"What?" Candace's blouse was wet for the second time that day, and Connor's eyes drifted to the telltale sign as if drawn by a magnet.

He shook his head, a shudder passing through his powerful frame. "Never mind. I've got work to do. I can't think straight."

Candace blinked and looked away, her cheeks flushed with hectic color. A rush of sanity overwhelmed her. What had she been trying to prove? She realized belatedly that

Connor was more interested in keeping his job than in taking her to bed. A sensible man. But right now she didn't want a sensible man. She wanted a passionate one, one who couldn't help devouring her.

Which was crazy, considering that the only man she'd ever slept with was Jeff.

"Hey." His knuckles softly grazed her cheek, but that only made Candace feel worse.

"I'm sorry I didn't tell you about Jeff," she said stiffly. "It was no reflection on you. Honestly."

"Oh, Candace, don't tighten up on me now."

He sounded world-weary, but she couldn't help herself. "I know you must think after this that I'm...available and—" her voice shook "—easy, but I'm not normally like this. It's just that..."

"Wait!" he said, trying to stop her pain.

"...it's been a terrible day. There are things in my life right now that I can't bear, and I came here looking for someone to love."

He didn't say anything. His expression was impossible to read, so Candace went on haltingly. "My father wasn't here, but you were. Do you understand?" She looked up appealingly, feeling more like a child than a woman at that moment.

His hand rubbed his jaw. "You don't want to pursue this, then?" he asked carefully.

Relief washed over her. "No, I don't. I just want to block this out of my mind."

He nodded stiffly. "I see."

Candace frowned. This wasn't quite the way she'd pictured him reacting, but she was too grateful to figure out what was wrong. "I—I've got to go now. I've made a fool of myself and I just want to evaporate."

He released her but said nothing.

With the little dignity she still possessed, Candace turned and walked to the door. She let herself out without a backward glance and half ran down the hall, through the glass doors and into the elevator, then collapsed against the wall.

What is wrong with me? she asked herself dazedly as the car lurched downward. *How could I act this way with him?*

She drew a long breath, thought about Connor and decided she didn't want to analyze her feelings for him too closely.

The heat hadn't abated by ten o'clock that evening, and Con drew a breath of stale air as he cut across Edward Faulkner's yard, let himself out through the gate at the end of the sloping lawn and climbed into his blue vintage T-Bird. He clenched and unclenched his hands around the wheel, hot and frustrated. Mr. Ed was arrogant and smooth, with a poker face that Con had wanted to run his fist through. The interview had not gone well from the beginning to end, and though Con had the law on his side, he sensed that he'd lost this skirmish.

And Candace McCall was to blame.

He started then raced the engine, grinding gears and wincing at the sound as he drove away from the Faulkner mansion and whisked through the light evening traffic to Lake Oswego. The T-Bird's top was down, and the wind rushed past his face, cooling his skin. His mind was still a fevered tangle, however, and by the time he was threading his way down the twisting road above the lake that led to his condominium, Con sensed he wasn't going to get much sleep tonight.

He clenched his teeth. Had he lost his mind? A date or two with Candace was what he'd originally had in mind— once he'd learned who she was. But back there, at the office, when it had been just the two of them— He made a choked sound of disbelief. How could *that* have happened?

He cut the engine and yanked on the emergency brake, listening to the sounds of the evening. Waves lapped gently at the dock at the condominium's west end; a cricket kept up a noisy harmony; a car bumped over the wooden bridge around the bend.

At least little Janice was back and in her father's care. Con had seen to that. Edward Faulkner must have had to move heaven and earth to get her back by tonight, but the child was home and safe. That was worth something.

Con sighed and let himself out of his car, slamming the door behind him. He walked up the steps to his front door, seeing through the beveled squares to the paneled entryway. The building had once been one huge, rambling home, but an eager developer had turned it into four spacious condominiums. Con's was on the corner, its back den surrounded by windows that looked over the lake.

Now he walked aimlessly down the planked hallway, his hands in his pockets, until he reached the den. There he stood under the low mahogany beams, his gaze on the black, restless water a good four stories below. He could see the path that switchbacked through shrubbery and rock gardens that were now heady with the scent and color of alyssum and rock cress, could see the string of small lanterns which lighted the way to the dock. Con opened his back door and walked down the path, still sweating.

At the end of the dock he stood silently, watching the play of light on water. He shouldn't have kissed Candace. Good Lord, he'd acted like a teenager. It had barely been in his power to pull back.

What if he hadn't?

He shook his head. It didn't bear thinking about. "Holy moley," he muttered in disgust, his voice echoing across the water. Around him, the houses were dousing their lights; only a few remained on. As if in tandem with his thoughts, the lights along the pathway were suddenly extinguished, the night timer switching them off.

He was alone in the dark. With a brief thought for Mrs. Collingwood, a widow twice his age whose glances his way were full of disapproval and who right this minute might be standing by her window watching him, Con stripped off his clothes and dived cleanly into the silky water.

Let her get an eyeful, he decided. He needed the cold water to cool him off.

It was with trepidation that Candace reported to work the next day. She had to screw up her courage to even walk inside, but she managed, and Terri must have noticed nothing amiss because she pointed to Pamela's empty chair and said, "Please. Help. I'm drowning."

"Anything specific I can do?" asked Candace.

"Pray?"

Smiling, she inquired, "In addition to that?"

"Just look at the pile on Pamela's desk. If that doesn't scare you off, nothing will."

Terri was right. Candace could see thick files stuffed with white papers stacked almost to the top of the computer monitor. As she settled in to work she reflected ruefully that sometimes you got what you asked for—in her case, enough work to make her forget her other problems.

She was poring over a particularly indecipherable handwritten note from one of the attorneys when Con pushed through the glass doors.

"Messages?" he asked Terri.

"Only one." She handed him the pink slip.

His reply was a snort that could have meant anything.

Candace's pulse was fluttering annoyingly. She trained her eyes straight ahead at the blank screen, but against her will they stole a peek at Connor. Her heart jolted when she found him watching her.

"Morning," he said offhandedly. "I see Pamela's still missing."

"Praise the Lord," Terri muttered.

So it's business as usual, Candace thought. He looked tired, though; there were lines around his mouth, and his blue eyes were more serious, as if there was a weighty problem occupying his mind. "I'm beginning to think this office would just close up without her," she said, gesturing to the growing work pile. As if to emphasize her point, Dan Morrison sailed up to her desk and thumped another file down on top of the stack.

"Looks like you're going to be busy for a while," he said. "No time for lunch?"

"Uh, no. Sorry." Candace flushed. Now why did she feel so guilty?

"Well, I'll see you all later," Con said, and strode off in the direction of his office.

Dan, however, leaned his elbows on Candace's pile of work. "I saw Jeff yesterday," he said softly.

The hairs on the back of her neck rose. "Oh?"

"Yep." He hesitated, as if unsure how to proceed. Cocking his head in Terri's direction, he said, "I'd like to talk, Candace. Think you could squeeze in some time for me?"

The last thing she wanted to do was talk to Dan about Jeff. "I thought you were in court today? The Tempe case?"

"Bart Tempe buckled under at the last minute. He struck a deal with his son's creditors yesterday. So I'm free as a bird." He smiled. "So, how about dinner tonight?"

"I can't tonight. I'm busy."

"And tomorrow?"

Candace bit her lip. There was no earthly reason she couldn't accept, apart from the fact that she didn't trust Dan.

"Well, I guess that's my answer," he said tightly, his neck turning a dark red.

"Wait, Dan," Candace said. She couldn't bear to have anyone humiliated because of her. "Maybe . . . next week. I have some free time."

"How about the company picnic?" he suggested suddenly—so suddenly, in fact, that Candace wondered if this had been his intention all along. "Leave it all to me. I'll make a picnic basket and bring the wine. Or would you rather have champagne?"

"Either's fine," Candace said hesitantly.

"Okay." He winked on his way out of the office. "See you then."

"That's a mistake," Terri murmured to the room at large once the door had closed behind Dan. Before Candace could retort, the phone rang and Terri blithely picked it up.

She doesn't have to tell *me*, Candace thought with a sigh, and with a grimace for life in general she went back to trying to read another lawyer's scrawl.

Con tossed the pink slip onto his desk, and it fluttered and skittered over the edge. Linda again. He jerked on his tie and with a savage growl yanked the whole thing off his neck. Flopping into his chair, he squeezed his nape, more out of sorts than he could remember ever being when he'd been working for Pozzer, Strikeberg and Carmen. In fact, even when he'd worked for Linda's father he'd never been this short-fused and testy. Work had always been a panacea. But not anymore.

His phone buzzed. Scooping up the receiver, he announced, "Connor Holt."

Terri's voice said, "It's Linda on line 1. Want me to put her through?"

"Never. But I'd better take it anyway."

She laughed. "Okay."

There was a click, and then he heard the fuzz of a long-distance connection. "Connor?" Linda asked, her low tones familiar and still disturbing.

"Hi, Linda. What's up?"

"Nothing, really. Same old thing." She paused. "I was thinking about coming up to Oregon to see you."

Con sat up straighter. "Why?"

"Now, don't sound like that. I'm having a rough time and I miss you, Con."

He counted to twenty.

"Are you still there? Con?"

"I'm here. What happened to Burden?"

"Burton," she corrected. "As you well know. Our relationship is over. Kaput." He heard her take a long breath. "He went back to his wife."

"Nice of him."

"Oh, Con..."

"Look, Linda, I'm sorry. Really. I want things to work out for you. I just don't know how I can help you. We're divorced, remember?"

"We shouldn't be, Con," she said swiftly, as if this were just the opening she'd been waiting for. "Remember when you were down here last? There were a lot of feelings between us."

All he could remember was that they had poked and prodded through the ashes of their relationship, occasionally turning over a hot coal of pain that refused to quite die. He didn't love Linda. He never truly had. He'd married her for all the wrong reasons, just as his sister, Maggie, had said, and he'd paid the price by hurting Linda and himself.

"I'm not interested in starting over," he said, not unkindly.

"I'd like you back here. Dad would like you back here."

"No."

She was crying, but he couldn't tell if it was put on for his benefit or not. Con gritted his teeth. She had a way of getting to him even now. "What do you want me to say, Linda? I'm not going to lie to you. You're only calling me because you're upset with Burton. You know it and I know it."

"You're so damn blind!" she shouted, then hung up.

Con replaced the receiver, searching his feelings. There was an emptiness inside him—the remnants of what might have been if he and Linda had ever been truthful about how they'd felt about each other. But that was all. No love, no pain, no pathos.

Grimacing, he realized he felt worse over what had happened with Candace yesterday.

He couldn't—wouldn't—let *that* happen again. After all, that was how he and Linda had gotten started, wasn't it? A stolen kiss in his office, a meeting after work, a dinner out with her father, a senior partner of the law firm he worked for . . .

He blotted out the memories. If he was going to make mistakes in his life, let them be different ones. He'd already married the boss's daughter. He wasn't going to take a chance on doing it again.

At lunchtime Marion mentioned to Candace that her father seemed upset about Jeff opposing Forsythe and Company on the Brinkwood custody case. Her father had always been fond of Jeff, Candace knew, and her mind kept worrying the idea all afternoon.

Finally, just before closing, she approached her father's office. He was on the phone, and he waved her impatiently toward a chair as he wound up the conversation and slammed down the receiver.

"What is it?" he growled without preamble, searching through the papers strewn across his desk.

"Jeff."

He stopped short. "What about him?"

"I heard about the custody case he's involved in."

Joshua grunted. "Con can take care of him."

"That's not what I meant," Candace said, a bit frustratedly. "I just know how you felt about Jeff, and I wanted to say I'm sorry."

"Save your apologies." He waved a hand in the air. "Jeff's a bright young man. He knows what he's doing. He's probably jockeying for position in his new firm and taking a case against us to show his new loyalty."

"How can you stand it?" Candace asked, shaking her head in disbelief. "He was your son-in-law. He sold out. *How can you stand it?*"

Joshua Forsythe tented his fingers under his chin, studying her. "Does it bother you that much, honey?" he asked softly. "Try not to let it."

Candace propped a fist on her hip. This wasn't going the way she'd planned at all. "I don't care about Jeff. I don't," she stated fiercely when she saw the sympathetic look that crossed her father's face. "But it really set me on fire to see the way he used you and me to get where he is."

A smile slowly drew across Joshua Forsythe's lips. "It's nice to see you showing a little emotion," he said thoughtfully. "Maybe Jeff is doing us a service after all." He paused, continuing to regard her intently. "Don't worry, Candace. Jeff McCall will get what's coming to him," he assured her. "You just wait and see."

"Then you're not sitting here going over what could have been?" Candace asked, frowning in bafflement. "I thought you'd be hurt."

"More like disgusted. With myself, mainly, for allowing Jeff so much free rein." He chuckled. "Are you up for some good old bloodthirsty revenge? Watch what Connor does to him in court. I guarantee you I'm going to get a front-row seat."

Candace's lips parted. This was a side of her father she'd never seen before. He'd always been so gruff, so austere, so cold. "You're awfully sure about Connor."

"Anyone who calls Edward Faulkner 'Mr. Ed' has got my vote." He roared with laughter. "I'm glad you don't care what happens to Jeff. That was the only blight on this whole case."

Candace regarded her father with unabashed amazement. "And what about the little girl?"

"Candace, Con wouldn't have taken on this case if he didn't have the child's interests at heart. And that's why he's going to nail Ed Faulkner to the wall. Because he has to."

Joshua Forsythe met Candace's startled gaze with shrewd, calm eyes. "Don't ever let me be on the wrong side from you," she said on a whisper, and her father leaned back in his chair and smiled.

Chapter Six

Candace pushed through the revolving door of the Forsythe Building into the late-afternoon sunshine. She had some shopping to do, and she wanted to get it done now, before she left for home. Shorts, she thought with a grimace. For the company picnic she'd promised Dan she'd attend.

She paused to search through her purse for her sunglasses, and once again encountered the paper with Susan Woodwin's phone number on it. For days she'd pushed thoughts of her condition out of her mind, but now they reared up in front of her, forcing her to think about the future.

No children, she told herself. *None of your own. Well, that's okay. Lots of women don't have children. Ever.*

She slipped the sunglasses on her nose and looked up at the dusky blue sky. What would it be like to take a lover? she wondered idly. A man willing to give her a child. No strings attached. Could she handle that? How could anyone?

Her thoughts danced like dust motes in a gentle breeze. If she could pick a man—any man—what would he be like? Tall, dark and handsome. With a sense of humor, and a serious side, as well. Someone who listened. Someone interested in her hopes and fears.

She smiled, seeing a hazy image of her imaginary lover in her mind's eye.

"Candace?"

She jumped at the sound of her name, whipped around to see Con walking toward her somewhat diffidently. It was clear he was as uncomfortable with what had happened as she was. "Hi," she said awkwardly.

"You looked like you were a million miles away," he remarked, squinting against the sun's bright glare.

"I guess I was," she admitted. Feeling some explanation was in order, she added, "I was thinking about going shopping. What are you doing?"

"Looking for the coldest, tallest beer I can find." He paused, narrowing his gaze. "Care to join me?"

The invitation was so sudden that Candace was taken aback. "I, uh . . . well, sure."

"I'd like to talk to you about the Brinkwood case, but if you don't want to, I'll understand."

She bent her head. "Just tell me how I can help you," she said.

"By giving me a woman's point of view" was his rather disturbing answer. He led the way to the Front Street Café & Bar and held the door open for her. Candace preceded him inside, her shoulder brushing softly against his shirt as she made her way into the narrow bar. A din surrounded them, making conversation nearly impossible. Con inclined his head toward a table at the far end, but just before Candace reached it, another couple sat down.

"I guess it's the bar, then," he said in her ear. He held out a stool for her to sit on.

Candace climbed onto the leather seat, tucking her legs along one side. Her skirt inched upward, showing more thigh than she wanted to, and when she tugged on it she felt Con's eyes watching her. She glanced up, but he was looking elsewhere, a tension around his mouth that hadn't been there before.

"What did you mean by a woman's point of view?" Candace asked as Con signaled the bartender. "Somehow I thought you'd ask me about Jeff."

"Jeff comes later. I've got a more immediate problem. My custody case involves a woman who doesn't want her child. In my experience, that's rare. What do you think?"

Candace swept in an involuntary breath. He couldn't know what a nerve he was scraping. "Yes. I'd say that is rare."

"When I'm in court, I'm going to point out why Janice's father is the better parent. To do that, I've got to show Michelle's failings. So I wanted to know, what would make a woman not want her child?"

"You're asking the wrong person," Candace choked out.

"You can't think of one reason?"

"Not right now."

The bartender came and glanced inquiringly at Con. "A draft for me," he said, turning to Candace. "What about you?"

"Uh . . . the same."

"I didn't know you drank beer," Con said. "You don't seem the type."

"You just don't know me very well."

"I know you're a woman," he said, as if that explained everything, then tossed back half the foaming glass the bartender set in front of him.

Candace took an experimental sip. In point of fact, she didn't usually drink beer, but it had sounded refreshing. She took a long swallow, hoping to clear her head, and was pleased to discover it was ice-cold.

"I suppose we should talk about what happened between us yesterday," he added, twisting his glass around.

"Do we have to?"

He darted her a swift look. "No. Not if you don't want to. We can act like it didn't happen, I suppose, although I must admit, it's been on my mind."

"It was a mistake, that's all," she said quickly. "I don't know what came over me. It won't happen again." She swallowed, then forced herself to meet his eyes. She could tell he didn't believe her, so she tossed her head, her gaze cool and even. Inside she was a melting, quivering mass of jelly.

"Well, I'm glad we got that straight," he said ironically.

"Me, too." Candace drank thirstily from her glass, then ruined the moment by coughing as the carbonation burned her throat.

"You okay?" he asked.

"Fine. Really." Annoyed with herself, she asked, "You wanted to talk about Jeff, didn't you?"

"Yes, the inimitable Jeff McCall. I've been doing a little bit of research on him."

"Believe everything you hear. He's all that and more."

"Are you still in love with him?"

Candace practically choked. "Good grief, no! Whatever gave you that idea?"

"It was just a theory. You seem so raw about him."

The loss of her marriage suddenly filled Candace with sorrow, rendering her speechless. It wasn't Jeff she cared about. But she missed being part of a family, being someone's wife. "I'm not in love with Jeff," she said distinctly. "If you want the truth, I doubt I ever was."

Con was silent as he studied her. At length he asked, "What's he like in court? This custody case has been hovering around on the back burner for months. All of a sudden the Brinkwood case is dumped in my lap and I'm facing Candace Forsythe's ex-husband in court in less than two weeks. What do you think about that?"

"I think someone's been pulling strings." She half smiled. "Possibly...Mr. Ed."

Amusement gleamed in his eyes at her choice of his irreverent nickname. "Who've you been talking to?"

"Father."

Con finished his beer, wiping his lips thoughtfully with the back of his hand. "Well, I think you're right. Someone has been pulling strings. But I'm going to win."

"That's what Father said."

"Well, Father knows best."

She laughed. She couldn't help it. And the sound carried above the noisy crowd, causing more than one head to turn. "You really are funny sometimes, you know that?"

"So I've been told," he answered wryly.

"No, I mean it. You're so direct. You take my breath away."

It wasn't what she'd meant to say, and when she heard it she was horrified. He paused, weighed her words and asked quietly, "Do I?"

"I think I meant that differently than you're taking it," she said in a rush.

Con's gaze focused on his empty glass, then on her face. "I've changed my mind. I don't want to talk about your ex, or the trial. I want to talk about you."

"Me? Not my favorite subject these days," she admitted with a forced laugh.

"Why not? Most people like to talk about themselves."

She just shook her head. With a sort of slow-motion fascination she watched his hand slide over to cover hers. The color of his eyes seemed to deepen, to intensify, causing her heart to lurch uncomfortably.

"What do you really want out of me, Candace?" he asked quietly. "I don't get it. The woman in my office yesterday was not the Candace McCall I met several weeks ago."

"How do you know?" Her voice was a squeaky parody of itself.

"How do I know?" he repeated. "Because you wanted me to make love to you yesterday. You would have let me."

The boldness of his words made her cringe. And he was right! She bent her head, certain everyone could hear. "Con . . . please . . ."

"Why did you want me?"

"Why?" she repeated in disbelief. This conversation was getting way out of hand!

"I just don't understand what's happening. I want to know what's going on inside that beautiful head of yours. It's driving me crazy."

"Con, please. I'm a mess. I've got—things on my mind." Candace felt near panic for no reason she could name.

He withdrew his hand and sat back. "I don't know what you want out of me, lady, but I don't think it's anything I can give."

He needed some kind of explanation; she could see that. But what explanation could she give? He'd been there last night when she'd needed a shoulder to cry on, and though it had all gotten mixed up with sex, she'd just wanted someone to take care of her for a while.

Her jaw clenched and unclenched as she worked up the courage to tell him the truth. "Con, yesterday I just wanted someone . . . to want me."

How pathetic she sounded, even to herself. Dying inside, she braced herself for his response.

She heard him draw a breath. "Candace, you've got to know there are innumerable men out there who would want you."

"I'm not talking about sex," she said unevenly. "I just wanted someone to care about me, that's all." She gave a short laugh. "I was looking for my father. And then you were there, and so angry, and I was upset. . . ." She let the words trail off, unable to go on.

"What were you upset about?"

I want a baby and I can't have one. "Nothing. Nothing I want to talk about."

"So all you wanted yesterday was a friend," Con said. "I see. Well, maybe that's for the best." He sighed. "Anything else would be a mistake."

His brows were drawn together; his lean face looked dark and dangerous when it was so serious. Candace saw the sweep of his black lashes against his cheek and, caught between them, a thin line of cerulean blue. She realized with a start that she wasn't being completely honest at all. She wanted *him*! She, who had never wanted any man—not even Jeff, really—wanted Con with a passion she'd heretofore thought only existed in fantasy.

The realization hit her like a blow to the stomach. She could barely think, and she missed half of what Con was saying. She surfaced at the words " . . . like to get together and talk about Jeff some more."

"Pardon?" she asked blankly.

He smiled. "Which part did you miss?"

"I don't know. You said something about . . . Jeff?"

"If you have some time in the next week I'd like to go over this custody case with you, find out how you think Jeff will proceed. Your father seems to think he's taken the Brinkwood case to prove a point at his new firm. What do you think?"

"I would guess that's right. Jeff's—" she searched around for the right word "—determined. Single-minded. Tough. And selfish." She shrugged. "If it'll help Jeff, who cares about the client?"

Con didn't seem surprised by her cynical analysis. Thoughtfully he said, "Mr. Ed doesn't have a case. Michelle took that child over a state line; I'm sure of it. If I have to I'll requisition Faulkner's phone bill and prove it. I think he called Michelle and told her to bring Janice back. I bet he was furious with her for messing up his campaign."

"What does it matter if Michelle took Janice over a state line?"

"Michelle gave Brinkwood temporary custody until the hearing."

"How strange. Why is she fighting for custody now, then?"

Con gave a snort of disgust. "She isn't. Her father is. Michelle doesn't want Janice. The poor little kid is just a pawn for Mr. Ed."

Candace stared across the bar, her vision blurring a bit as she thought about Michelle Faulkner. She couldn't put herself in the woman's shoes at all. Not now. Not when she was throwing away the one thing in life Candace truly desired. Filled with resentment toward both Michelle and Edward

Faulkner, she said intensely, "If there's anything I can do to help you, just ask."

Con smiled, and it was a smile of genuine friendship. "Good. I may need your help. I'm glad we . . . understand each other now."

Candace regarded him obliquely. "Right," she murmured, but couldn't help being disheartened at the way his brow cleared.

"We'll forget about yesterday," he said lightly. "It was just one of those things."

Her mouth quirked in a semblance of a smile. *Just one of those things.* The kind that happened to her once in a lifetime.

A week later Candace stood in front of her mirror, checking her reflection, a scowl darkening her face. Why had she ever consented to go with Dan to the company picnic? She would have given her mother's pearls to change the past, but here she was, in a pair of white shorts and a sky-blue summer top, her hair pinned loosely away from her face, a tennis racket twisting nervously between her palms.

The last thing she wanted to do was spend five hours trying hard to have fun.

She wondered if Con would be there. He'd brought it up once in passing, but nothing more had been said, though he and Candace had spent a lot of time working together over the past few days. Once Con had found she wasn't trying to start a relationship, he'd begun treating her like a friend, bouncing ideas off her, asking advice. Though she was flattered he considered her opinions important, she was also deflated. He'd been so eager to nip their relationship in the bud. Where had the man who'd dogged her heels at the Christmas-in-July party gone? She wouldn't mind seeing him again. Being Con's girl Friday lacked an important element she needed right now.

The doorbell rang. Dan, she thought with a grimace as she grabbed her purse and headed for the door.

Dan was in a white-and-red tennis outfit, looking fitter than she'd given him credit for. "Hello there," he said, sliding an appreciative glance up and down her long legs. "You ready?"

"Uh, yes, just a minute." She locked her door, pocketed her keys and fell into step beside him. The black Jaguar was sitting in the driveway, and Dan admired it as they walked to his car.

"You just leave it right out there for anyone to ruin?"

"Who would ruin it?" she asked.

"God only knows. Anything could happen. Teenagers could throw things at it, lightning could strike, someone could steal it."

Candace shook her head. Beneath his teasing she detected an element of envy. That was Dan's problem, she thought. He put too much value on inanimate objects and not enough on people. "I'll take my chances."

"Whoa." He stopped short, examining her fender. "What happened?" His voice was filled with horror. "It's been scratched."

"Harold," said Candace with a flicker of amusement.

"Harold?" he asked blankly. "Who's Harold?"

"A friend. Don't worry about it." She walked to his pale green Porsche and opened the passenger door before Dan could help her.

"Well, you'd better put the screws to this Harold," Dan said once they were under way. "He ought to pay for doing that to a piece of art."

Candace only grinned.

* * *

The picnic was held at the Lakeside Country Club, of which Joshua was member. Though many of the employees of Forsythe and Company had brought their own picnic baskets, there was additional food supplied on gleaming silver trays held aloft by the staff of the club. The lake sparkled like jade through a veil of drooping cedars. To one side were the tennis courts and a row of tables specifically set up for the occasion. Beyond were the sloping fairways, a ripple of manicured green ribboning around a curve of firs.

Dan laid out a blue-and-black checkered blanket and plunked a wicker basket down on it. "Don't you want to use the table?" Candace asked.

"When I can have you here?" He patted a spot beside him. "I'd have to be crazy."

Most of the others were already seated at the tables, and Marion motioned Candace over. "I'll be right back," she murmured to Dan, easing quickly away.

"What are you doing over there?" Marion asked. "There's lots of room here."

"I don't know. Dan's idea." Casually she glanced around. Con was nowhere to be seen.

"Well, let me talk to him." Marion marched over to Dan, rooted him up and succeeded in dragging him—basket, blanket and all—to where they were seated.

He emitted a long-suffering sigh and said to the table at large, "Just when I finally got her on the blanket. Don't any of you have a heart?"

There was a smattering of laughter, but like Candace, most of the others were embarrassed. Candace's smile felt strained, and luckily Terri challenged Dan to a game of tennis, breaking the tension.

Candace had just seated herself beside Marion when a streak of blue glimmered through the trees. A vintage

Thunderbird. Her eyes were riveted, and her foolish heart began a beat of its own as Con stepped from the driver's seat. He was dressed in khaki shorts and a black polo shirt, and Candace's lips had already curved into a smile of greeting when a dark-haired woman alighted from the other side of the car.

The woman grinned at Con and said something Candace couldn't hear, and Con reached into the back and pulled out a cooler. He tried to hand it to his companion, and she gamely held it for a few moments before setting it down with a thump. They both laughed.

Candace bit her lip and glanced away. Con was with a woman. It wasn't really surprising, she supposed, yet it hurt far more than it should have. She was still trying to gain control of herself when Con and the woman walked up the hill from the parking lot to their table, Con holding the cooler, his companion carrying a small picnic basket in which Candace could see various cheeses wrapped in cellophane and a loaf of French bread. Simple, elegant, inexpensive... Candace's throat tightened unexpectedly, and she glanced at the pâté and truffles and Dom Perignon in Dan's basket.

"Hi, all," Con said, tucking his hand under the woman's elbow. To a chorus of greetings he introduced her, saying, "This is Gayle Kempwood. *Dr.* Gayle Kempwood." He gave her a courtly bow, his eyes sparkling.

"He's always teasing me," Gayle said tolerantly. "Half the time he acts like he's impressed, the other half he pretends I'm not a real doctor. I'm a psychologist," she added by way of explanation.

Candace's heart had plunged to her stomach. She found herself staring at the plastic tablecloth, short of breath. They knew each other well. It had never occurred to her he might be seriously involved with someone else. No wonder he'd made such a point of pushing her away.

"Candace." It was Con's voice, and she drew on her courage, lifting her head to smile and greet Gayle as if nothing were wrong.

"So you're the lady I've heard so much about," Gayle said. "From the way Con tells it, he couldn't do anything without you."

There was no rancor in her tone, no envy. She was secure enough not to be threatened by Con's praise. Which made Candace feel worse.

"It's nice to meet you," Candace said formally.

Con raised his eyebrows at her.

Gayle was immediately swept into the group, a dozen questions fired at her. Where do you work? What made you decide to become a doctor? How long have you know Con?

To this last question, she answered, "Con's sister, Maggie Baines, introduced us about a year ago, when Con first moved from Los Angeles. Maggie's a nutritionist at Briar Park Hospital, where I work."

I like her, Candace thought dully. But then she'd liked Renée Southfield, too.

Dan came back, wiping sweat from his brow, breathing hard. "Greetings," he said heartily, assessing the situation with Con and Gayle in one glance. He smiled widely.

Con's lashes narrowed. "Greetings, Morrison," he said coolly.

"Why don't you introduce me to your... friend?" Dan suggested in a tone that implied an intimacy between Con and Gayle.

What Con thought, Candace couldn't tell, but Gayle shook Dan's hand and dutifully answered his probing questions. Dan's joy in meeting Con's date was clear to

Candace. What was also clear was that Dan felt Con had been some kind of competition for Candace's affection.

The next few hours were excruciating—doubly so because Dan kept shortening the distance between them, acting more and more like a lover. His attitude grew in relation to his alcohol consumption, as did Candace's icy stiffness. The limp arm tossed carelessly across her shoulders was enough to make her want to scream. She could barely consume one bite of his gourmet salads and canapés, mortified by his sloppy familiarity.

"Want to play some tennis?" The words were spoken behind her head, and she turned to find Con watching her steadily.

"I'd love to," she said in relief.

It was with a certain amount of finesse that she extricated herself from Dan's arm and followed Con to the courts. She drew a long breath and sighed, not seeing the flicker of a smile that crossed his lips.

"It might be a few minutes," Con said as they watched the couples on the courts bat the ball back and forth across the net.

"Fine with me." She didn't really feel like playing, anyway. She'd just wanted to escape Dan's clutches.

"Gayle's a longtime friend," Con remarked, his gaze following the whizzing tennis ball.

"Dan's a pushy attorney," Candace answered, her heart feeling lighter.

Con laughed. "So am I."

"I'd say just the opposite. Thanks." She chewed on her bottom lip.

"For what?"

"Rescuing me, among other things." She lifted her shoulders expressively. "I've been thinking about the way I've acted toward you, and I wouldn't blame you if you thought I was beyond help. I'm not usually so hot-and-cold. I'm usually...just cold." Her breath expelled on a short laugh.

"That I don't believe." He grinned lazily, in a way that melted something inside her. "But never mind. I like being your friend, Candace McCall. It sure beats anything we've tried so far."

She smiled uncertainly, wishing she felt the same way.

"What made you decide to come with Dan?" he asked, curious.

"It just happened." She shaded her eyes, watching the tennis ball zigzag back and forth.

"The Brinkwood hearing date is next Wednesday. I hope you're coming."

"Wouldn't miss it. Neither would Joshua."

"Do you suppose you and I could get a bite to eat together afterward?" he asked unexpectedly. "To celebrate?"

Candace's heart somersaulted. "You're awfully sure of winning, aren't you?"

"Well, if I don't win, then you can help me lick my wounds." He waited for her answer.

Her palms were sweating. Proceed with caution, she told herself. Could she really go on a date with him as a friend? Could she be another Gayle Kempwood to him?

"I'll tell you what," Con said persuasively, the lean planes of his face hiding a smile. "If I win, we go out to dinner somewhere posh and extravagant. And if I lose...we go out to dinner somewhere posh and extravagant."

"I accept." She laughed.

"Good." He swept his racket toward the now-empty tennis courts. "Now, give me your best game."

It was over before it had even begun. Though Candace kept up with him, he had her running all over the court. Con loped back and forth, easily returning her balls. At the end of the second set she begged off, wrapping a towel around her neck, her face glistening with a sheen of perspiration.

"You toyed with me," she said accusingly.

"Maybe," he answered immodestly.

"You're awfully good at tennis."

"I had a good teacher." He frowned, as if the memory displeased him.

From somewhere behind them, Dan said, "There you are." Candace glanced back to see Dan advancing on them, his expression grim. She looked nervously to Con, whose own mouth was quirking into a smile. He seemed to be handling Dan's appearance with equanimity. "I was wondering what happened to you," Dan remarked, tucking a proprietary hand beneath Candace's elbow, leading her to one side. She had to force herself not to yank her arm away.

"I'll see you both later," Con said. He waved to Gayle, who was seated with Marion and Terri, Candace noted, and seemed to have no such insecurities. Ironically, Candace realized she'd rather be with Gayle than with Dan.

The rest of the afternoon was nearly unbearable. Dan, whose ego had apparently been bruised by Candace's game with Con, made it clear she was *his* date and *his* alone. He kept her pinned to his side, though the way she involuntarily froze up whenever he touched her finally penetrated his skull and he kept his hands to himself.

Contrarily, Con had a wonderful time. Gayle was quick and fun and amusing, and everyone at the office seemed to fall in love with her. It was a bittersweet experience for Candace. The best she could say about it was that she applauded Con's taste in women; the worst was that she couldn't see any reason Con wouldn't eventually fall in love with Gayle. It was depressing to always like the women who were her rivals, Candace thought. Where were the scheming witches with greed and avarice on their minds? Where was someone she could really hate?

"What're you thinking about?" Dan asked as he drove them through the early twilight to her home. Candace had sat silent and brooding throughout most of the journey.

"Nothing much."

"It doesn't have to do with Connor Holt, does it?"

Surprised, she had to school herself not to react.

"I saw the way you were watching him. And so, I imagine, did he."

"I don't know what you're talking about."

He laughed, but there was no humor in it. "Oh, come on. You would have rather been at the party with him."

Candace gave him a sidelong glance. His jaw was thrust forward with bulldog determination. For the first time she wondered just how much he'd had to drink. He'd seemed to sober up later in the day, or she wouldn't have climbed in the car with him. But now she wondered if she'd made a mistake.

They drove in silence the rest of the way. When they finally pulled into the driveway, safe and sound, Candace exhaled in relief. Her fingers were already on the handle when she felt his arm steal around her shoulders.

"Aren't you going to invite me in?" he asked.

"I'm sorry, Dan. Not tonight. I'm beat."

"Is my touch that repulsive to you?"

He was looking for an argument. The air was charged with tension and aggression. *How do I get myself into these things?* Candace asked herself woefully.

"I'm just tired."

"You wouldn't give me a dance at the last party, now you won't even give me a kiss. I'm beginning to get a complex."

"Dan, you're a friend of mine. I'm not looking for anything else right now."

"Except with Connor Holt."

Candace wouldn't even dignify that with an answer. She thrust open the door and let herself out into the sultry night. "Good night, Dan," she said pointedly. She was tired of him moving in on her, circling like some bird of prey.

"Okay, fine. Go. I don't need the abuse." He slumped back into his seat. "But don't think Holt's such a knight in shining armor. He was married before, you know. To the boss's daughter. And after he'd worked his way up as far as he could go in the law firm, he divorced her." He snapped his fingers. "Just like that."

"Sounds like you've got him confused with Jeff McCall," she answered tightly.

"Check the statistics. I'm not lying."

"Maybe not, but you're trying to sow the seeds of discontent." She walked away.

"They're alike, Candace." Dan's voice drifted after her. "Jeff and Con. I'm afraid you're going to find out the hard way."

She was seething by the time she shoved her key into the lock. Not that she believed Dan for a minute. She knew Con well enough to understand what kind of man he was. What was disheartening was that Dan—who was more like Jeff than Con could ever think of being—was the man who was interested in her.

She slammed the door behind her and drew a deep breath. One of these days, she thought. One of these days it'll all fall together.

She stood in the silence for long moments, thinking over the events of the day. Her heart lightened and a slow smile spread across her lips. She had a date scheduled with Con. Right after the hearing. Mentally crossing her fingers, she hoped everything would turn out right—for little Janice, and for herself.

* * *

It had to be the hottest day so far, Candace thought wearily as she sat in the stuffy courtroom. The crowd was a waving mass as people fanned themselves with pieces of paper, their hands or whatever else they could find. Candace was wedged between her father and a stranger, and she was sweating. It amazed her that Con, who had held the room's attention through most of the hearing, could look so cool.

He was dressed in a gray suit with a white shirt. His dark face was set in sober lines, and his gaze was clear and direct whenever it swept the courtroom. As she watched him, Candace felt a sense of pride that was completely out of place. But it didn't matter. All that mattered was that the hearing was almost over—and Con was winning.

Beside him Tom Brinkwood, bearlike and uncomfortable in his blue suit, was huddled down in his chair, as if he hoped to sink right through the floor. It was obvious he was nervous and unused to being the center of attention, in total contrast to his ex-wife, whose sophisticated black suit and diamond earrings revealed more about her taste and personality than words could have expressed. How had those two gotten together in the first place? Candace wondered, although she had to admit there was a gentle, loving quality about Tom that was very attractive.

And then there was Jeff. Candace's gaze shifted to the trim attorney in the camel suit sitting next to Michelle Brinkwood. There was a perpetually ironic set to his expression, a condescension that seemed embedded in his personality. Why hadn't she ever noticed before? She'd lived with him for nearly two years, yet today it was like a bolt from the blue. Jeff's face was thin but handsome, and his eyes were as dark as Con's were blue. While she'd watched the events of the hearing unfold, Candace had searched her feelings and realized she cared nothing for him. There were no bittersweet regrets or thoughts of what might have been. He was simply an attractive man she'd once known—a selfish, ambitious, greedy but attractive man, she thought with an inward smile.

But no matter how adroit an attorney Jeff was, he couldn't bring out the motherly side of Michelle. No convincing argument could hide the fact that Michelle's heart was in her pocketbook. There was a feral, self-serving quality about her that made it hard to believe she cared a whit about her little girl.

As for Janice herself, Con had explained tersely before the hearing had begun that she was waiting in a room down the hall with Tom's sister. The judge had already made it clear that he would talk to Janice in chambers if need be. Con, however, was hoping the issue could be settled without putting the child on the stand. Janice was already overly grave and introverted. Having to choose between her parents would be tough.

Now, as everyone in the room awaited Jeff's closing argument, Candace felt her father's hand sneak over and give hers a hard squeeze. It was such an intimate gesture that she darted him a startled look.

"Don't worry," he whispered, apparently oblivious to his unusual display of affection. "It's in the bag."

Candace wondered where her father's heart was. With Janice? Or with the interests of Forsythe and Company? The best she could hope for, she supposed, was a little of both.

All eyes swiveled to Jeff and Michelle, whose heads were close together, their eyes darting around the courtroom almost guiltily. Candace felt a fresh sense of injustice. Why couldn't Michelle just give in and let Tom have Janice? What did she care?

Automatically her gaze narrowed on the beefy frame of Edward Faulkner. The man's superior attitude set Candace's teeth on edge, and she knew Con felt the same way. Edward nodded his head at Jeff and Michelle with false benevolence, as if to commend them for being obedient children.

The judge was looking inquiringly at Jeff, who half rose, his every movement suggesting that he was cognizant that people were watching. "We're ready with our closing remarks, Your Honor."

"Go ahead."

He walked to the center of the room, taking his time, an actor through and through. She could almost appreciate the performance. Almost. A part of her could never forgive him.

"The issue here is the bond between parent and child," Jeff said loudly. "Specifically, the mother-daughter bond. Statistics have shown that should this bond be broken, serious social difficulties can arise in the life of the child...."

Candace tried not to listen. Jeff was eloquent, she had to give him that, but his glibness couldn't disguise his shallowness. Michelle was hardly a role model for the mother-daughter bond, and Candace almost grew bored when he expounded on "the importance of financial responsibility." She knew for a fact that if she had walked into this courtroom cold, without knowing any of the principle players, she still would have cast her vote for Tom Brinkwood.

As soon as Jeff was finished, Con stood up. He glanced at the opposing attorney, his jaw set. Unlike Jeff, he started in without any conscious dramatics. "We're here to select a parent," he said in a normal voice. "A parent for a little girl who's been used as a pawn in a dangerous game played for the benefit of others. She doesn't want to have to choose.

She told me that, and I don't think it comes as any big surprise. All she wants is a happy, loving home." He paused. "That's what we should want for her.

"Happiness and love are emotions. They have nothing to do with the size of a person's bank account. Love is as much a father's emotion as a mother's. I dare anyone to argue that the father-daughter bond can't be as close as the mother-daughter one."

Candace stared at Con with new respect. He had no set speech. He was reacting to Jeff's closing remarks with feeling and passion. Her own heart started to pound.

"The issue here is who's the best choice for Janice. It has nothing to do with sex. It has nothing to do with money, as long as there's enough to provide for her. All it has to do with is who can love and care for her best, most fairly. Unfortunately, a choice has to be made. And it's become the court's responsibility to decide. But the basis of the decision must remain what's best for Janice. Nothing else matters."

Con glanced from Michelle to Tom. "I believe the choice should be an easy one. Thank you, Your Honor." Con walked back to his seat.

The gavel came down with a sharp crack that nearly brought Candace to her feet. A buzz of excited babble rose in the courtroom like a bubble. Candace turned blindly to her father, feeling somehow disoriented as the judge swept from the bench to his chambers to make his decision and the courtroom began to empty. Joshua was already heading forward to talk to Con. Candace tried to follow, but as she squeezed around several people, she ran straight into Jeff.

"Candace!" His face registered surprise, and she couldn't blame him. She'd never come to one of his trials.

"Hello, Jeff."

He recovered himself admirably. "Showing a united front?" he asked in the casual tone he'd perfected over the years. He inclined his head in the direction of her father. Joshua had reached Con's table and was talking rapidly and forcefully.

"Something like that," Candace admitted. She felt Con's eyes on her and glanced back, giving him a wink of encouragement.

"You're looking good," Jeff said.

She laughed. "That's like saying, 'Nice day if it don't rain.' Tell me, do you ever really feel anything? I mean, way down deep?"

He frowned. "I don't have time to talk right now. Maybe we can sometime later. I'd like to sort of smooth out the rough edges between us."

"They're smooth, Jeff."

He was already turning, but something in her tone stopped him. Giving her a searching look, he said, "You seem different."

That was the most honest thing he'd said all day. "Thanks, Jeff," she replied levelly. "I'll take that as a compliment."

But he was already gone, swept up in his other life, the one he'd stepped over her to achieve. To be charitable, he probably hadn't meant to hurt her. He'd just used her. Her feelings really hadn't entered into it at all.

Candace worked her way toward Con. Joshua was talking rapid-fire, dissecting everything he'd done, every word he'd uttered. Con, for his part, accepted this with a tolerance Candace hadn't known he possessed.

She cut through her father's torrent of words. "You were wonderful," she told Con, shooting a glance that said "Behave yourself" to her father. Joshua snorted and looked unrepentant.

"I hope the judge feels the same way," Con said. "He didn't ask to see Janice in chambers."

"I'm glad," Tom Brinkwood burst out, his words fast and clipped, as if he were afraid of being cut off before he finished. "It would have broken her heart to stand up against her mama."

"When will the judge reach his decision?" Candace asked.

"Soon, I hope." Con turned to Tom. "If you want to go see Janice, I'd do it now."

"Think I won't be getting her, then?" Tom asked, worried.

"Let's hope for the best. Michelle didn't portray the image of sainted motherhood her lawyer would have liked her to."

"I'd say it's no contest," Joshua put in, and Candace could have kicked him for raising false hopes. If things didn't turn out as they all hoped, Tom could be shattered.

Candace walked with Con, her father and Tom Brinkwood out of the courtroom. Everyone was standing in the hall. Jeff came over and said a few words to Joshua, and Candace caught Con eyeing him curiously.

"So what do you think?" she asked.

"You don't want to know." He smiled, his blue eyes lighting with amusement and, she could have sworn, affection.

"Father's right. You're a better lawyer than he is. It's obvious you believe in what you're doing."

"This is a far cry from your first opinion of me," Con pointed out dryly.

Candace tossed her head. "Well, maybe I've learned a thing or two."

It didn't take long before the bailiff opened the doors to the courtroom and called everyone back inside. As the judge sat down at the bench, Candace held her breath. *Please,* she thought. *Please make the right decision for Janice.*

He started in without preamble. "I have weighed the matter of Janice Brinkwood's custody and come to a decision. As Mr. Holt so eloquently stated, money is not the issue." He smiled faintly. "Janice needs a guardian who will look out for her best interests. Ideally that would be both of her parents, but since that's impossible, I award custody to Thomas Brinkwood."

There was half a beat of stunned silence. Then Michelle Brinkwood rushed out of the courtroom, her face a mixture of emotions, the main one anger. The door slammed behind her, and everyone started talking at once.

Edward Faulkner stood up, his neck crimson with fury. He glared at Con, who didn't even notice. Con was too busy dealing with Tom Brinkwood's arm-pumping enthusiasm.

"Well," Joshua said, pleased. He chuckled. "Well, what do you know? Looks like I got a winner in Mr. Holt."

"Don't act so proprietary," Candace murmured, smiling and squeezing past him. "I don't think he'd appreciate it."

"And how would you know?" Joshua's brows lifted.

"I know a little bit about Mr. Holt myself."

She let him chew on that one as she approached Con and Tom Brinkwood. Tom's eyes were suspiciously moist. "I can't thank you enough," he was saying over and over again to Con.

"You were the one who impressed the judge," said Con. "A lawyer is only as good as his client."

Tom shook his head at Con's humility. "I'll talk to you later. I've got to find Janice."

"Sure." Con turned to Candace. Seeing her expression, he laughed. "What is this? I would almost believe you'd changed your opinion of the legal profession as a whole."

"Something like that." She grinned. "I'm really glad for Tom and Janice. And for you."

Con was dumbstruck by the beauty of her glowing face. Where was the unhappy woman of three weeks ago? He could almost see her developing strength right before his eyes. "Looks like we're going to be celebrating tonight, rather than commiserating."

Joshua poked his head between them, his bushy eyebrows drawn together. "What's this?"

Candace didn't know whether she could deal with her father's interference right now, but Con said smoothly, "Your daughter's promised to help me celebrate. We're having dinner together."

Candace groaned inwardly at the look of pleasure that crossed her father's face. "Wonderful," he said, beaming and clasping Con's hand enthusiastically. Con slid Candace a wry glance. "Have you picked a restaurant? The Bayside has wonderful food. Why not take my boat out? You can dock right in front of the restaurant."

"Father—" Candace protested.

"Can you drive a boat?" Joshua asked Con, undeterred. He snapped his fingers and made a face. "You need a license to operate one on the lake. I forgot."

"As a matter of fact, I have a license," Con drawled. "Thank you, Joshua. I might just take you up on your offer."

"Good, good." He clapped him on the shoulder. "And congratulations on the outcome of the hearing. I never had any doubts. You've made Forsythe and Company look good."

"Is that right?" He picked up his briefcase. "Well, that was my primary aim," he said sardonically.

Joshua wasn't put off. "Now, Con, what's important is that Tom Brinkwood gained custody of his daughter. But you have to admit, this win didn't hurt the firm, either."

"No, it didn't," Con agreed.

They were almost out the door when Jeff McCall approached Con. He thrust out his hand. "Looks like Forsythe and Company has another bright star."

"Thank you," Con said carefully, and Candace held her breath.

"I'm sure we'll meet across a courtroom again. Maybe next time it'll be over something bigger."

"Oh, I don't know. A child's welfare is a pretty big issue to me."

Jeff's composure didn't falter by a hair. "If Edward Faulkner has anything to say about this decision, I'm sure I'll see you sooner than you expect."

"Edward Faulkner is a meddling outsider whose selfish interests don't have any place in this issue. You can quote me." Con's smile was cold.

This lack of regard for one of Portland's most influential citizens obviously surprised Jeff. He eyed Con with something akin to horror.

Candace walked ahead, her stomach churning at the thought of more confrontation, but when she passed through the courtroom doors to the blistering afternoon heat she found Con beside her.

"Let's get the boat and fly," he said in her ear. "For once I agree with your father wholeheartedly. I want to feel wind and sun and water. I want to go somewhere and breathe. And I want to do it with you."

She heard someone inhale sharply and turned to see Jeff narrowing his gaze on Con, his handsome mouth an unhappy, purposeful slash. A rival, thought Candace in surprise. All Jeff had wanted was a rival for her affections.

How shallow. How shallow and sad.

She looked at Con. His eyes were very blue, and in them was a restlessness she felt stirring in her own breast. "Let's get out of here," she said feelingly.

He grinned, tucked her hand in the crook of his elbow and led her down the tiered steps.

Chapter Seven

Wind screamed past Candace's face, tangling her pale hair, making it impossible to do more than grin as she and Connor skimmed across Lake Oswego's choppy green surface in her father's boat, the *Elizabeth K.* She sat beside Con, her white cover-up pressed against her body, the sleeves flapping wildly. Ahead and to the left was a small inlet, and Con careened the boat around in a tight circle before suddenly straightening their course and pulling back on the throttle. The boat rocked on high swells and floated toward shore.

"Are we stopping?" Candace asked, clutching hard to the gunwale. They'd been running at full speed for about half an hour, laughing in exhilaration. She hated to see it end.

Con flashed her a grin, his white teeth a contrast to his dark skin and black polo shirt and trunks. "Do you know where we are?" He inclined his head toward the curving shoreline. A white wooden boathouse stood at one end, its flat roof fenced and turned into a sun deck. Con guided the boat toward the dock and cut the engine. They drifted slowly inward, bumping gently against the wooden pilings.

"Is this where you live?" Candace looked around her. An imposing three-story home stood on the ivy-covered bank above.

Something about the place seemed familiar, and as she tried to put her finger on it, Con said, "It's the Baines house. Tanner and my sister live here now. I imagine Maggie will just be getting home from work." He jumped lithely onto the dock, tying the mooring rope with quick, efficient strokes. "Do you mind? I thought we'd just stop for a minute."

Candace's lips parted. "No...I don't mind." She swept a glance over herself and tried to comb her fingers through the ruins of her hair. His sister. Maggie.

Something must have shown on her face, because Con said, "They don't bite. At least Tanner doesn't. Maggie might have gotten me once or twice when we were kids."

"You make her sound more interesting by the minute." Candace smiled.

He shrugged. "She's all right." He stretched a hand to her, and she stepped onto the gunwale of the boat, grabbed his fingers and leaped to the dock—and nearly straight into his arms. For a moment his hands seemed to close around her, his palm spreading against the small of her back. But as she gained her footing, he released her.

"You said you and Tanner were friends when you were kids. Did you introduce him to Maggie?"

"In a manner of speaking. When she was fifteen I made her climb up the tree outside his bedroom and deliver a message to him for me. She fell for him. Pretty hard, I'd say. She never married, and after his first marriage fell apart and he moved back to Lake Oswego, they got together again."

They walked up a worn path to the deck that surrounded the back of the house. "She fell in love at fifteen?" Candace murmured. "She must be a woman who knows her own mind."

"She is. I can guarantee it."

Candace was a little afraid to meet her. What if Maggie didn't like her? She could sense Con's deep love for his sister, and Candace, for reasons she couldn't explain, was afraid of not measuring up.

"What if we can't get in this way?" Candace asked, glancing at the glass door that led from the deck to the kitchen. "The door's probably locked."

"And I know where there's a key." Con flashed her a grin. To one side of the deck there were several flowerpots brimming with a profusion of lobelia and petunias. Small pebbles lined the soil, and from beneath one larger stone Con produced a key. He was in the act of inserting it through the back door lock when a woman's figure was suddenly framed in the window.

Candace froze as the door opened.

"Well, you could have at least waited until I'd completed my break-in," Con said accusingly. "Candace, meet my little sister, Maggie Baines. Maggie, Candace McCall."

"Hi, Candace." Maggie was direct, her eyes as green as Candace's own, her hair a lustrous chestnut. She wore a white lab coat that bore her name, followed by the letters R.D. "Registered Dietitian," she said, answering the unasked question.

"Hello," Candace murmured, shaking hands with her. She had the terrible feeling she'd been right to worry: she wasn't going to pass muster with Con's sister. It was silly. But there was something about the way Maggie looked at her that made her nervous.

"We're just going out to dinner," said Con, "and I thought I'd stop by for a minute."

"Whose boat?" Maggie asked.

"My father's," Candace answered, then was uneasy at the look that suddenly shot between Maggie and Con.

"Some things never change," Maggie remarked in a tone edged with irony. "You're not the Candace whose father owns the law firm Con works for, are you?"

Feeling as if she were way out of her depth, she said on a short laugh, "Guilty as charged."

To her surprise, Con slipped his arm over her shoulder protectively. "I'm trying to overlook the fact that she's a Forsythe," he said lightly. "It's not easy. I mean, the woman drives a Jag, for crying out loud."

"Your father owns the island in the lake?"

Maggie was trying to be polite, Candace could tell. But it was difficult for her, and Candace began to feel defensive. "That's right," she said. "Ostentatious, isn't it?"

Maggie smiled, but Candace could see the worry simmering in her eyes.

Con glanced past Maggie to the interior of the house. "Tanner's not home?"

"He should be here any minute. Would you like a drink or something? It's so hot and muggy."

"Iced Tea?" Con asked. "Or maybe a beer?" he added hopefully.

Maggie grinned, and Candace saw the resemblance between brother and sister. "Come on in the kitchen and look for yourself."

"I'll be right back," Con said to Candace, following his sister.

Glad for the respite, Candace let out a long breath. Whatever undercurrents had been passing between Con and his sister were gone, and the crisis had been resolved for the moment. She didn't understand exactly what was going on, but she knew it had something to do with her.

Maggie doesn't approve of you.

The idea, once formed, refused to be rooted out. Candace's uneasiness gave way to anger. How could Con's sister judge her so quickly? Was she one of those jealous sisters who tried to control their siblings' fate?

Rubbing moist palms down her white cover-up, Candace made a wry face. She'd known Maggie would be a stumbling block. She'd sensed it. And it all had to do with the fact that she was Joshua Forsythe's daughter.

Deciding she would just have to change Maggie's image of "the boss's daughter," Candace headed for the kitchen, too. Her footsteps were muffled by the carpet, and Candace could hear Maggie and Con clearly as she approached. Their conversation stopped her in her tracks.

"... just like Linda," Maggie was saying. "Doesn't anything penetrate that thick head of yours? My God, Con. I thought you'd gotten over that phase."

"Now wait just a minute." Con's voice had lost its tolerant edge and had deepened with anger. "I have a date with Candace, that's all. I don't care that she's the boss's daughter. She's nothing like Linda."

"But you're doing it again, Con," Maggie said. "You're letting yourself get seduced by the wealth and power."

"Is that what I did with Linda? Go ahead, Maggie, spell it out for me. I'd really like to know just what I do and what I think. It's great you can tell me those things."

"Oh, for pete's sake." She made a sound of disgust. "I can't talk to you."

Candace eavesdropped unabashedly, her own anger mounting.

"Maggie, I like Candace," Con said bluntly. "She's a friend. Stop trying to be my conscience." He started to laugh. "You think *you* were hard on her because she's a Forsythe? You should have seen me."

Candace heard ice being dropped into a glass and realized Maggie was nearly finished making the iced tea. Not wanting to be caught eavesdropping, she walked back to the deck, stepping out into the slanting evening sunlight.

Her mind was churning with new information. Linda was Con's ex-wife. Could this be the same Linda who had been calling him at work? And what kind of woman had she been that Maggie was ready to put Candace into the same slot without even giving her a chance?

"Well, hello there," a male voice drawled behind her. "And who, may I ask, are you?"

She whipped around to see a silvery-blond man eyeing her carefully, the corner of his mouth lifted in greeting. He was one of the handsomest men she'd ever met, and the cool way he was assessing her increased her nervousness a hundredfold. "Candace McCall," she said, holding out her hand. "You must be Tanner Baines."

He inclined his head, reaching out a hand to clasp hers. Her heart lurched at the crisscross of scars that covered his right hand. The accident, she remembered belatedly.

"Don't worry, it doesn't hurt anymore," he said with a touch of irony. "Maggie practically fainted when she saw it the first time. You are a friend of Maggie's, I assume."

"Con's. I'm a friend of Con's."

His eyebrows lifted thoughtfully, and at that moment Maggie and Con walked back onto the deck. By this time Candace was thoroughly unnerved, and the flush on her face revealed her feelings.

"A Jag, huh?" Maggie said, but there was no rancor this time, only an amused twinkle in her eye. Tanner gave his wife a kiss of greeting on the crown of her head.

"It was a gift from my husband." Why not explain? "I'm getting rid of it."

"Why?" Maggie was curious.

"Because—" She felt all eyes on her and said with a twisted smile, "Because I don't feel comfortable with my father's wealth, either." She turned to Con. "How's that for honest? Sorry, I eavesdropped on you."

"Why, you little sneak," he said teasingly.

"Uh-oh." Maggie's gaze switched from Candace to her husband. "I think I put my foot in my mouth again."

"Don't worry." Tanner's smile was wry. "There's still room for the other one."

Jabbing him in the ribs with her elbow, Maggie said to Candace, "If you overheard Con and me, I apologize. Con used to big-brother me to death, and I guess I'm little-sistering him the same way. My only defense is, I have his best interests at heart."

Con groaned. "Oh, pllleeeze..."

"Stay for dinner," Maggie said suddenly. "I've just got fresh fruit salad, cold cuts and rolls, but we could sit out here and get to know each other."

"See that?" Con gave Candace a sidelong glance. "Now she's trying to salve her guilty conscience." He shook his head. "Thanks, Maggie, but we're heading to the Bay-side."

"Then you'd better hurry," Tanner observed. "It's going to rain later tonight."

Candace glanced at the sky. There were clouds clustered on the horizon, but they looked puffy and harmless. The air, however, felt close and dense.

"Are you going to make me beg?" Maggie demanded.

Con touched Candace's arm. She realized he'd declined the offer because he wanted to make sure she felt comfortable. In truth, she would have liked to be alone with him, but she was determined to change Maggie's impression of her, and there was no better time than the present.

"Do you mind staying?" Candace asked Con, and had to hide a smile at the look of surprise and delight on his face.

"How do you do it?" he asked Maggie. "You're rude and obnoxious and people forgive you. It's not fair. It's never been fair."

She just smiled and tucked her arm through Tanner's. The way Tanner looked down at his wife's auburn head, his feelings clear though his expression had changed very little, made Candace's heart swell with longing. His love for Maggie could almost be felt, and it made her realize what a sham her own marriage had been.

As Maggie dragged Tanner off to the kitchen, Con bent his head close beside Candace's. "We didn't have to stay."

"You wanted to, didn't you?"

"Is that why you agreed?"

"No. Well, maybe. But I'd like to make your sister eat her words."

His lashes narrowed. "How much did you hear?"

"Enough to know that having money is a fate worse than death."

Con studied her so intently that she felt she'd said something wrong. But then he smiled and, to her joy and amazement, kissed her swiftly on the lips. "You're okay, Candace McCall. I don't care what anyone says."

"Thanks," she said wryly, and sat down beside him on one of the blue canvas deck chairs, propping her elbows on the glass-topped table, tenting her fingers under her chin. Con regarded her lazily, but there was something different in the way he was watching her, and when his fingers involuntarily grazed her cheek her breathing quickened.

I want you, she thought, wondering if he could read the message in her eyes.

* * *

Dinner was over and the dishes cleared, and a brass oil lamp had been brought outside and placed in the center of the table. Twilight shadows had deepened to purple night, and the clouds Candace had seen on the horizon had moved in with ominous stealth.

"Time to go," Connor said, gazing at the sky. A half-empty glass of Scotch sat before him, and he twirled it absently on the tabletop.

"I wish you hadn't come by boat," Maggie said. "You could stay later."

Con's lips curved in amusement. "Don't worry, I'll be back to cadge another meal off you."

Candace stirred herself from the feeling of lethargy that had come over her. Tanner had given her a snifter of brandy, and the hot liquid had brought a weakness to her limbs and a general sense of well-being. She'd enjoyed the evening immensely, a melancholy part of herself comparing Con's family life to her own childhood experiences. She'd missed so much, she realized.

It was a pleasure to feel Con's hand guide her down the path to the boat. From the dock they waved to Tanner and Maggie, a gust of hot wind clearing Candace's senses a bit. She stumbled as she climbed into the boat, however, and was glad for Con's tight grip on her arm.

Unlike herself, Con seemed in complete control, and it was clear to Candace that his mind was sharp, his reactions swift. With a roar the engine turned over, and Con guided the boat to the darker waters, opening the throttle wide as soon as they were away from shore.

"Let me know if you see lightning," he said tensely.

Candace blinked. "Do you think we will?"

"I doubt it. Those clouds look more like rain, but with this hot weather..."

Nothing could have cleared her head more quickly. She let the wind race past her hot cheeks and kept an anxious eye on the lowering cloud cover. They sped in the direction of her father's island, but it was at the far end of the lake, several miles away. Before they were halfway there, the clouds opened and a torrential sheet of rain poured from the sky, soaking them both instantly.

Con swore, softly and distinctly, and Candace wiped rivulets of water from her hair. The cool rain revitalized her, and she inhaled deeply, laughing as Con shook his dark head, sending a spray of water everywhere. He flashed her a white grin.

"We've got to get out of this!" he shouted above the rain.

She nodded, then grappled for a hold as he suddenly swung the boat toward shore. Shooting him a questioning glance, she hung on tightly. They were still a long way from her father's island.

Minutes later he cut the engine, and the boat rode a series of swells as he maneuvered it toward a narrow wooden dock. Before the boat bumped gently against the mooring Con was on the dock, working fast to secure the boat, lashing it down with quick, hard strokes, then grabbing Candace's hand and hauling her up to join him. She slipped on the slick dock, clung to his arm, then tried to help as he pulled the gray cover tarp from beneath the back seat and hastily snapped it on to the boat.

Candace stood up, pulling back her lank hair. Rain had soaked her white cover-up to her skin, and it stuck to her bare limbs, outlining her blue one-piece swimsuit. Con grabbed her hand, and they raced together up the dock, slipping and laughing, until they found a drenched, muddy path that led upward, illuminated by yellow lanterns.

"Where are we?" Candace asked.

"My place. Quick! Wave to Mrs. Collingwood." He lifted his hand to his forehead in a snappy salute, spoiled only slightly by the water-soaked hair hanging in his eyes.

The curtains twitched behind one of the corner windows of the stately Victorian home that rose before them. "Who's Mrs. Collingwood?" Candace asked.

"Our resident Peeping Tom. Or Tomasina. The house was divided into condominiums, and she lives in the one on the end. I'm on the other end, and since our neighbor in the middle is in his twilight years, I'm her only source of vicarious thrills. Come on."

Candace hurried after him, holding on to his hand. Rain poured down furiously, and she huddled close beneath the narrow eaves above the back door as Con searched for his keys.

"Damn. We're going to have to break in."

"Break in? How?"

He laughed. "I can see there are big gaps in your education. Don't worry. There's always a way. Wait here."

She started to shiver as soon as he left. It wasn't exactly cold, but she was wet and it had grown very dark. The rain was so intense it bounced off the pavement, pouring off the roof and down the choked downspouts, pummeling the hapless flowers into the ground.

Glancing behind her, she saw lights on the water: other boats, moving slowly through the summer storm, their visibility reduced to just a few feet. No lightning, though, she thought with relief, searching the black sky. It should be safe on the water.

The door suddenly opened, and Con beckoned her into the room with a sweep of his arm. "Come in."

"How did you get in?" she asked, looking down at his bare feet and the water still running off his muscular legs.

"I climbed onto the roof and came in the second-floor window."

"In this rain? You could have fallen and killed yourself."

"Could have, but didn't."

He led the way through the den into a small living room with a marble fireplace, its ornately molded mantel painted white, the mirror above reflecting Candace's appearance.

"Oh, my God," she said in horror. "Look what the cat dragged in."

Con was behind her. He glanced up, catching sight of both their reflections. "You look pretty good to me," he remarked, his gaze skating over Candace's breasts, outlined soft and lush against the thin fabric.

"This hair," she protested weakly, picking up a strand and letting it fall limply against her neck.

"Stay there. I'll be right back."

Candace watched him leave, wondering what was on his mind. He walked with a slight limp, she realized. Had he hurt himself somehow?

"You lied to me about not getting hurt," she said when he came back with a fluffy white towel. At his blank look, she pointed to his right foot. "You're limping."

"Oh, that. I broke it skiing one year, and it likes to give me trouble every now and then." He placed the towel around her shoulders and smiled. "All right, I confess. I twisted it a little when I was on the roof."

"Aha!" Candace laughed, then gasped when he suddenly lifted the towel and began rubbing her head.

"You'll be dry in no time," he said, as if his actions were as natural as the beating rain.

Candace let him towel her hair, catching sight of herself in the mirror whenever part of the towel wasn't in her eyes.

He worked systematically, as if drying her hair were the most important issue at hand.

He finished with a flourish, and when she looked at herself, she groaned. Her hair might have been tangled before, but now it was a total disaster.

Con was grinning at her, but when he swiped at his own wet mane Candace deliberately pulled the towel from his hands. "Bend down," she said. "It's my turn."

Obediently he lowered his head. Candace rubbed the towel briskly until his black hair was nearly dry. Several times her fingers encountered the silky thickness of it, and she wanted to run her hands through the damp waves. But she managed to resist. She and Con were friends, nothing more.

Straightening, Con ran an experimental hand through his hair. She watched the black strands ripple around his fingers. "Nearly dry." He eyed her clinging white cover-up. "You're soaked. Let me get you something to change into."

"Maybe I should just . . . go home." She glanced at him uncertainly, plucking at the wrapper, trying to pull it away from her skin.

"Maybe you should," he agreed, but the deepness of his voice suggested he felt something else. "How about another brandy first to warm you up?"

"I'm warm. Really." Her smile hurt. "And I couldn't drink anything more."

"Do you want to leave?"

The seriousness of his tone made her catch her breath. "Well, I don't know. Maybe—" she licked her lips— "Maybe I could have a soft drink. . . ."

"Coming right up."

Candace sat down gingerly on the corner of the couch, trying not to dampen the soft tan fabric. Raindrops ran down the outside windowpanes, closing off the room, making it seem far too intimate.

When Con returned it was in a dry shirt, still unbuttoned, and a pair of low-riding faded blue jeans. She saw the dark hair arrowing down from his navel and had to drag her gaze away.

He set a tray down on the table and handed her a glass of orange juice. "It was all I had," he explained. "A bachelor's life, you know. You were lucky to get it. Oh, don't worry about the couch. It's one of Maggie and Tanner's rejects that I inherited. I'm a little short on furniture," he admitted. "I haven't bothered to get anything. This is about it, apart from a kitchen table, a few chairs and, well, I do have a bed."

Candace didn't answer. She had a sudden mental image of Con's bed.

"My wife ended up with the house and furniture after we were divorced," he said with equanimity. "Which was lucky, because it was god-awful."

"The house, or the furniture?" Candace tried to settle the wet wrapper around her legs but it was impossible to keep the couch dry and her legs covered. She saw his gaze skate to her bare skin. In the glow from the dimly lit lamps her limbs had a warm, peachy tone.

"The furniture. It was very chic. Black lacquer, red tassels, lots of murals. Not the kind of place you'd curl up with a dog at your feet. Are you sure I can't get you something dry to wear? You look so uncomfortable."

"I'm fine. Really."

"Here." He shrugged out of his white shirt and handed it to her. His skin was a burnished copper color, and muscles rippled beneath it like well-oiled machinery when he moved.

"I..." She could peel off the wrapper, she supposed, but then she'd be sitting in her bathing suit, covered only by Con's shirt. Now he held out the selfsame shirt to her, and she accepted it, feeling the warmth of it in her hand.

"I could leave if it would make you more comfortable."

She gave a shaky laugh. "Now that's ridiculous." She pulled her wrapper over her head, then quickly thrust her arms through the sleeves of his shirt, pulling the lapels close around her breasts. Shooting him a glance, she thought that the way his gaze was narrowed at the window was unusually intent.

She tucked his shirttail around her leg. "What were you saying about your ex-wife's taste in furniture?" she asked, trying to put the conversation back on track.

But the mood was spoiled. Con seemed to drag his thoughts back with an effort. "Just that it wasn't my taste."

"What is your taste?"

His blue eyes met hers briefly before settling on her mouth. "Oh, I don't know," he drawled.

Snug within the folds of his shirt, Candace slid him a look from beneath her lashes. There was a fine tension around his mouth, even though he tried to disguise it. "It's warm in here," she said when the silence stretched to the breaking point.

"I could open a window."

He did so without another word, and the beating rain created a soft stirring of air through the room and a rushing, elemental background roar. Con stared into the inky night, and Candace slid from the couch to stand silently beside him.

"Con," she whispered, hardly aware of what she was doing.

He didn't turn her way. She saw his jaw tighten, and he kept gazing through the window. "I worked for Linda's father," he said conversationally, as if picking up where they'd left off. "I met her one day in the office. She was there to see Daddy Warbucks. One thing led to another, and we went to bed together."

Candace shivered. Maggie wasn't the only who'd been comparing her to Con's ex-wife. "Did you love her?" she asked with difficulty.

Shaking his head, he said, "I never did. I married her because I—" He cut himself off, then finished with, "Well, because it seemed like the thing to do."

"That's hardly a reason to get married."

"It's no reason at all." He slid her a measuring look. "Why did you get married?"

She opened her mouth, then closed it, smiling sheepishly. "Because it seemed like the thing to do."

"I'm not good at lying to myself about my feelings. I like you, Candace. And I'd like to sleep with you. But I'm not interested in marriage," he added softly.

"That's fair, I guess." Candace swallowed, aching inside.

His hand cupped her chin, turning her face toward his. His eyes smoldered with a blue flame, and she realized they were fast approaching the point of no return. "And what do you want?" he asked in a voice that throbbed with undercurrents of emotion.

"I want—something else, Con. I want a man who loves me, and a home, and a family." Her pulse had quickened, her breathing light and shallow. "But I don't think I'm going to find it."

His palm slid over the skin of her neck, beneath the shirt's collar, to stroke her collarbone and shoulder. Lips trembling, she waited for him to make a decision. "You're honest. And if that's what you want, I'm bound to disappoint you."

"I don't expect anything."

"Oh, yes you do. All women do."

She would have liked to argue that point, but his head slowly lowered, his mouth exploring hers in a slow kiss. Con seemed determined to make this as slow as their first love-making had been fast. Candace stood before him, neither hastening nor slowing down the speed of his sensual invasion. His hand moved convulsively against her skin, the other wrapping around her, pressed against the small of her back, but his lips were gentle, urging her into a response.

Tentatively she slid a hand up his bare arm, resting it against the wall of his chest. His heart was like a hammer.

He shifted, drawing her nearer. His belt buckle dug into her abdomen, but she felt the rising pressure of his passion and instinctively moved closer.

"Candace," he breathed in a ragged whisper, sliding his lips down her neck and sending shivers of delight up her spine. "Candace," he repeated achingly, and buried his lips in hers again.

That was all she needed to hear to fantasize that he was in love with her. She moaned softly, meltingly, and he pulled her tightly against his rigid arousal, cupping her bottom, groaning with primitive desire.

Her legs were trembling, and suddenly he swept her into his arms, looking into her flushed face with glittering sapphire eyes. He was breathing hard, and she felt the slight tremor in his hands as he carried her from the room.

Candace could do little more than lie weakly in his arms. She stared at him with passion-glazed eyes, returning to her senses briefly and clinging tightly to his neck as he began to mount the stairs.

"Am I too heavy?" she asked in a breathless voice.

"No." He walked carefully, swore when he brushed his hand against the wall, then laughed at the ridiculousness of it all.

His bedroom overlooked the water, and the light from the string of lanterns on the pathway below created a dim glow through the small rectangular windowpanes. Con laid her softly on the bed, leaning over her, his hands planted on either side of her. His gaze probed hers, hot and smoldering, but he said softly, "Are you sure?"

For an answer she laid her hand against his cheek. She'd realized sometime during the evening that what she'd considered her infatuation with him was really love. The words sprang to the tip of her tongue, but she held them back. He'd said he couldn't love her; he'd told her not to hope for it.

He turned his mouth to her palm, kissing it, his tongue tasting her flesh. *It's nothing but sex,* Candace reminded herself, but she didn't believe it. She couldn't.

Gently he removed his shirt from her shoulders. Then the straps of her bathing suit were sliding down her arms, the garment slipping over her hips and off her legs. Con kissed her neck and the hollow between her breasts, and Candace closed her eyes, aching with longing.

She heard him take off his own clothes, then felt his weight settle on the bed beside her. He lay against her, and her flesh felt on fire where it melded with his. Tenderly he kissed her closed eyes, moving against her in a way that made her clutch the covers of the bed.

"Candace," he whispered huskily. "You're so tense. Open your eyes. You act scared to death."

"I'm not." She swallowed and opened her eyes, gazing into his beloved face, overwhelmed by the fact that she cared so much for him so soon. Her tension was fear of their uncertain future. To him this was a passing thing, a fling, a moment of insanity. He'd been painfully clear about that, yet she couldn't walk away.

His mouth found hers again, slanting back and forth in a fierce, wildly arousing kiss. Candace wound her arms around his neck, feeling his chest hair against her taut nipples, her flesh awakening as his hands slid over her hips, exploring, delving downward between her legs. She automatically stiffened, but his touch was like velvet and she was lost in the wonder of his lovemaking, distantly realizing how poor Jeff had been at understanding her needs.

His kisses deepened, and she found herself moving beneath him, her body possessed of a will of its own. Then his knee wedged between her legs. Gasping, she pulled back, but his kiss intensified, and when his tongue thrust into her mouth all her resistance melted.

"I want you," he whispered harshly, moving his hips against her in a gentle grinding motion that had her digging her fingers into his buttocks, soft moans issuing from her lips as her body opened to him.

He plunged into her partway, then eased back, plunging deeper the next time. Candace wrapped her legs around him, one hand sliding over the sinewy muscles of his back, the other lost in the silky pelt of his black hair. She kissed him wildly, with dizzying hunger, and the groan she wrung from him sent her senses soaring.

It was only with a great deal of effort that he held himself under control. "I didn't ask," he panted, "about pregnancy."

Candace's blood was running too hot for the words to wound. She thought of the women with her condition who'd turned up sterile. She felt somehow that this would be her fate, too. How ridiculous to worry about contraception when she wanted a baby more than anything in the world, could never have one.

"Candace," he whispered urgently, his body moving within her. She shuddered in need, her head tossing on the pillow, and he took her silence to mean there was no reason to worry. Steadily he increased the tempo of his thrusts, until her body was molten fire, her low cries lusty and wanton.

"Con!" she cried, just as shooting fires plunged through her, bursting into flames, burning her with a desire so intense a scream tore from her throat.

Con's control evaporated. He drove into her one last time and met the same fiery oblivion, amazed by the magnitude of her power.

"I love you," Candace whispered drowsily, her eyes closed as she snuggled close beside him. But later, when Con was lying awake beside her sleeping form, he thought it must have been a trick of his imagination.

Candace drifted to wakefulness, an evocative scent she couldn't quite put her finger on teasing her nostrils. She turned over into the pillow and realized the seductive smell was Connor's masculine odor clinging to the soft fabric.

Her eyes flew open, but she was alone in his bed. She sat bolt upright, wrapping the sheet around herself, memories from the night before tumbling over themselves, each more frantic than the last.

Something inside her melted and she sank back down, color staining her cheeks as she recalled her wanton ways. It was so unlike her! Good grief, after making love to Jeff she'd always been half-glad it was over. But Connor had made love to her twice more, once in the deep hours of the night when she'd felt his hand reach for her and she'd turned into his arms, tangling herself up with him, and once more in the gray of dawn, her own hands seeking him out, her own body riding on his, forcing him to meet her insatiable demands.

"Oh, God." She flung her arm over her face in embarrassment.

The sudden cessation of sound made her realize Con had been taking a shower and had just shut off the taps. Quickly she pulled the sheets more tightly around herself, tucking herself in like a mummy.

When he walked through the door to the bathroom, a towel slung across his lean hips, he stopped dead in his tracks, quirking an eyebrow at her maidenly retreat. "What's this?"

She was speechless, her eyes wide and shimmering. He'd told her he didn't love her, for pity's sake. He'd made it clear his feelings weren't involved. And yet she'd made love to him. Moreover, she'd begged for what he could give her. She was beyond embarrassment.

"Candace?" His gaze swept her wrapped form, his mouth forming into a grin.

"I'm...I'm..."

"You're—you're what?" he asked when she couldn't go on. He laughed at the hectic color that rose in her face and sank down beside her on the mattress. "Don't tell me you're embarrassed?"

She couldn't answer, nor could she meet his eyes. She was too overwhelmed with the person she'd suddenly become— a stranger to herself—to deal with him on any level.

Con didn't intend to let Candace wallow in regrets. He brushed back the tousled blond locks that lay fanned on the pillow, kissing her gently on the forehead. "It's too late to be embarrassed."

"I know that."

"And wrapping yourself up like this is too much of a temptation to resist."

"What do you mean?" she asked automatically, but his rich chuckle was answer enough.

Slowly he began pulling on the sheets, letting them slide away from her little by little. His blue eyes teased her, but she saw desire flare in their depths. "Make love to me, Candace. Like you did last night."

"Don't," she said, mortified, her arms rigid against her sides, attempting to hold the sheets down.

"Oh, Candace. You're so funny. Stop tightening up. That's not the woman I know."

"It's the woman *I* know," she said frantically.

"You really are a liar. I bet you know more about this other woman than you've ever let on." Con kissed her hard, then pulled back, reading her expression. Her eyes shimmered emerald green, passion smoldering. "Come on, Candace," he said, more intensely. "Show me."

Her treacherous body was responding in spite of herself. What are you fighting? she asked herself. Why do you care? Take what he has to offer and let the future unfold any way it will.

But still she resisted. "I don't want you," she said, tempting him with the very sound of her voice.

He laughed low in his throat and climbed over her, the towel slipping off. There was a desperate struggle between them for the sheets before they were finally tossed on the floor. She squirmed and fought and laughed, and then he was kissing her in earnest, licking her skin until she moaned and writhed on the sheets and he entered her in one smooth stroke.

"You're going to be the death of me," he muttered as the tempo steadily mounted.

Candace barely heard him. She was too wrapped up in a cocoon of love and fulfillment, and she couldn't think beyond the fact of pleasing him and pleasing herself.

Chapter Eight

Candace stood on tiptoes, searching through the top file drawer. The files were so jammed together that she could barely get her fingers between the folders to pull one out.

The sound of knuckles rapping softly against the open door caught her attention. Fingers still in the file drawer, Candace twisted around to see Con's dark head ducked inside the door.

"You busy tonight?" he asked.

The corner of her mouth twitched. She'd spent the last six nights with him, and he knew her schedule better than she did. She wasn't busy. She only wanted to be with him. It amazed her that she could be so abandoned with him, yet carry on at work as if nothing unusual were happening in her life. "I don't know— I'll have to check my calendar."

"Really. Well, try to pencil me in somewhere if you can." He leaned in farther and whispered, "I'm your slave."

She laughed, and Con drew back out of sight, his footsteps receding down the hall. Unspoken between them was the understanding that they would meet after work, have dinner or go out to a play or something, then end up back at his place to make love until they were exhausted. In the morning Candace would get up, fly back to her place, change and get ready for work, then see Con in the office and act as if nothing had happened. Except that every time she looked in his eyes she read their shared secret . . . and sometimes she thought she read something more, something deeper, something lasting.

Finding the file she needed, she shut the drawer, drifting back to the reception hub in the same cloud of happiness she'd walked around in ever since she and Con had first made love.

"What are you grinning about?" Terri asked suspiciously as Candace handed her the file.

"Oh, I don't know. Life, I guess. Funny, isn't it, how things can turn around just like that?" She snapped her fingers.

"I've never known that to happen, myself," Terri said. "What about you, Pamela? Has your life ever suddenly turned around?"

Pamela's normally dour face was hidden behind a tissue. She coughed, shook her head and turned her attention to her work.

"So what's the big change?" Terri asked.

"Nothing I want to talk about." Candace saw several pink message slips with Con's name on them and asked innocently, "Want me to take those to him on my way back to the file room?"

"These?" Terri held up the messages. "Well, now, I could do it." She started to laugh, and Candace snatched them out of her hand.

"Troublemaker," said Candace, smiling, and Terri gave her a look that said, "Who me?"

She started to stride down the pearl-gray hallway when Terri added, "Don't you even want your own message?"

"There's one for me?" Candace asked blankly, slowly turning on her heel.

"Right-o." The pink slip was passed to her, and Candace stared down at Dr. Evinrud's name and number.

Fear moved within her. It was all she could do to act normally as she thanked Terri and walked toward Con's office.

It wasn't that she'd forgotten about her condition; far from it. But being with Con had pushed her troubles to the far corners of her mind. She had better things to think about, much better things.

Knocking on Con's door, she glanced down at the message on top of the stack and her blood froze. It was from Linda.

"Enter," Con yelled, and Candace pushed open the door.

"Terri had a few messages piled up she hadn't given to you yet," Candace said. "I thought I'd bring them by."

"What's wrong?"

His ability to read her so easily unnerved her. "Nothing," she said, and he shot her an ironic glance as he accepted the small pile of pink slips. Glancing down at them, he shot her another look, his eyes alight with humor. "Is this the problem?" he asked, waving the message with Linda's name on it.

"Of course not."

"Yes, it is. I can tell by your face."

"You are so conceited," Candace blurted out, and was rewarded by his deep laughter.

"It's true. I am conceited. I'm also only interested in one woman. You."

Grateful for his sensitivity, she was also determined to make him understand she wasn't the jealous type. "I didn't mean to pry. It was just the note on top, and it surprised me."

"Linda means next to nothing to me."

"You don't have to say anything. It's okay—"

"Candace, shut up." His tone was gentle. "I'm trying to tell you something, and I want you to hear it. Linda's making noise about coming to Portland. Just for a visit. I thought you ought to know. But our relationship is long dead."

Candace stared at him, trying to school her expression not to reveal all the emotions racing through her. She hadn't realized how much she'd let Con become a part of her life. The thought of his ex-wife making a visit to Oregon to see him filled her with terror.

"Come here." He moved toward her, clasping her hand, pulling her into the security of his arms. "I met Jeff and didn't fall apart. You can meet Linda, if it comes to that."

"Are you going to...tell her about us?" Candace hadn't even had the courage to let her father know that she'd become seriously involved with Con, even though he asked her what their relationship was every time he saw her.

"How do you feel about that?" Con watched her closely.

Candace appreciated his understanding of how much the gossip concerning Jeff and Renée had hurt her. He'd made it clear a dozen times that it was up to her whether to let the rest of the office know about their affair. Affair. Lord, how she hated that word.

"I don't know how I feel," she admitted, her eyes suddenly stinging with tears. What was wrong with her? How could she be so happy one minute, devastated the next?

"We're dating, Candace. That's all anybody has to know. I'll play this any way you want."

She turned her back to him, needing to pull herself together. *I love you,* she thought fiercely. *I'm scared.* "I think Terri already has an idea how I feel about you," she said unevenly. "Maybe we should let people know we're...dating."

"Candace, I care about you." She felt his hands descend lightly on her shoulders. "I don't ever want to hurt you."

You are already. "I know."

Con's line buzzed, and Candace used the moment to escape. She walked blindly toward the file room, then veered off into the empty office near the end of the hall. She hadn't expected to face the impermanence of their relationship so quickly.

Deciding to get all the bad news over with at once, she dialed Dr. Evinrud's number.

"I was just checking on our next appointment," the doctor said when Candace had been put through. "I'm going to be out of town for a few weeks, so you may want to come in early."

"Can I wait until after you get back?" Candace asked, feeling as if she'd been granted a temporary reprieve.

"Well, let me see..." Candace heard her flipping through her book. "You were here on the twenty-sixth, and now it's near the end of August. I'll be back on the seventeenth. I'll schedule you then."

"Thanks."

"Oh, Susan Woodwin called me. She said you stopped by."

"Yes, I did. And she was great. It was nice to talk to someone who's been there, so to speak."

"She's awfully worried about your car. Something about her dog scratching it?"

Candace managed a laugh. "Oh, for goodness' sake. Yes, Harold nicked it a bit. I'd better call her and try to stop her worrying so much."

"Okay. I'll see you September seventeenth."

Candace found Susan Woodwin's number and placed the call. Susan answered on the fifth ring, sounding harassed and out of breath. "Hi, Susan, it's Candace McCall."

"Have you got an estimate on the car?" she asked before Candace could say anything more.

"No, I really don't care about the car. But since you're so worried about it, I have an alternate plan: how about if you take me to lunch as repayment?"

"But it's not enough! I don't know how much fixing your fender will cost, but I'm willing to bet—"

Candace cut in. "It's all I'll accept. Take it or leave it."

Susan sighed, and in the background Candace could hear Scott's loud wails. "I would love to go to lunch," she admitted. "Let me see if I can get a sitter and I'll call you back."

"Great." Pleased, Candace gave Susan her office number, and when Susan called back fifteen minutes later, saying she could meet Candace in the middle of the following week, Candace marked it on her calendar. Then she stared at the date, wondering when Con's ex-wife planned to breeze into town.

"What are you so worried about?" Con asked her later that evening. They were sitting on his back deck, drinking iced tea and watching the boats slice through the clear water of the lake.

"Who says I'm worried?" She focused her gaze on the sparkling water, sliding her sunglasses up the bridge of her nose.

"You do. Every time I look at you." He reached over and turned her chin, making her look at him. "It couldn't be more clear if you shouted it to all the world."

Candace tried to pull away, but Con forced her to meet his steady gaze, pulling off her sunglasses to probe the depths of her green eyes.

"The truth is, I don't know if I can deal with this," she heard herself say with a trace of defiance. "Letting it be known that I'm divorced and you and I are dating is one thing. Seeing you every night and making love—" she swallowed "—with no commitments... It's too hard for me. It's not how I want my life to be."

There, she'd said it. The worry that had been following her like a black cloud since the first glorious time Con had taken her to bed.

"How do you want your life to be?" he asked quietly.

"I want a family someday." This time, when she pulled her chin away, he let her go without resisting. *And I want you,* she thought with unhappy clarity. She loved Connor. Deeply. And it hurt so much to know it was one-sided.

"Well, I want a family, too. But I'm willing to take it one step at a time."

Hope rushed through her in a joyous wave, but she carefully contained her feelings. Was he talking in the abstract, or could he possibly be thinking about a family that included her?

"Candace," he said quietly. "We've got all the time in the world. I'd like to spend some of it getting to know you. I'm not willing to make another mistake."

She felt his fingers explore the curve of her cheek and she leaned her face into his palm. She didn't have all the time in the world, and somehow, someday soon, she was going to have to tell him.

* * *

The restaurant Susan Woodwin chose for lunch was a funky downtown pizza parlor with no decor but great food. Candace stopped at the window before entering, watching one of the employees skillfully toss a wheel of dough in the air and catch it as it spiraled downward into a perfect pizza shape.

Pushing through the door, she spotted Susan seated near the back. Susan waved as Candace wove her way through the tables.

"Pizza by the slice," Susan said when Candace was seated. "They've got pepperoni or double cheese. Which can I get you?"

"Uh...pepperoni, I guess."

"And a beer?"

Candace shook her head. "Make it a root beer," she suggested as Susan headed for the counter.

Stretching, Candace realized her mauve linen dress and her strand of natural pearls were far too sophisticated for the pizza parlor's regular clientele. She stood out like the proverbial sore thumb.

Susan returned, carrying a small tray laden with pieces of pepperoni pizza, a root beer for Candace and a beer for herself. "The service is lousy, but the food's good." Smiling, she added, "Although I suppose this isn't what you're used to."

"Now what does that mean?" Candace demanded, biting into the pizza.

Susan shrugged. "Your life-style's a great deal different from mine. I thought you might enjoy slumming a little."

"This is hardly slumming. This is the best pizza I've ever eaten."

Grinning, Susan said, "You seem different this time. Less tense. Has something good happened?"

Candace wiped her chin. "Where's your crystal ball?" she murmured.

"Something good *has* happened. I knew it! Don't tell me, you've decided to have a baby after all."

Candace nearly choked on her root beer. "No. There's just not enough time to have a relationship, decide on pregnancy and make it happen before it's too late. And I've got this feeling that even if everything worked out I'd find out I'm barren."

"What a pessimist!" Susan proclaimed.

"Two of the women Dr. Evinrud's treated for this never conceived. I'm just being realistic."

"So if it's not the baby, then what's happened to you?" Susan asked, watching Candace's changing expression. "You've met someone," she whispered with growing excitement. "That's it, isn't it?"

"Well, yes, I've met someone," Candace said, feeling suddenly shy. "But he's not interested in getting serious."

"Have you told him about your problem?"

"We've just started seeing each other," Candace protested.

"Well, don't waste any time," Susan said matter-of-factly around a bite of pepperoni pizza. "This is it, Candace. Your chance. Grab it."

"No." She wanted to clap her hands over her ears. Susan made everything seem so possible, but there were too many obstacles. How could she tell Con she would never have a baby when they'd barely started their relationship? How could she tell him about the surgery she faced?

Sighing, Susan shoved her plate away, her expression serious. She wiped her hands on a napkin and asked, "Is this guy the type who would run for cover at the mention of a baby?"

Candace thought of Con, of his teasing ways and the deeper emotions she felt she was just beginning to touch. She couldn't shake the foundations of their relationship. She just couldn't. She was too scared.

"I appreciate how much you're trying to help," she told Susan softly, "but my friend has made it clear he wants to take one step at a time. I won't have a baby," she said firmly, as much to convince herself as Susan. Thinking otherwise was much too dangerous. "But I might have Con, if I'm lucky. Now," she said briskly before Susan could open her mouth again, "how about another piece of pizza? Then tell me everything you can about Scotty. And don't leave out any details. . . ."

It was much later, as Candace was driving back to the office, her errands completed, that Susan's remarks crowded back into her thoughts. Should she tell Con about her condition? What good would it do? She had the strong feeling that hitting him with too much, too soon, would be a mistake—and it wouldn't change anything anyway.

Candace nosed the Jaguar into her parking spot in the underground lot and pulled on the emergency brake. It was almost closing time, and she was beginning to feel anxious. This was the first day in the last three weeks she hadn't made some kind of prior arrangement with Con. He'd been in court all morning and she'd been gone all afternoon. She hoped he was either still at the office or had left her some kind of note. She didn't know how she'd feel if she had to go home alone without any word from him at all.

"You've got a message from Mr. Holt," Terri said as soon as Candace pushed open the glass door to the Forsythe and Company offices.

Candace's face split into a smile of relief. "Oh?" she asked innocently, and Terri sent her a sidelong glance that said she was wise to her.

Handing her the note, which read, *I'll be at the Front Street Café & Bar until 6:30. Join me if you can*, Terri murmured, "That sure sounds like a date to me."

"Well, maybe it is," Candace countered saucily.

"Oho." Terri laughed. "Well, then, who's the brunette he walked out with? She didn't look like a client."

"What do you mean?"

"What do *you* mean?" Terri repeated, her mouth still curved into a grin. "I was just teasing. She must be some client of Con's. I figured you were meeting her, too. The dark-haired woman?" she added, seeking to jog Candace's memory.

But Candace just shook her head. She was certain that if Con had wanted her to meet one of his clients he would have said so. "I've been gone all afternoon," she murmured. "I don't know."

"I thought she was an acquaintance of yours or your father's. She was very intense."

Candace felt as if someone had reached a hand into her chest and squeezed her heart. Her mouth went dry. "Maybe she is," she replied, not wanting Terri to see how the slightest comment about Con could affect her.

Ten minutes later, she walked out of the Forsythe building on legs that felt like lead. It was quite possible the woman Con was with was a client. There was certainly no reason for her to think otherwise. He would hardly have asked Candace to join him if this mysterious other woman was a threat.

Her hand on the door of the café, her fears suddenly coalesced into one thought: Linda. Con had said his ex-wife was coming to Oregon. This woman could very well be Linda.

Candace felt the strength drain from her. She wanted to turn around and bolt. But then sanity prevailed and she reminded herself that if it was Linda, the woman was still no threat to her. Con's relationship with his ex-wife was over.

Stepping inside the café, she heard Con call out, "Candace, over here!"

He was at a table in the corner, one hand raised so that she could spot him easily. The brunette Terri had mentioned sat across from him, her back to Candace, but even from this distance Candace could see the luster of her hair, the shimmer of real gold at her ears, the sleek cut of her black dress.

Drawing on her courage, Candace resorted to the icy veneer that had been her trademark during most of the first part of the summer. She'd learned long ago how to be polite and remote even when she was dying inside.

Con held her chair, scooting it toward the table, seating himself next to her. "Candace, I'd like you to meet Linda Holt," he said in an even voice. "Linda, this is Candace McCall."

So it was true. Candace stared into Linda's clear blue eyes and thought, *She's even more beautiful than I imagined.* Linda, in turn, assessed Candace with a watchful curiosity that could only be described as suspicious. But then she smiled in such an open, friendly way that Candace was momentarily taken aback.

"Linda's visiting for a few days. She stopped by the office just before closing," Con explained, and Candace, who was beginning to know him well, heard the deeper tenor of his voice that meant he was not as much in control as he would have liked to appear.

"Hello," Linda said, extending her hand.

Candace cracked a smile. "It's a pleasure to meet you," she answered, her own hand clasping Linda's cool one.

"You work for the same company Connor does, then?" Linda asked politely.

"Yes."

Linda glanced at Con, who was leaning back in his chair, his brow creased into a frown. "Connor used to work for my father's company," she said, never taking her eyes from him. "But I suppose you know that."

Candace wondered what Linda would say if she told her Joshua Forsythe, founder of Forsythe and Company, was her father. "Con mentioned it," she murmured, sliding Con a look beneath her lashes that said, "So you kept that a secret, huh?"

His answer was a faint lifting of his eyebrows and a quirk of his lips.

Candace had no fear of liking Linda too much, she decided. Though the other woman was polite and was even trying to be friendly, she obviously felt Con was still her property. Lines had been drawn long before Candace had arrived. Candace didn't know what Linda's game plan was, but her feminine instincts were abuzz with worry. Whatever it was, it involved Con.

"I've tried to get Con to come back to Los Angeles," Linda said in the long silence that followed. She sent him a smile that was full of remembered intimacy. "But he seems to like it here."

"You don't really want me back in L.A.," said Con.

"It's not just me, Con. Dad wants you back just as badly." Linda sighed and ran her finger around the top of her wineglass. "You always liked L.A."

"I did then," Con admitted. "But I like Portland, too." His smile didn't quite reach his eyes.

Buoyed by Con's disinterest in Linda's offer, Candace's confidence returned. "Do you work at your father's law firm?" she asked politely.

"No. I made it a practice early on to stay out of my husband's business. Isn't that right?" she asked Con.

"Except that you didn't keep to it," he answered dryly.

"What do you mean?" She was more flattered than angry. "I was a good wife. You always said so."

Con didn't answer. His eyes narrowed reflectively, his gaze on Linda's porcelain face. Candace had the distinct feeling that he remembered things differently.

"Well, hello all," a voice drawled. Candace glanced around to see Dan Morrison leaning against the oak bar. He smiled and sauntered over, his eyes telling Candace that he was still sorry for acting like an oaf at the picnic and that he hoped she'd finally forgiven him. She offered him a watery smile.

Linda turned to assess the newcomer. "Don't tell me," she said with a grin. "Someone from the firm."

"Half the people in this place are from Forsythe and Company," Dan agreed easily. "So, Con, aren't you going to introduce me to the lady?"

Linda glanced expectantly at Con, who offered somewhat reluctantly, "Dan, I'd like you to meet Linda Holt. Linda, this is Dan Morrison."

"Holt?" Dan questioned, his eyebrows lifting.

"Con and I used to be married," said Linda with the perfect ironic inflection, letting Dan know the divorce had been inevitable but amicable. Candace wondered just how true that was. "I'm trying to talk him into coming back to our firm."

"Our firm?" Dan was obviously intrigued.

"My father's."

A wave of realization passed over Dan, and a slow grin spread across his lips. "You gotta hand it to this guy," he said, gesturing in Con's direction. "He knows how to meet the women who count." At Linda's puzzled look, he said, "Didn't you know Candace's father is Joshua Forsythe?"

Candace wanted to drop through the floor. She shot Dan a furious glance, then looked anxiously at Con. Con, however, was staring blandly at Linda, whose own face mirrored surprise and, just for a moment, defeat.

"You're kidding," she said when she'd pulled herself together.

Luckily, Con was more amused than angry. As Dan pulled up a chair, he said, "Which really doesn't make a damn bit of difference. I wasn't coming back to Los Angeles anyway. Tell Charles I appreciate the offer, but I'm happy here."

Linda tried her best to smile, but the realization of who Candace was had knocked the stuffing out of her. Candace almost felt sorry for her. She must have wanted Con pretty badly to swallow her pride and come after him. But Candace's pity disappeared in a rush when she caught the bitter resentment in Linda's ice-blue eyes.

Linda swept up her black purse. "Well," she said, "I guess I've made my pitch. I'll leave you two be." She stood up and so did Con, his own blue eyes wary. Apparently he was surprised by her capitulation. He escorted her to the nearby door. At the last moment she twisted around, and Candace could hear her ask hesitantly, "Could I talk to you tomorrow... alone? Maybe we could meet for lunch. There are some things I want to get straight."

Dan was watching their exchange with interest, and Candace wished she could think of a subtle way to smash her fist into his face. Didn't he realize how transparent he was?

"Call me at work," Con said, but the look on his face wasn't encouraging.

"Nice meeting you," Linda remarked vaguely toward Candace and Dan, then tossed her head as she walked out the door.

Dan's mouth curved in lazy amusement. "Pretty woman," he observed as Con sat back down.

"Wealthy, too," said Con. "And single. Also, she likes lawyers. Unlike others I could name," he added with a smile for Candace. "You ready to go?"

She nodded, swept by a rush of love for this man who was so sensitive to her feelings.

Dan heaved a dramatic sigh. "Candace, you wound me to the core," he said. "I'm not a good loser."

"I think you'll survive," she said wryly. She followed Con into the soft summer night, glad that Dan was smart enough to know when to give up.

"I'm sorry about Linda," Con said as they walked to the underground garage, holding hands like teenagers. "I didn't know what to do with her."

"You're very polite to each other."

"Not always," Con admitted. "But she wants something, so she's on her best behavior."

"She wants you."

He shook his head. "No. She thinks she wants me. She'll find something she wants more pretty soon, and she'll get out of my hair."

Candace wasn't so sure. "I think she's on a campaign to win you back," she said lightly, warningly. "She seems . . . determined to me."

"She is determined." A hard note crept into his voice. "But then, so am I."

They took separate cars back to Lake Oswego, dropping Candace's off at her home, taking his T-Bird to a small lakeside bistro that grilled steak and seafood on an outside barbecue. They sat under one of the red umbrellas, neither of them mentioning Linda again, but the dark-haired woman hovered over Candace's thoughts like a pall.

Candace barely tasted her salad and grilled salmon, and finally she thrust her plate away, feeling depressed and exhausted. When the waiter brought the dessert tray around, her stomach lurched and she shook her head, declining coffee, as well.

Con, who'd given up trying to draw her into conversation, sensed what she was feeling and said quietly, "Linda and I are through. Completely. It wouldn't even matter what happened between you and me; I wouldn't go back to her." He sighed. "I really don't like her very much anymore."

Candace's green eyes shimmered in the soft light. She plucked worriedly at the edge of the tablecloth. "But you were in love with her once," she said softly.

"No." He grimaced. "Of course, I thought so at the time, but now..." His voice trailed off, and the corners of his mouth tightened, turning downward. "She lied to me to get what she wanted. When I found out, I realized I'd married a woman I didn't even know."

Although Candace was dying to know what he was talking about, she refrained from asking. Whatever it was, it was between Con and Linda. But she was relieved it prevented Con's feelings for Linda being reignited.

An incredible weariness stole over Candace as Con drove through the star-studded night to her house. He pulled into the driveway, turned off the key and glanced over at her. "You're tired," he said.

"Exhausted."

He leaned over and kissed her, and Candace felt the unspoken question. He wasn't certain whether to come in or not.

In point of fact, she wouldn't mind an evening alone, she realized. She was tired through and through. Yet she didn't want to give him up, either.

She let him kiss her again and again, deeper each time, and slowly wound her arms around his neck, savoring the moment. Their relationship had changed, she realized. They were beginning to know each other in the intimate way lovers do, an idea she found both frightening and exciting.

Con's mouth was in her hair. "Do you want me to leave?" he asked huskily, the mounting tempo of his heartbeat making her aware of his own desires.

She lay passively in his arms, half dreaming. No, she thought, I don't want you to leave.

His lips moved to her ear. He pressed tiny kisses against her flesh, and she turned toward him as a flower turns toward the sun. She shivered as his tongue sent electric flashes along her nerves.

"Are you cold?" he asked, gazing down at her.

She shook her head and sighed contentedly. "No."

"Come on. Let's go in."

As soon as she was on her feet, she wished she was sitting down again. She was glad for the support of his arm around her shoulders. Her own arm was curved possessively around his strong back beneath his sport coat.

"Candace, are you all right?" he asked at the door, tipping up her chin.

She smiled up at him, her eyes half-closed, her face a soft blur in the moonlight. "Always, with you."

He kissed her hungrily and she responded, but her limbs felt weighted down, as if by lead bricks. She was content merely to receive his lovemaking, clinging to him when she felt him pull her tight against his hips, his tongue darting in and out of her mouth.

Suddenly he threw back his head and laughed. "You're done in, aren't you?"

"How can you tell?" she murmured, wrapping her arms around his chest, wishing she could just fall asleep next to him.

"Believe me, I can tell." His tone was rich in amusement. "Okay, I can take a hint." He whisked the keys from her fingers, unlocked the door and gave her a gentle push inside. "I'll see you tomorrow."

"You're leaving?"

"I think you need a good night's sleep. And I'm afraid I couldn't give it to you. I'll see you at work tomorrow."

Suddenly afraid, Candace said, "And tomorrow night?"

"Tomorrow night we'll pick up where we left off here. Good night, love," he added as he walked away, his voice a soft caress that drove away Candace's fears.

Closing the door, she leaned her head against it, hearing the echo of his words. *Good night, love. Love . . .*

The stairway loomed before her. Candace straightened, forcing herself to cross the small square of oak flooring, reaching her hand for the rail. Two steps up, she suddenly knew she wasn't going to make it to the top. Her forehead broke out in a cold sweat. Her heart raced and her stomach revolted, and she ran for the bathroom, retching violently over the toilet.

When the storm had passed she gasped for air, then washed out her mouth with cold water. As she stared at her ghastly-white reflection in the mirror, her heart nearly stopped.

Pregnant?

She pressed hard fingers to her trembling lips, shaking so badly that she sat down on the bathroom floor. It couldn't be. It couldn't!

But it's possible. More than possible.

She shook her head, her eyes widening, her heart hammering. But it couldn't be that easy. She'd made plenty of mistakes with Jeff and had never turned up pregnant.

But then she'd never had such sustained, abandoned lovemaking with her husband.

Mind racing, Candace could barely think straight. She wanted a child so badly. So badly . . .

It might just be the flu.

Her stomach was better now, just a flutter of queasiness left. Deliberately Candace prepared for bed, washing her face methodically, brushing her hair with careful strokes, slipping on her silk nightshirt.

She lay in bed alone for the first time in several weeks, eyes wide open, staring at the ceiling. She was afraid to be pregnant—afraid because she wanted it so badly, and afraid because it might mean the end of her relationship with Con. What if she was pregnant? What would he do when she told him?

She turned over, burying her head in the pillow. Her mouth was dry. She wanted Con as much as she wanted a baby. What if realizing one dream made her lose another?

Chapter Nine

The Claremont Room, the five-star restaurant at the Claremont Hotel, was as renowned for its clientele as for its cuisine. Many of Portland's most famous faces could be found lunching or dining at the Claremont, and Joshua Forsythe was notorious for arranging impromptu business meetings at a moment's notice, sending the staff scurrying to find an extra room. Out-of-towners who queried Portlanders about which restaurants were the city's finest were sure to hear the Claremont named. Its reputation was flawless, its decor rose and oyster-white, its elegance memorable.

And the place never failed to make Con feel uncomfortable.

"What's the matter?" Linda asked, sipping from a cut-crystal champagne glass. Her heavy bracelet—solid gold, he'd have bet—clinked gently against the stem of the glass.

"You mean besides the fact that we're meeting at the Claremont and discussing the remains of our marriage like jackals over a long-dead carcass."

Linda grimaced. "You really have a way with words, don't you?"

Con shrugged. "There's nothing left. You know it as well as I do."

"Why are you so obstinate? You won't even try to listen to me."

Con lifted a hand in surrender and was immediately accosted by a waiter who leaned over him with a tray full of sausages, bacon and croissants. "No thanks," he said with a faint smile.

"I was going to tell you something yesterday," Linda went on, "but your girlfriend showed up before I had a chance."

He let that one pass. If Linda was fishing for information about his relationship with Candace, she could keep on casting her line. He wasn't biting.

"Con, if you come back to the firm, Daddy's willing to make you a senior partner," Linda said in a tone of someone delivering unbelievably good news. Her mouth was drawn into a triumphant smile, and her eyes glittered with excitement.

Con stared at her. *She thinks I'm going to grab for it,* he realized with a sense of self-loathing. Had he given her that impression once? he wondered uncomfortably. That success was all that mattered? That he could be bought for a price?

And the price, in this case, would be going back to Linda—at least until she grew restless again.

"Linda, I wouldn't give a damn if your father offered me half the state of California. I'm not going back."

She went red with embarrassment, then white with fury. Settling back in her chair, she pinned him with angry, snapping eyes. "You sure are arrogant for someone who has nothing!"

Inclining his head in agreement, he said simply, "Yep."

"Dan Morrison was right. You're after Forsythe's daughter. I'm too late."

"Linda, as always, you overestimate yourself. You tricked me into marriage, now you're trying to buy me back to California. Maybe you ought to ask yourself why. I'm certainly not the kind of man for you."

"You sonofabitch." As furious as she was, there was reluctant admiration in her tone. "You're exactly the kind of man for me."

Con scraped his chair back, keeping his gaze directed at his wily ex-wife. He almost smiled. "Give up. You're going to make my life miserable, and your own, as well. It's not going to work. It didn't last time."

"I used to matter to you," she said wistfully. "I used to be able to get to you."

"Last summer. Not this summer."

"This summer you've got Candace."

"Candace isn't the issue between us, Linda. You and I just didn't work well together."

"I've never loved anyone like I loved you."

For a moment Con was diverted by the seriousness of her words. She believed them, he realized, whether they were the truth or not. "You're speaking in the past tense," he told her gently.

"It could be the present." Her eyes brightened with hope. "I'm in room 714, Con."

"No."

"Con..."

"Goodbye, Linda. Have a nice flight back." He tossed a hundred-dollar bill on the table, saw her bent head and, knowing he was being ridiculously softhearted, gave her a quick hug before leaving.

Candace sat in her father's office, staring unseeingly across his empty desk. Her mind was a million miles away, and she'd barely roused herself all morning. Marion had come and checked on her twice, her face drawn into lines of concern.

"Your father won't be back until after lunch," she'd said the last time she'd entered. "What's wrong, Candace? Isn't there something I can do?"

"A cup of tea," Candace had managed to answer. "I could use a cup of tea."

Now she sat with the teacup cradled between her palms, the tea long since having gone cold. Twice she'd called Dr. Evinrud's office, intending to make an appointment for a pregnancy test even though the doctor wasn't there, and twice she'd replaced the receiver, her hands sweating.

She was afraid to find out. She wanted to be pregnant so badly she could hardly think. Yet what would happen if by some miracle she was?

She'd spent the morning in a fever of indecision. Last night she'd been certain she was pregnant, but today she felt fine. Was it just a bug? Had she eaten something wrong? Good God, she'd go crazy if she didn't learn the truth soon.

Setting the teacup on Joshua's desk, she paced his opulent office, stopping by the sloping windows to stare at the minuscule traffic far below. *If I'm not pregnant I'll die of disappointment. If I am, I'll die of anxiety.*

"Oh, good grief." More from momentum than decisiveness, she snatched up the phone and dialed Dr. Evinrud's office. When the receptionist answered, she said, "This is

Candace McCall. Could I schedule a pregnancy test today, please? I know Dr. Evinrud's gone, but it's very important.''

"Well...if you could come now we might be able to fit you in," she said reluctantly.

"I'll be there in twenty minutes."

"Okay."

Candace replaced the receiver and was halfway down the hall before her brain really clicked in. Distracted, she nearly ran into one of Forsythe and Company's most famous trial lawyers. Mumbling an apology, she dodged past him, collected her purse and pushed through the glass door to the elevator.

The elevator doors slid open, and there was Con. Candace froze.

"Hi," he said, smiling. "How're you doing today? Better?"

"Um...yes." She felt her lips quiver as she returned his smile.

"Are you on your way out?"

"Yes...I am." The elevator doors were closing, and Candace resisted the urge to dive into them, away from Con, who was so adept at reading her mind.

He flicked back his cuff and checked his slim silver wristwatch. "Got a minute? I'd like to talk to you."

"No, I'm sorry. I'm late. I've got to go." She edged toward the elevator.

Con was watching her so assessingly that Candace began to grow warm, feeling the treacherous flush of guilt creeping up her neck.

"Are we still on for tonight?" he asked carefully. "In case I don't see you the rest of the day."

"Oh, yes. Absolutely." She nodded jerkily. "Come by my place after work. I...don't think I'll be back today."

"Candace, are you sick? You look pale."

"I'm fine. Really." The elevator bell dinged and the doors opened again, admitting several other people into the hallway. Lifting a hand, Candace fled, glancing back to see Con's grave blue eyes a second before the doors whispered shut.

She nearly collapsed against the wall. A quivering in her stomach reminded her of where she was going and why. If only... she thought fervently. If only... if only... if only.

She couldn't even express her wish to herself.

The next hour and a half were a blur. The nurse at Dr. Evinrud's office extracted her blood and told her to call back around five o'clock for the results. Candace left the Briar Park offices, feeling as if she were walking about six inches above the ground. The late-afternoon sun soaked into her skin, and she stood on the steps outside Dr. Evinrud's office for several moments, gazing across the verdant parkway that separated the medical offices from the hospital, drawing in deep, calming breaths.

"Candace," a woman's voice called to her, and Candace glanced around, seeing an auburn-haired woman in a lab coat coming around the corner of the building.

It was Maggie, Con's sister.

A thrill of fear shot through her, and she stared wide-eyed at the woman walking toward her. Maggie's hands were in the pockets of her coat, and she had a puzzled smile on her face. She greeted Candace amiably. "Hi there. You look like you're in a fog. I wondered for a minute if you were even going to hear me."

Candace fell back to earth with a bang. "I was just thinking."

Maggie glanced to the door behind her. "Are you a patient of Dr. Evinrud's?"

Could she lie? She didn't think so. And really, there wasn't any need. Maggie couldn't know how things stood between her and Con. "Yes, er... I had an appointment."

"But Kathleen's not back yet, is she? I thought she was going to be gone until the middle of the month."

"You know Dr. Evinrud?" Candace asked faintly. Belatedly Candace remembered Maggie worked at the Briar Park Medical offices. And her husband, Tanner, was administrative head of surgery at Briar Park Hospital.

Maggie nodded. "My office is right around the corner. Kathleen's my gynecologist." She shrugged, a bit self-consciously. "Tanner and I are thinking of adding to our family."

"Adding?" Candace glanced longingly toward her car.

"Tanner has a daughter, Shelley, from his first marriage, but she's a teenager now and hardly ever home. I'd really like a child of my own." A smile teased her lips, and she added, "Confidentially, I think I might be pregnant and I just couldn't wait until Kathleen returned to find out."

Candace felt faint. "Well, I hope you get good news."

"Me, too."

Silence fell between them, and Candace waited helplessly for her chance to escape. Would Maggie ask what *she* was doing at Dr. Evinrud's office? She could almost feel the questions beginning to form in her mind.

"Well, I should get along," Candace murmured. "I've got a lot to do."

"Are you seeing Con tonight? He's been notoriously absent around our place the past few weeks."

"Uh, yeah. We're meeting after work."

Maggie was watching her in that same assessing way Con had, and slowly Candace saw the puzzlement on her face change to dawning comprehension. Her lips slackened, and Candace felt her own pulse begin to race.

"Candace," Maggie said abruptly. "Why are you here? Did you have some tests run?"

Her mind was a blank. She couldn't think of one plausible reason for being at Dr. Evinrud's office, though there must be dozens. She just couldn't think. She stared at Maggie through the dull eyes of a condemned person waiting for the ax to fall.

Maggie grabbed her arm with tense fingers. "Candace," she said unevenly. "I don't normally pry into anyone's private life, but Con's really important to me. I've hardly seen him these past few weeks, and whenever I call and ask him what's up, he says he's made plans to be with you. Are you here because of—because of him?"

Candace exhaled a shaky breath. How could this be happening? "As a matter of fact—" she managed on a choked laugh.

Maggie was dazed. "I've never known Con to be so wrapped up in anyone," she murmured, almost to herself. "He has a tendency to keep his distance." She shook her head as if to clear it. "Wow. I can't believe this." Staring at Candace as if she'd never really seen her before, she inclined her head toward the park and asked, "Would you care to sit down on those benches over there? I'd really like to—to get to know you."

The last thing Candace wanted to do was confide in Con's sister, especially since she didn't know the truth yet herself. "Don't you have to have the pregnancy test run?"

"This'll only take a minute. Please. If you don't mind..."

Like an automaton, Candace walked with Maggie down the brick pathway that led to the circular benches surrounding the nearest maple tree. She sat down carefully on the edge of her seat, tense and afraid, aware that Maggie was already armed with enough information to kill her relationship with Con if she so desired.

"Are you in love with Con?" Maggie asked unexpectedly.

The question took Candace's breath away. "You Holts certainly are direct." She laughed uneasily, shading her eyes and turning her face to the breeze that fanned her hot cheeks. "Yes. I'm in love with Con."

Maggie moved in surprise. "I didn't really expect you to tell me the truth."

"Why not?" Candace slid her a look. "Can't wealthy women be honest, too?"

Emotions ranged across Maggie's mobile face: surprise, bafflement and regret. Sheepishly she said, "You must know my brother pretty well."

"I know that he distrusts me because my father's Joshua Forsythe. It bothers him. And I think he sometimes sees me as another Linda."

"You know about Linda, then."

"I've met her."

"You've met her?" Maggie repeated, surprised. "She's here in town?'

Candace nodded. "She wants Con to go back to Los Angeles."

"He'll never do it," Maggie said swiftly, fiercely. Hearing herself, she smiled crookedly and said, "He's through with that life." Candace didn't remark, and Maggie asked, "Have you told him how you feel?"

She sank farther back on the bench. There was no way to avoid this confession, she decided. "In many ways, but not in words. Maggie, you don't understand. He doesn't love me. He made that very clear at the onset."

"Well, I wouldn't be so sure. If he doesn't love you yet, he might be well on the way." Glancing back at Dr. Evinrud's office, Maggie chewed on her lower lip, at a loss for words. Finally she sighed and said, "I hate this, but I'm going to just barrel right in. Are you pregnant? Dr. Evinrud won't be back for several weeks, and unless you have some problem I don't know about, I can't see any reason you'd schedule an appointment with another doctor." She lifted her shoulders apologetically. "It's not my business, I know. But I—" Pressing her hands to her cheeks, she finished shakily, "Oh, I don't know. I just want things to turn out right for Con, that's all."

Birds circled and chattered among the tree limbs above her head. Candace didn't move. She was stripped bare. Neither Maggie nor Con pulled punches. If they wanted to know something, they just asked.

"I had a pregnancy test taken," Candace admitted tonelessly. "I won't know the results until later." She thought about going further, telling Maggie about her cervical problems, then let the matter slide away. She'd revealed more of herself than she wanted to already.

"Oh, my God." Maggie was stunned.

"If I'm pregnant, I'm keeping this baby. I want this baby."

"Does Con have any idea that—"

Candace cut her off. "No."

"Candace." Maggie's voice was urgent. "Did he tell you he had to marry Linda? She told him she was pregnant, and he believed her. When it turned out to be a lie, it was too late."

Candace stared at her, her head reeling. She remembered how he'd cut himself off when he'd started to tell her why he'd married Linda. "No," she said weakly. "He didn't tell me."

"You've got to tell him right away about this, as soon as you learn the results. Take him to Dr. Evinrud's office if he needs to be convinced, but whatever you do, don't keep this from him. He'll never forgive you. Do you understand?"

Maggie was so intense that it almost scared Candace. Already she felt strange and disoriented, but this loaded on top of it made her heart palpitate as if she'd run ten miles. "I'll know tonight," she said in a strange voice. "I'll tell him tonight, one way or the other."

Suddenly Maggie leaned forward and hugged her with real affection. "I believe you do love him," she said. "Just don't hurt him."

"Hurt him?" Candace choked out. Her flesh broke out in goose bumps. She had a feeling Con wasn't going to be the one who got hurt.

"Do me a favor, as soon as Con knows, would you call me? I'd like to know whether I'm going to be an aunt or not."

Candace heard the tenderness in her voice and wanted to cry. Here was a woman who hardly knew her, who'd only met her twice, and yet she sensed in Maggie a deep compassion and understanding she'd longed for all her life. "I'll call you," she choked out. "Thanks, Maggie."

"Good luck," she said gravely, her laughter vanishing. "This is a really sensitive issue with Con, and sometimes he can be unpredictable."

"You think he'll be angry, then?"

"It takes two to make a baby," Maggie answered dryly. "But it might be necessary to point that out to him."

With mixed feelings, Candace watched Maggie head up the stairs to Dr. Evinrud's office. This wasn't going at all as she'd planned, but then, if she'd planned it, how would it have gone?

Love, marriage and a baby—in that order.

Squaring her shoulders, Candace started determinedly for her car. She didn't really care what order it was. She just hoped she was pregnant.

And she hoped Con would be happy about it.

* * *

The night was dark and velvety. A breeze that had grown steadily stiffer all evening scattered the cloud cover, letting the stars shine down bright and diamond-hard.

Con drove with the top down, his black hair flying wildly in the wind. He felt a little uneasy about Candace. Their relationship had been like a train without brakes, and he had the hair-raising sensation that he was heading for a huge crash. Linda's presence in Portland hadn't helped. She reminded him of all the foolish mistakes he'd made in his lifetime.

Wrenching the wheel, he whipped around the curving streets that ran above the lake, seeing the water glimmer black beneath the moonlight. He was eager to see Candace. He wanted to assure himself she was all right; she'd looked so strange and frightened this afternoon. But he also wanted to see her for more selfish reasons. Just thinking about her brought about an instantaneous physical reaction that never ceased to amaze him.

He pulled into her driveway and leaped over the door of the car like a teenager. What the hell. He felt like a teenager.

As he pressed his finger to the bell, a wry smile touched the corners of his mouth. He'd once wanted Tricia Wellesley with an all-consuming passion—or so he'd thought at the time. It had taken him years to figure out he'd wanted her just because she'd been out of reach. And Linda had been an extension of that same need to be accepted by a different social class. What a waste. He'd been so flattered by Linda's attentions at first, and so let down in the end.

Candace was something different. He didn't *want* to want her. She embodied everything he distrusted in women: beauty, wealth, prestige. Yet she was also warm and soft and vulnerable in a way neither Tricia Wellesley nor Linda had ever been. He desired her with a fierce, hot longing that refused to be quenched and, miracle of miracles, he also enjoyed just being with her, talking to her. He kept searching for some flaw, some minor imperfection that would prove him right, show her to be just like the others, but so far it hadn't happened.

Could she really be all she seemed?

The door opened and Candace stood in the hallway wrapped in a blue satin bathrobe, her blond hair spilling over her shoulders, her green eyes wide and moist, as if she'd been crying. But she was smiling, her mouth trembling with happiness, and seeing him she suddenly shot straight for him as if the devil were at her heels.

"Whoa," he laughed. "What kind of a reception is this?" Her arms were around his waist, and her face was pressed against his shirt.

"I'm happy," she said in a muffled voice. "And I'm scared."

"Happy and scared," he repeated, tilting her chin up to look into her face. Smiling, he asked, "Why? What's happened?"

Her eyes shone with excitement, and his breath quickened as he looked at her. His arms tightened around her of their own accord, and his body ached with longing. "You're beautiful," he breathed against her mouth, feeling her lips quiver and respond.

He didn't know why he'd received such a warm greeting, but he wasn't about to argue with the Fates about his good fortune. Swinging her into his arms, he murmured softly, "I thought this day would never end."

She lay nestled in the crook of his arms like a child, but the way she clung to him was anything but childlike. Her soft laughter was breathless. "I love you," she said. "I love you so much."

Con nearly stumbled on his way upstairs. For a moment he wondered if he was hearing things. But this was real. Candace had just told him she loved him, openly and joyously, and her lack of reserve when she made such an important admission set off red warning lights inside his head.

Gently he laid her on her bed, then stood looking down at her, into emerald eyes filled with love and trust. Con was silent. He could think of nothing to say.

"Come here," she whispered, pulling him to her, and as he lay beside her he felt her shaking limbs.

"Candace," he muttered, somewhat alarmed.

"Love me. Please, love me. I love you so much."

Sensing there was more here than met the eye, Con tried to keep a cool head. But her hands were everywhere, touching him, begging him, seducing him. He felt her mouth hot against his throat and groaned, his own fingers pulling aside the lapels of her robe, molding the soft curve of her breast, teasing her taut nipples.

"Good God," he muttered, laughing, tugging off his own clothes. "If this happens after one day, I'd hate to think what being separated a week might do."

She rained kisses on his face and he covered her body with his own, capturing her mouth with an ardent kiss, groaning as her legs gripped him while he, unable to prolong the moment, moved into her with a quick thrust, then battled raging need to keep from demanding his own fulfillment.

All of a sudden she was crying, and Con was amazed and shocked by the change. "Candace, are you all right?" he rasped, concerned. "What is it?"

"Oh, Con, I'm just so happy, and I'm afraid you're going to shatter that happiness."

"I am?" he asked blankly. She moved in a way that made him clench his teeth to keep his mind on their conversation.

"If you want to talk, you've got to stop doing that," he growled, pinning her arms to her side.

"I don't want to talk," she breathed.

Con would have liked to argue, but Candace had other things on her mind. Her hands slid down his back, her silky limbs twining around him, her mouth softly touching and retreating until he felt a roaring in his ears and moved in a way designed to give her maximum pleasure. She arched and threw back her head, soft, mewing moans issuing from her throat. He plunged into her again and again, drawing out the movement until she reached a tumultuous climax, crying out. He crushed her to him and finally allowed himself his own release.

But as soon as the mists of passion had cleared she was brushing back his hair, smiling at him, only the tracks of her tears remaining.

"Candace," he murmured when she was tucked close to his side, her white-blond mane fanned across his chest. "What the hell is it?"

She drew in a long breath and held it. Con waited, tense, cautious—and suddenly sure he didn't want to hear it.

"I'm pregnant," she said simply.

In the moment that followed he sensed many things: the ticking of her bedside clock, the heat of her body, the eerie sense of déjà vu. His heart stopped for just a second. "Pregnant?" he repeated dazedly.

"I had a pregnancy test today, and I called back this evening to find out the results. It was positive. I've been numb ever since."

I'm pregnant, Con. I don't know how it happened, we've been so careful. I don't suppose you'd want to marry me, would you?

Linda's face swam before his eyes. A mistake. A terrible mistake. And it had all been a lie.

Con rolled away from Candace in one lithe movement, grabbing his pants in the next. He heard her hurt intake of breath but ignored it, shoving his foot into one pant leg.

"Con," she whispered achingly.

"You're sure about this pregnancy?"

Candace shrank against the pillows, wounded by the harshness of his voice. "Yes. You can call Dr. Evinrud's office tomorrow if you don't believe me."

He froze in the act of buttoning his shirt. "Why wouldn't I believe you? Is there some reason I shouldn't?"

Candace turned her head, trying to hide her tears. "Maggie told me about Linda. I realized you might—have your doubts."

"Maggie?"

"I saw her today, outside Dr. Evinrud's office. She guessed why I was there, and I told her the truth." Candace shivered, but Con's heart was too hard to melt. "She told me why you married Linda. She warned me about how you might take this news."

Her voice had grown so low he could barely hear her. He felt the blood pounding in his head. "I asked you if you were protected," he reminded her tensely.

"I thought I couldn't have children," she answered in a small voice.

"You *thought* you couldn't have children?" The depth of her deception left him speechless. He stared at her huddled figure and felt nothing but a chilling fury.

"There were reasons. Jeff and I weren't always careful, yet nothing happened," Candace said, defending herself unevenly. "And there were other things."

Impotent rage flooded through him, directed mostly at his own gullibility. "You could have told me this," he said tightly. "You could have warned me."

Candace's lips parted, and anger flared in her eyes. "As I recall, you weren't exactly interested in stopping long enough to hear all the particulars about my use of birth control!"

"You set me up," he said in dawning comprehension.

Candace bounded off the bed so quickly it took him by surprise. She struggled into her robe, fighting the sleeves, swearing in frustration until her arms were free. Yanking on the sash, she said clearly and intently, "Go ahead and be upset, but I won't take all the blame. It happened. I'm not sorry. If you never want to see me again, that's your choice, but I'm keeping this baby—*our baby*—and you can damn well grow up and try to be happy about it!"

Chapter Ten

Candace met Con's bright, accusing gaze squarely. She'd had about all she was going to take. She'd told him she loved him. She'd explained about the pregnancy, and all he could do was act like a spoiled little boy who wanted to throw a tantrum just because he hadn't gotten his way.

He raked his hand through his hair. "Jeez," he muttered, looking suddenly lost.

Clasping her hands in front of her, Candace said, "I didn't mean it to happen. I know it's going to cause problems. But I'm happier about having this baby than I've been about anything in my life."

It was true. Once the full import had struck her she'd been delirious with joy. She was going to have a baby—her baby!—after all. In her mind it was nothing short of a miracle, and even her love for Con was pushed aside in the elation of the moment.

Con's gaze raked over her small form and proud, flushed face. "Forgive me if I don't feel the same way," he said harshly.

"Fine. I'd rather you didn't lie." Candace swallowed, secretly disappointed that he wasn't at least a little bit happy. But then, what had she expected? He was in shock. *She* was in shock, for pete's sake. "You don't have to pretend you're as delighted as I am. But I didn't set you up, as you so crudely put it."

Con could only stare at her, and some of her anger melted at his total stupefaction. She'd expected too much, too soon. She'd forgotten his past.

"Why did you say you loved me?" he asked hoarsely.

"Because it's the truth."

"Because you're pregnant."

She didn't like his tone; it was as if he had everything all worked out. "I don't expect you to love me back."

"Do you expect me to marry you?"

"You bastard," Candace said with feeling, hating his cold tone. His cruelty tore her apart.

Something must have finally penetrated the wall of his emotions, because he came to her, his hands on her shoulders, his fingers digging into her skin as if they had a will of their own. Then his hands were entwined in her silvery-blond hair.

"I don't understand you at all," he muttered.

"I love you. You just can't believe it."

He pulled her head back, his narrowed gaze searching her eyes. "I never heard you say you loved me before you found out you were pregnant."

She sucked air between her teeth. "Well, I have. You're just so wrapped up in the idea of never loving anyone that you don't hear."

"You have an answer for everything, don't you?' "

Candace was mildly surprised. *He* was the master of the quick retort. Staring into his eyes, she saw molten desire simmering there, ready to explode into flame. But then he closed his eyes in self-disgust. "God," he muttered, running his hands down the silken fabric of her robe, resting them on her hips. "I don't believe this."

Candace was silent. She recognized the very real possibility that he was about to reject her. She believed, however, that he would not reject his child. But that would be hollow compensation. She wanted him. As much as she wanted this baby.

Her breath caught as he undid the tie of her robe and her gaze flew to his, hopeful. Trembling, she waited as he pulled back the lapels to reveal her satiny limbs. But his appraisal was hardly admiring. His hands encircled her abdomen, and Candace felt abused and humiliated at the way he moved his thumb searchingly over her skin, as if touching her could make her pregnancy not be true.

Abruptly he pulled her robe closed. His face was drawn and haggard. "I've got to go," he said, striding blindly for the door. She heard his footsteps on her stairs, and a minute later the front door slammed shut with sharp finality.

Only when the roar of his engine had faded away did she allow herself to collapse. Knees shaking, she sank onto her bed and buried her face in her hands.

Con stamped on the accelerator, the T-Bird whining in protest as he tore around the lake. The trees flashed by in a blur of black and green, and his wheels thumped over one of the small bridges that divided the main lake from the bay.

Only when he was climbing toward Skyridge Drive did he begin to slow down. Pregnant. Candace was pregnant *with his child*!

The Baines house appeared on his left, and Con pulled into the drive behind Maggie's car, heart pounding as if he'd run a marathon. Switching off the engine, he sat taut and unmoving in the still night, his hands clenched around the wheel, his mind a jumble of turbulent emotions. A baby. His baby.

"God..."

He let himself out of the car and walked toward the oak tree he'd helped Maggie climb years before to reach Tanner's bedroom window. Leaning against the bark, he closed his eyes. His strength left him in a powerful rush, and he sank to the ground, his hands on his knees.

He didn't know what to do.

A light came on behind him, illuminating a dry patch of ground in a yellow rectangle. Then a door slammed and footsteps approached. Expecting Maggie, Con said bitterly, "I haven't learned a damn thing, but I don't want to hear about it from you."

"All right," Tanner said easily.

Con stiffened, then glanced at his brother-in-law, managing a sick smile. "Sorry. I thought you were my sister."

"She's on the phone to Candace."

"Great." Con laughed uneasily. "She called."

"Maggie called her. Apparently they ran into each other at Briar Park, outside Dr. Evinrud's office."

Tanner had always been a man of few words, and now he simply stood and waited. Con, who was more inclined to speak first and think later, both resented and admired his tact. "Candace is pregnant," Con said unnecessarily.

Tanner nodded.

"I don't know how the hell I feel about it."

"Maybe you should figure out how the hell you feel about Candace."

"What are you, a psychiatrist?"

Tanner smiled. "There's an added complication I think you should know about. Maggie had a pregnancy test today, and it turned up negative. When you talk to her, remember—this is not the time to be less than enthusiastic about having a baby."

"Having a baby," Con repeated dazedly.

At that moment the door slammed once more and Maggie, her arms crossed rigidly beneath her breasts, walked up to her husband. Tanner drew her into the protection of his arms, but her eyes were focused on Con—and they were full of anger.

"You are such a jerk," she told him furiously.

Con's own sense of rage and injustice had been bubbling just below the surface, searching for an outlet. Now he rolled to his feet and glared down at his little sister. "I don't need this from you."

"She tells you she's pregnant and you walk out on her! If I were her I'd kill you!"

"And what would you have me do?" he demanded tensely. "Lie to her, pretend I'm happy about this?"

"Yes," Maggie said flatly, her eyes filling with tears. "For the moment, yes."

Tanner coughed significantly. "Come on in the house, Con. I'll get us all a drink. I know I need one," he muttered under his breath.

Feeling like a lamb being led to a slaughter, Con followed Tanner and Maggie. When they were all assembled in the den—Maggie with a snifter of brandy, Con and Tanner with neat Scotch—Tanner drawled, "And now I think I'll leave before this gets bloody." He kissed Maggie on the top of her head and said on his way out, "I'll be upstairs working, if you need a doctor."

Maggie, who'd been holding herself stiff and tight, suddenly dropped limply into one of the wing chairs. "I'm sorry," she said, but her voice was still angry.

Con sighed. "Maggie, I can only be what I can be. I'm stunned. Shaken. I don't know what to think."

"She's keeping the baby, you know."

He nodded. "That's what she said."

"Well, what are you going to do about it?"

Con shook his head slowly.

"How do you feel about her, Con?" Maggie demanded. "Do you love her?"

"No."

"How do you know?"

"Because I—" Con cut himself off, remembering as if from a great distance how he'd felt about her earlier that evening. He'd been so eager to see her, restless for her, dying for her.

"She loves you," Maggie said softly.

For just a moment Con felt a rush of affection for Candace that staggered him. He wanted to hold her in his arms and bury himself in her, make love wildly and furiously. He wanted to beg her forgiveness.

"She's not Linda," Maggie said, watching him. "I know that now. I like her, Con. She's as undone over this whole thing as you are."

"I can't marry her," he said tonelessly.

"Who's talking about marriage? For God's sake, Con. You've got to act like a reasonable adult first." Maggie thought a moment and added, "And why can't you marry her, anyway?"

He looked at her as if she'd lost her mind. "Among other things, she's Joshua Forsythe's daughter."

Maggie tilted her head. "So what?"

"You of all people know the answer to that," said Con through his teeth.

"I know my big brother has a problem believing rich people are just the same as poor people. I've had the same problem. But I love Tanner and I always have, and he's your friend. You used to hang out with him when we were kids. Remember? Racing around the lake in his boat. He taught us both to water-ski, and he taught you to play tennis."

Con eyed her watchfully, tossing back the rest of his drink. The last thing he needed was a lecture from his sister.

"And then you didn't like Tanner anymore because you thought he'd hurt me. So you decided to become better than the lake people. Richer. You became a lawyer and married the boss's daughter. Only it didn't work out so well. It wasn't really you," she finished softly.

"And Candace isn't really me, either."

"Maybe she is, maybe she isn't. I don't know how you feel. But I do know your feelings for her are being clouded by your feelings for Linda. You're afraid you're making the same mistake."

"You bet," Con said feelingly.

"Put it aside, Con. Think about now. Think about Candace and think about that baby."

Maggie had gotten to her feet, and now she stood at the window, staring restlessly into the dark night. Regret slid over Con as he remembered her own disappointment of the day. He stood behind her and dropped a brotherly arm around her shoulders. Drawing a deep breath, he said, "I've already made a mistake."

"Which one is that, oh brother dear?"

He smiled crookedly. "I've hurt you, and I've hurt Candace."

"I'll survive," Maggie said. "Will Candace?"

Con didn't answer. In his mind's eye he remembered how he'd last seen her, the way he'd wounded her.

And the hell of it was he didn't know how he felt about anything.

A cool breeze snapped Candace's robe around her knees as she stood on the back deck, staring at a sliver of pearl-white moon. She tried not to examine her feelings too closely, afraid she'd break apart and shatter if she relived the evening. Con's desertion hadn't been unexpected; she'd taken him completely by surprise, and it really would have been odd if he'd acted any other way.

Or so she kept telling herself.

She turned her face skyward and closed her eyes. She knew she was going to be miserable tomorrow, but for the moment she was holding on to the joy of having Con's baby growing inside her.

She managed a weak smile. Con's baby. She couldn't have found a better man to father her child if she'd looked for one. Though her future with him was uncertain, she would always have this part of him. It would be enough. It would have to be. He'd made his feelings abundantly clear.

Hearing a noise from inside her house, she turned to look through the closed window. Nothing. The breeze tousled her hair, and she tossed the wayward strands out of her eyes, gazing once more across the water, touching her hands to her abdomen, awed by the future.

Behind her the back door opened. Candace froze, then whipped around. "Con," she breathed, surprised.

His face was shadowed. "I'm sorry," he said crisply.

Something broke inside Candace. She ran to him on winged feet, moaning with delight at the sweet crush of his arms around her. He was kissing her, her face, her hair, her neck.

"I'll marry you," he said. "We'll have our baby together."

Abruptly Candace was chilled. She pulled back, searching his face, reading the taut line of his jaw. He didn't love her. He was doing his duty.

With all the dignity she could muster, she pushed herself away from him. "No, thank you," she said distinctly. "You can leave the way you came in."

Chapter Eleven

Candace walked quickly across the polished marble of the Forsythe Building's street floor, checking the huge clock face on the wall. She was late, and though no one checked her hours, she hated anyone thinking she was abusing her privileges because she was Joshua Forsythe's daughter.

Harry Pendergrass greeted her from his desk near the elevators. "Hello, Mrs. McCall."

"Hi, Harry. I'm late." She smiled.

"So am I," a voice said behind her.

She glanced back and saw Dan Morrison walking toward her, as tidy and together as she felt rumpled and undone. Not that she was. Her cream cotton skirt and blouse were just back from the cleaner's, a silver belt cinched her waist, and her hair was brushed to fall in lustrous golden waves to her shoulders. But she'd spent a long and restless night, twisting and turning on her bed, reviewing every moment of the evening before. She'd overslept and had barely had time to dash into the shower. As a consequence she could still smell Con's scent on her.

He'd left, just as she'd asked him to. But as soon as the door had closed behind him she'd wanted to call him back. Pride was a wicked enemy, yet how could she even consider marrying him when he'd only offered marriage as a result of her pregnancy?

"You look great," Dan remarked as they rode up the elevator together.

"Thank you." Candace pinned a tired smile on her lips.

"I just had breakfast at the Claremont. You'll never guess who I ran into."

"My father?" Candace watched the numbers of the floors flash by.

"The ex Mrs. Holt. We sat at the same table."

"How nice." The bell dinged for the thirty-second floor, and Candace practically shot through the door to the inner office. She couldn't bear to hear about Linda today.

"She's sticking around awhile, I guess," Dan went on, undeterred, dogging her heels. "She's an interesting woman. Very bright. Any messages?" he asked Terri as Candace swept past him in her eagerness to escape.

Linda. Connor. Candace shuddered. She had to stop thinking about everything or she'd go crazy. Yet how could she stop thinking about Con when she loved him? When he worked right down the hall from her? When he could cross her path at any given moment?

She was already halfway down the mirrored hallway. A few more steps and she would be in front of Con's door. Should she talk to him now? she fretted anxiously. Try to make some kind of sense of the madness that surrounded them? At least so they could work together?

Raising her hand, she knocked rapidly on his door, biting into her lower lip. The door swung inward on its own.

Con wasn't at his desk, and the room had the cold feeling of disuse.

"He hasn't come in yet," Marion told her as she whisked from the coffee room, heading in the direction of her office.

"Oh."

"I'm glad you're here, I've got a ton of work for you," Marion said over her shoulder.

Candace got her feet in gear and accepted the pile of letters and reports Marion needed help typing. Her arms full, she walked back to Pamela's desk, asking when she could use her computer terminal.

"Now," Pamela said gruffly, stuffing a lozenge in her mouth. "I'm going home."

Terri lifted her brows angelically. "So soon?"

"I don't know if I'll ever get rid of this bug," she said huffily slamming books together as if it were Candace and Terri's fault that she'd been suffering so long.

"Maybe it's all in your head," Terri remarked, which earned her a glower from Pamela on her way out.

"You don't exactly encourage her friendship, you know," Candace said as she sat down heavily at Pamela's desk.

Terri was philosophical. "I used to try to be nice, but it was a waste of time. She's the same no matter what I do. I just gave up."

"Do you know where Con is?" Candace asked, trying to sound offhand.

Terri sent her a sly glance. "Well, now, let's see. He's at the Claremont, I believe."

"The Claremont?" Candace felt the blood drain from her face. Dan had said Linda was at the Claremont. "With whom?"

"I don't know. Your father, I suppose."

Of course. Relief washed over her in a mad rush, and she was instantly angry with herself for assuming the worst. Just because Linda had been at the Claremont didn't mean Con was with her. Why should he be? He was not the kind of man to race into his ex-wife's arms just because of the fight they'd had the night before.

Candace turned to her work, trying to slow her desperately racing heart. Of course, their fight had been anything but ordinary. Maybe Linda didn't look so bad to him now. Maybe she was much more attractive now, less of a threat....

"Stop it," she said harshly.

"Pardon?" Terri asked.

"Nothing," Candace muttered, giving the computer all her attention.

At one o'clock Con suddenly strode into the office. There were new lines on his face, and a grim set to his lips that made Candace's mouth turn to cotton. Right behind him was her father, and before Candace could even say hello, Joshua began a stream of animated conversation about Con's latest case that allowed no room for interruption. Con, for his part, responded with monosyllabic answers, his gaze catching Candace's for one long, heart-stopping moment. But he glanced away, bending his head toward Joshua as if the case they were discussing were all he cared about.

With mixed feelings, Candace watched them walk down the hallway to their respective offices. She was relieved Con hadn't been with Linda, but her stomach still churned whenever she thought of what lay ahead.

Near closing time, Candace was bent over one particularly hard-to-decipher letter when sweat broke out on her forehead and she knew she was going to be sick again. At that very moment the outer door swung open and a cool, feminine voice inquired, "Is Connor Holt in? I'd like to see him, please."

Candace felt a jolt of recognition even before she glanced up to find Linda standing beside Terri's desk. Today she wore a beige crepe suit, her thick, dark hair lying softly against the fine fabric.

Terri was gazing at Linda with something akin to awe. "Mr. Holt's in a meeting right now," she said. "Would you care to wait?"

Linda's gaze flickered to Candace's white face. "Hello again, Mrs. McCall," she said. Turning back to Terri, she added, "Yes, I'll wait. But tell Con it's important I talk to him." Smoothing the back of her skirt, she settled into one of the reception chairs.

Terri shot Candace a surreptitious glance that asked all kinds of questions, but Candace could wait no longer. She hurried abruptly to the bathroom, bathing her forehead with cool water. As she stared at her hollow-eyed expression, her lips twisted. She looked awful. Her color was slowly returning, but even so, her skin was drawn, her eyes tired.

She nearly ran into her father on her way back to Pamela's desk. Seeing her, Joshua frowned. "You look pale, Candace."

"I'm sick," she admitted.

"Then you should go home. Do you want someone to drive you? As soon as Con and I are finished, I'll take you."

Shaking her head, she said, "It's not that kind of sick."

"Oh?"

Suddenly it seemed imperative that she tell him what was happening to her. "Father," she asked urgently, "could I talk to you privately? There's something I've got to get off my chest."

Joshua's head snapped up and she sensed his retreat—a reaction she'd long since grown used to whenever some sticky personal issue arose between them.

"I'm kind of busy right now," he began, but Candace, flooded with surging feelings, refused to give up.

"I know you're busy. You're always busy. But do you think you could find just a few minutes for me? It's almost closing time and I need you."

Running a hand around the back of his neck, he cleared his throat, eyeing her speculatively. "Come into my office in fifteen minutes," he said reluctantly, then added suddenly, "This doesn't have anything to do with Jeff, does it?"

"No," Candace answered, a bit hysterically. "It has to do with me."

Nodding, Joshua moved away, as if expecting her to unravel right before his eyes. Candace stared after him helplessly, wishing just once he'd embrace her problems as his own and treat her as more than just an awkward burden.

Linda was still seated in one of the reception chairs when Candace returned. "Did you talk to Connor?" she asked casually.

"No." Candace was abrupt. It burned her that Linda would naturally assume she would run to Con with the news that his ex-wife wanted to see him. Con was his own man. Terri would give him the message; Candace didn't have to interfere.

"Do you know how long Connor's meeting might be?" Linda persisted.

Realizing she was talking to her, Candace shook her head. "He's with my father. It shouldn't be too much longer."

"Oh." Pulling a compact out of her purse, Linda checked her lipstick. "I don't have a lot of time. Maybe I shouldn't wait. Looks like he's busy with your family."

Under normal circumstances Candace would let a remark like that slide by, but these weren't normal circumstances. Linda was needling her, and Candace was in no mood to be needled. "Yes, it looks that way," she said flatly.

Gathering up her purse, Linda said, "Just let him know I want to see him. He knows my room number at the Claremont."

Candace stared at her. She could think of nothing to say. Linda regarded her solemnly for several moments, then remarked, "People don't change, you know. Con likes success. He always takes the quickest path to it."

"For someone who used to live with him, I don't think you know him very well," Candace choked out.

"I know him better than you think."

Terri's eyes were wide with amazement as she looked from Candace to Linda. Inhaling sharply, she muttered something under her breath that sounded suspiciously like a prayer. Ignoring her, Candace rose to Con's defense like an avenging angel. "Then you ought to know," she said to Linda with cold deliberation, "that Con's a complex and sensitive man who can't abide anyone with such shallow ambitions. He'd hardly be that way himself." She rose to her feet and strode to the door, holding it open. "Good evening, Linda. I'll let him know you stopped by."

Linda's mouth was an O of surprise. Whatever she'd expected to achieve, this obviously wasn't it. Stiffly she marched through the door, her back a ramrod of fury. Only when the elevator had swallowed her up did Candace sink back against the wall.

"Wow," Terri said, exhaling a pent-up breath. She blinked. "Is she really Con's ex-wife?"

From down the hallway a deep voice remarked, "Yes, she really is."

Horrified, Candace watched as Con appeared, saying casually to Terri, "Any more messages?"

Gulping, Terri handed him the one she'd scribbled down. "Just this one."

"Linda Holt, hmm?" Though he spoke lightly, his face reflected none of the humor in his voice.

"She wants to see you. She's staying at the Claremont."

Con slid a look to Candace. "Is that right?"

Candace answered with a brief nod and a sick smile. He had to have heard everything.

"Well, then I guess I'd better find out what's on her mind." He walked up to Candace, pushed his arm against the door, then paused, his face bare inches from her own. "Thanks for the defense, counselor," he murmured as he let himself out.

"Well," Terri said. "Well, well, well."

Candace, her heart fluttering with renewed hope, said between her teeth, "You tell anybody about this and you're dead."

"Are you kidding? That woman deserved everything you gave her and more."

"No, no." She closed her eyes in mortification. "I shouldn't have said anything. Believe me, that was not the done thing."

Terri snorted with delight. "To hell with 'the done thing.' Connor appreciated it."

Candace didn't offer further argument. Yes, Connor had seemed more amused than angry, which lifted Candace's spirits immensely. But then he'd gone to meet Linda, and Candace's ears were burning already, just imagining what kind of things she would be telling him about the ill-mannered Mrs. McCall.

A few minutes later Candace left Terri and headed for Joshua's office. Dan beckoned to her as she passed in front of his open office door, but luckily he was on the phone and she shook her head and smiled. Whatever he wanted could wait. She'd made a date with her father, and though now, sensing that Con was beginning to accept her pregnancy— at least he didn't hate her for it!—she didn't feel quite the urgency to confess all her problems, and she was determined to follow through and meet Joshua anyway. For all his faults, her father loved her and would continue to love her no matter how many mistakes she made. For that reason alone, she decided to force a father-daughter talk. As Dr. Evinrud had told her more than once, she needed someone to confide in, someone on her side. For better or worse, that someone was going to be her father.

"Candace," Joshua said with a faint smile as she opened the double doors to his office. "I'm not quite finished here. Could you give me a few more minutes?"

"I could, but I won't, because then you'll find some other method of evasion."

His eyebrows shot up. "Well, all right, then," he said slowly. "This must be important."

She sat down in a chair across from him. Only the width of the desk divided them, but it might as well have been a chasm as deep and impassable as the Grand Canyon. Twisting her hands, she admitted, "I don't know how to start."

Joshua sat like a stone. He rubbed one hand across his chin. "Just lay it out for me," he said quietly.

He must think I've committed murder, she thought, a bit hysterically, recognizing the way he braced himself for bad news. "I'm pregnant," she expelled. "Con's the father, and he asked me to marry him but I turned him down."

He blinked twice, rapidly. She had to admire the stoic way he absorbed her shocking confession. "You don't want to marry him, I assume," he said carefully.

"Dad, I don't know what I want."

"Did he offer marriage solely because you're pregnant?"

"Yes." Candace's voice was self-mocking.

"You're sure?"

"Oh, yes." She got wearily to her feet, pacing across the room. "But it's so much more complicated. Con doesn't even know the half of it."

The phone on Joshua's desk purred. "Damn it all to hell," he muttered, snatching up the receiver. "No more calls, Terri!" he blasted out. "I'm through for the day. Tell them I'll call them tomorrow." He slammed down the phone and said at the same time, "You'd better tell me everything, then, daughter. I want to hear it all."

Drawing a deep breath, Candace said softly, "Not long ago I learned I wouldn't be able to have children unless I had one within the next year or so. I was shattered. At the time I didn't even know a man I was willing to get close to, and then Con appeared and one thing led to another...." She moved her hands helplessly.

Joshua regarded his daughter with a degree of incredulity. "Back up," he said into the silence that followed her dramatic confession. "I want to hear more about why you think you can't have children. And then I want to hear more about Connor Holt." He shook his head. "My God," he muttered, and in his eyes Candace saw the reflection of some of her own pain.

Connor stood outside the black-and-gold-canopied entrance to the Claremont Hotel, resisting the urge to check his watch. Linda's blue eyes swam with a sorrow he had a feeling might be fake. "I've listened and listened and listened," he said, not unkindly. "There's nothing more to say."

"I'm not leaving town."

"Fine. Stay as long as you like. But it won't make any difference. I won't accept your father's offer."

"You're really in love with this Candace, aren't you?" Linda said pathetically.

Con sighed and counted silently to ten. "Why do you keep coming back to Candace?"

"Because she's the real issue. I'm no fool, Con. I can see how you feel about her, even if you can't. I can't say one word about her without you jumping all over me." She pressed her lips together.

"That's because you can't say one kind word about her," he retorted, amused.

"I wonder if you'd be so crazy in love with her if she was poor."

It was remarks like that that had kept Con's temper simmering all evening. Staring at his beautiful ex-wife, he wondered why he bothered listening to her at all. Guilt, he supposed. The basic underlying feeling that he'd treated her badly—which was ridiculous, since she'd been the one to crush the last crumbs of their marriage.

A taxicab pulled up in front of the hotel's awning and Dan Morrison stepped out, for once forgetting to check the crease on his pants. He paid the driver and, seeing Con and Linda standing on the sidewalk, said distractedly, "Oh, hi. Linda, I was hoping to see you tonight."

Con lifted his brows, glancing from one of them to the other. This was a wrinkle he hadn't expected.

Linda, however, looked less than thrilled at the other attorney's appearance. "I'm just about to go to bed," she said tautly.

Dan seemed to barely hear her. Con scrutinized him closely. He acted like a man who'd just received unsettling news. His mind was not where his body was. "How about a drink, then?" Dan proposed.

Linda made a sound of impatience. "I'm sorry. I'm just not interested."

Dan's eyes found Con's, and the look in them was so intent and calculating that Con froze inside. *He knows about Candace,* he thought with certainty. Somehow Dan had learned of her pregnancy.

But then Dan fell back into character, a lazy smile drifting across his lips. It happened so quickly that Con didn't trust his own instincts. Maybe he was overreacting, he told himself. The last thing Candace would do was tell Dan about her pregnancy.

Her pregnancy. Con had to drag himself back to the present, just as he had all day. All he could think about was Candace and the baby. And the fact that she wouldn't marry him.

Dan was saying, "...buy you both a drink. Ten minutes. That's all I want."

With Con's inclusion in his invitation, Linda was less decided. "Con?" she asked.

"Count me out. I've got somewhere to be."

He left before he found out the results of Dan's efforts, mentally betting on Linda to come out the winner. But Con's thoughts were filled with Candace. He'd spent a bad night and an even worse day. He'd asked her to marry him in all sincerity. Having her turn him down had been unexpected and, he'd found to his surprise, unacceptable. She was having his child, for God's sake. Didn't he have some rights where it was concerned?

He'd worked himself into a lather of injustice and had been preparing to confront Candace at the first opportunity when he'd suddenly come across the scene between her and Linda. It had knocked him sideways. For the first time he'd actually given some credence to her vow that she loved him.

Smiling, he jaywalked across a busy downtown street, raising a hand to the blaring horn and bright lights of a fuming driver. His mouth quirked ironically. So okay, you didn't want to marry her when you thought you had to. Now you want to when you think you can't. Hardly rational adult behavior, pal. Time to think things through more carefully.

Candace's Jaguar was not in the underground parking lot as Con walked through the echoing concrete building in search of his T-Bird. She was probably already at home or on her way there. He'd spent more than two hours fruitlessly arguing with Linda, he realized. Well, it was time to set things straight with Candace.

Traffic was a snarl of lights and noise as dusk deepened to night. The heat had abated, but only just, and after a few moments of consideration Con decided to go home and shower before he met with Candace. This could be the most important evening of his life, and he wanted to be cool, collected and persuasive. She was going to marry him, he decided arrogantly. If he had to drag her by her hair to the altar.

The condominium was dark when he arrived, except for Mrs. Collingwood's front porch light. Slamming his car door, his lips curved into a grin when he saw her shadow pass by the window. Would she be disappointed to learn he was getting married and settling down?

His key was in the lock when he heard those words in his mind again. He stood back for a moment, amazed at the way he embraced the idea. He'd thought he would never want to marry again, but now, the image of a life with Candace and their child stretching out ahead of him, he couldn't conceive of any other alternative.

You love her.

He let himself inside and ignored the light switch, guided down the dark hallways by his own familiarity with the condominium. He went straight to the bar and poured himself a glass of Scotch. Bringing the glass halfway to his lips, he suddenly stopped and set it back down on the small cupboard he used as a bar, staring unseeingly, dumbfounded, beyond the confines of the room to the skeletons of his own life.

You're in love with her, you idiot.

In total disbelief he sat down hard on the nearest chair.

Candace looked in her refrigerator at the remains of a meal she'd prepared for Con several days before and shuddered. She wondered if she would ever have an appetite again. Closing the door, she walked aimlessly from the kitchen to the living room, to the back deck, finally trudging up the stairs to her bedroom. She stripped down and turned on the taps of the shower, plunging her face beneath the hot, stinging spray, washing away the bad feelings of the day.

She didn't know how long she'd stood beneath the scouring water when she thought she heard the faint sound of her phone. Twisting the taps, she strained her ears, but all she could hear was the fan in the bathroom and the sound of water dripping from her hair and body.

She toweled off vigorously, bringing a pink tinge to her flesh. Brushing her teeth, she thought about what she'd eaten for the day and acknowledged that Dr. Evinrud would give her a tongue-lashing to end all tongue-lashings. Nausea or no, she needed to eat.

Cinching up her blue satin bathrobe, she walked barefoot downstairs, her toes curling into the luxuriant cream carpet Jeff had insisted on installing. For all his faults he'd been a man of taste, Candace grudgingly allowed, and she let herself enjoy the sensual feel of the plush carpeting and the cool caress of her satin robe.

Surveying the kitchen with a jaundiced eye, she finally decided on sliced cheese and apples. Maybe her stomach wouldn't rebel, and if it did, what could she do about it anyway?

She was cutting a thin wedge of cheese when the phone on the counter rang, startling her. Dropping the knife, she picked up the receiver. "Hello," she answered, somewhat diffidently.

"Hello there," said Con, and Candace leaned weakly against the counter.

"Uh . . . hello."

"I've been doing some thinking, Candace. A lot of it, as a matter of fact. And I've come to the conclusion that I was a bloody idiot last night."

Her knuckles were pressed to her lips, and a smile was forming beneath them. He wasn't angry anymore! "I came to the same conclusion."

He almost laughed. "Now that some of the, er, shock is over, I'd like to edit out some of the things I said last night and insert more positive remarks."

Candace wanted to cry, she was so relieved. "Such as?"

"Well, let's not drag them all up. Suffice it to say I'm sorry. For a lot of things."

"Con, it's okay. I'm sorry, too. I—"

"Shhh. Tell me when I get there. I want to look you in the eye and say some things I should have said last night." His voice deepened provocatively. "And do some things I should have done later last night, too."

It was going to be all right. He'd already forgiven her, and she'd forgiven him. "I'll be waiting," she said softly, and was rewarded with his amused chuckle.

Con had barely hung up when his phone rang beneath his hand. For half a beat he contemplated not answering it; he wanted to get to Candace and put all the misery to rest once and for all.

But then he thought she might be calling back with some important message. Picking up the receiver, he said in a monotone, "Hello. You've reached the Holt residence. At the sound of the tone please leave your name, number and the time of—"

"Con, it's Linda. I know you don't have an answering machine; you despise those things, so shut up and listen to me!"

It was the intensity of her voice that made him cut short his spiel. Impatient, he demanded, "All right, what? You caught me on my way out."

"It's Candace. I just talked to Dan Morrison, and he overheard a conversation between her and her father that involved you."

"Goodbye, Linda." He was in the act of pressing his finger down on the receiver when she cried, "Listen to me! If you hang up, I'll come to your house."

"I won't be here."

"Con, she had to get pregnant. She had to have a baby right away or she wouldn't have one at all. Are you listening? I don't exactly know what's wrong with her, but she told her father she set out to have a baby, and lucky you, she picked you for the father—"

He cut the line so quickly he was momentarily impressed by his own speed. Moments later it rang again and he picked up the receiver, severed the connection with his thumb and left the phone off the hook. To hell with her, he thought dispassionately. He'd been patient as a saint. She could take her vile accusations back to southern California.

Thinking of her threat to show up on his doorstep, he snatched up his keys and headed for his car. Mrs. Collingwood was on her front stoop, picking up her evening paper. Seeing Con, she gave him a curt nod of recognition, then scurried back inside.

He grinned and backed out of his driveway with a roar, deliberately revving the engine. She already thought he was a pervert, might as well be a disrespectful pervert into the bargain.

Candace's front porch light was on when he pulled into her driveway. For the first time since he'd learned the stunning news of her pregnancy, he felt ready and eager to change the course of his life. Twenty-four hours—that was about how long it had been since she'd told him. God. It seemed like eons.

The door opened before he could knock. Candace stood in the doorway, smiling shyly, her blond hair hanging straight to her shoulders. It was still damp and smelled faintly of coconut, and Con felt the familiar hot need rising in his loins. Words of love formed in his throat but remained there, unuttered, to be swallowed back. It was a new experience for him to feel so unsure. Not since his teen years had he been so fatally attracted to a woman.

"You got here fast," she said as he entered the hallway.

"I was in a hurry. Were you in the shower?" he asked with deceptive casualness. Moisture glimmered on the V of skin exposed above her bathrobe's lapels.

"I was already out when you called. I was just getting myself something to eat. Are you hungry?"

"Starved," he admitted lazily.

Candace's eyes were warm with love. She'd never looked so beautiful to him, her skin pink, her lashes so long they cast shadows on her cheeks. She had a mouth that invited kissing—trembling when she was angry, parting when her passion was awakened.

"Come on in the kitchen. I was having a snack of cheese and apples. My stomach seems to be acting up these days."

He caught her from behind, sliding his arms around the satiny folds of her robe, burying his face in the glory of her sweet-scented hair. Candace stopped short, her head cocked, waiting.

"We're going to have a baby together," he said huskily. "I'm not hungry for food."

Sighing, she leaned her head back against him. "Neither am I."

Her spine was curved against him, his hands free to roam over her stomach. He slid them beneath her robe, against the heat of her skin and down the bones of her hips until he felt her quiver from his touch. "Make love to me," he said in her ear.

"Right here?" she asked, amused.

He chuckled. "Well, I'm not opposed to discomfort if you aren't, but I was thinking more of a bed." Slowly he turned her to face him, his thumbs holding up her chin. "Although Mrs. Collingwood would think it was just par for the course, I'm sure, if I tossed you down on the kitchen counter."

"Whatever did you do to give her this impression of you?"

"A mad party or two." His grin was teasing. "One of the attorneys I used to work with at Pozzer, Strikeberg and Carmen stumbled into her apartment by mistake one night and crashed on her couch. It caused a minor sensation."

"I'll bet," Candace said on a laugh.

"If she thought I was getting married, I'm sure she'd have lots of advice to give the prospective bride."

Candace held her breath. "I don't recall discussing marriage."

"*I* recall that you turned me down," he murmured, pulling her hips inexorably toward his as he lowered his mouth to hers.

Candace was too blissfully happy to continue the conversation. He did love her. She could tell. And he wanted her as passionately as he had before she'd told him about the baby.

This time when he swept her into his arms he smiled down at her flushed face. "The hell with Mrs. Collingwood. I'm all for bed," he growled.

For an answer she slid her hand beneath the collar of his shirt, across the soft mat of hair that covered his flesh. He shuddered and carried her quickly up the stairs to her room, laying her against the soft cream coverlet.

She reached up for him, then gasped when he bounced down on the bed beside her. Laughing, he pulled her atop him, tangling his hands in her hair, dropping tiny kisses across her face, moving his hips in a purposefully slow circular motion that had Candace divided between amusement and desire.

"Oh, Candace," he breathed against her lips. "I've been such an ass." He pulled open her robe and ran his hands over the smooth mound of her buttocks.

"It doesn't matter," she said happily.

With a deep chuckle, he muttered, "I think Linda's finally gotten the message about how I feel about you."

How do you feel about me? "Oh? Why?"

"She called tonight with some outrageous story Dan cooked up about you—you have to give that guy an A for ingenuity—and I hung up on her."

"What story was that?" Candace asked, a little flame of fury licking through her. Dan's ambitions were beginning to really irritate her.

"Something about overhearing a conversation between you and your father. He said you were—well, basically you were looking for a man to help you have a baby. He made it sound like you'd gone over the list of hopefuls and decided on me."

Candace's blood ran cold, and she stiffened involuntarily. Con's eyes captured hers, questions hovering in their blue depths. He hadn't believed Linda, she realized, but he was smart enough to imagine there was some grain of truth to her accusations. Still, he expected Candace to be able to explain it to his satisfaction.

She licked her lips. She was stumped about how to tell him, afraid, deep down, that he might think her less of a woman somehow. Which was ridiculous. "I—it's true. I never thought I'd have a baby. This will be my only one. I've been trying to find a way to tell you, but with everything that's happened it got pushed back."

For the space of a heartbeat nothing happened. He looked more nonplussed than anything else. "What are you talking about?'' he asked, his hands suddenly still against her flesh, his grip tight.

Candace licked her lips. "I'm going to have to have an operation to remove my cervix. I'll be fine once it's over, but I—"

"When? When will you have this operation?"

"Well, there's no real set time," Candace answered, a defensive note creeping into her voice. "It all depends on whether..." The fury darkening his face made her trail off.

"On whether you find a suitable stud?" he asked softly, dangerously.

"Don't be ridiculous!" Candace gasped.

He pushed her off him, and she tumbled against the coverlet. For a moment he lay staring at the ceiling, his skin paling, his mouth a frozen line of disbelief. "My God, she was telling the truth. When did you find out?"

His tone couldn't have been more frigid and distant had he tried. "That I couldn't have children? I received formal notice the night of my father's Christmas-in-July party," Candace replied in a quiet voice, wondering why it would matter.

She found out only too soon. "So it was after you divorced Jeff," he said, his mouth curling scornfully. "That's why he wasn't in the picture. That's why you picked me."

"I resent what you're suggesting," said Candace tautly.

Con turned his head, his blue eyes blazing with a cold, dangerous flame. "Did you decide that evening? Was I a better choice than Dan Morrison?"

She slapped him so hard his cheek went white, then turned an ugly dark red. Horrified, she whispered, "I'm sorry. I didn't mean to—"

He rolled to his feet. "Don't worry about it."

"Con, I— You hurt me and I wanted to hurt you back." She climbed anxiously to her feet, trying to block his path to the door.

His smile was enigmatic. "You succeeded admirably, Candace."

"Con," she whispered desperately, but when she reached toward him he grabbed her wrist in midair.

"You're as much a crafty liar as she was," he snarled coldly. "Maybe worse. And you've got me in a worse position, because you really are pregnant. You wouldn't have gone this far if you weren't."

"How can you be so tender one minute, so cruel the next?" she whispered, her eyes moistening with tears.

"Years of practice." He dropped her arm and walked around her.

"What—what are you going to do?"

"I'm going to find Linda," he said without hesitation. "I need a woman right now," he added, and his meaning pierced Candace's embattled heart. But his next words frightened her to her very core. "And then I'm going to fight for custody of my child, Candace. And I'm going to win."

Chapter Twelve

In the small inner room of her medical office, Dr. Evinrud regarded Candace seriously. "You're losing weight," she pointed out. "Not a lot, but it's a definite loss."

Candace's heart lurched. "How bad is that?"

"Sometimes a little weight loss in the beginning is normal. You're not feeling well. Your body's readjusting. But I'd like to see it turn around soon."

Candace nodded. She was six weeks pregnant. It was time she started putting on pounds, not taking them off. "I'll eat pizza tonight. And a double dark-fudge ice-cream sundae. And a spinach salad," she added as an afterthought.

"Sounds tempting," Dr. Evinrud remarked humorously. "Don't worry. The baby's doing fine."

Candace smiled and, after making another appointment, walked out the door into the early-October sunshine.

It had been a complete surprise to the doctor when she'd come back from her trip to learn the news of Candace's pregnancy. But after her first few questions about the father had met with hesitation and long-drawn-out silences, Dr. Evinrud had wisely refrained from asking anything more about Con.

Candace herself tried not to think about him—a nearly impossible task, since she ran into him at work on a daily basis. His politeness was forced, his distance from her so obvious that Terri had remarked upon it. The tension had been so unbearable that Candace had nearly quit. After all, she didn't need the money, and soon her pregnancy would begin to show.

But then she'd hardened her heart and decided he wasn't going to make her turn tail and leave. Forsythe and Company was her father's business, and Candace had as much right to be there as Con. More. Besides, deep down she felt it would be good for Con to have to see her. She wasn't the scheming bitch he'd painted her to be, and there was no need for her to feel guilty.

Still, it wounded her soul to feel his unspoken scorn, to see the revulsion in his blue eyes whenever he looked at her. Though she was no coward, it took a certain amount of time to summon the courage to approach his office whenever she'd completed some work for him—which wasn't often, luckily, as Pamela had returned to the office full-time.

The only moment of satisfaction she'd felt during the past few awful weeks had been when Jeff had shown up unexpectedly, asking to take her to lunch. She'd been standing by the elevator when he'd tendered his invitation, and at that precise moment the doors had opened and Con had stepped out, just in time to hear Jeff's request.

The look on Con's face had done Candace's wounded pride a world of good. He'd been stunned and, yes, jealous. It had been just a dark flash across his face, but she'd seen it, and the scowl that had darkened his expression the rest of the day had made her want to hug herself with joy.

She'd accepted Jeff's offer out of spite, then had lived to regret it. Those couple of hours with him had been excruciating. All he'd talked about was how unhappy he was with Renée, how many wrongs he now wanted to right and how he hoped there was a chance for him and Candace in the future.

You were right, Marion, Candace thought. *He did come back.*

She'd had to tell Jeff candidly that she wasn't interested in him and that the divorce was, she now realized, the best thing for both of them. He'd taken the rejection well—too well, as it turned out. No, to Jeff, was just a preliminary to yes, and he'd persistently called her and tried to see her. Telling him she was pregnant with another man's child had been the key to ending his interest in her—she'd almost laughed at the look that had crossed his face.

Candace drove through the quiet fall evening, tugging her collar more closely to her neck. The heat of summer had been replaced by more bearable weather, yet she felt bittersweet about the change of seasons.

Jeff McCall hadn't been Candace's only would-be suitor during the past few weeks. Dan Morrison had done his best to ingratiate himself with her again, but Candace had coolly let him know just what she thought of his eavesdropping—and what her father would think if he ever found out. Since then Dan, too, had given her a wide berth.

Candace was less equitable, however, when it came to Linda. Con's ex had hovered around him like a bad smell from the moment Con had walked out on Candace. To her credit, Candace supposed, Linda had tried to hide her smugness behind a veil of friendliness, but Candace wasn't fooled. The woman was ecstatic that Con was through with Candace forever.

Stamping on the accelerator, Candace set her jaw. The image of Linda and Con together didn't bear thinking about, but whenever Candace recalled Con's cruel remarks about needing a woman she couldn't help seeing them together in her mind's eye. It was like sticking pins in herself—purposely torturing herself—yet she couldn't help running the scene of Con and Linda entwined together across the screen of her mind again and again.

Candace drove the remaining few miles to her home and pulled into the driveway, yanking the emergency brake and walking tiredly to her front porch. As if contending with Linda weren't enough, Con's threat to sue for custody kept flashing through her mind. It was a moot point until the baby arrived, but just the thought of it struck fear in her heart. Could he be serious? Would his anger at her sustain him that long? Knowing this baby would be her only child, would he truly battle her for it in court?

She shuddered. Con was devastating in a courtroom. If he truly planned to battle her, she'd need her father's entire law firm to help her win.

Her father. Candace inwardly cringed, thinking how Joshua had reacted to the news that Con had not only rescinded his offer of marriage but had shoved Candace completely out of his life. Taking his role of fatherhood to heart in a way he'd never done before, Joshua had practically ordered Con into his office the day he'd found out and had hollered at him so loudly and furiously that the rest of the staff had wandered around on tiptoe, wide-eyed, for the next week. Unfortunately, all her father's interference had accomplished had been to make Con grow more cold and distant. He was as unbending as Joshua—and as determined.

And he was doing his damnedest to make her pay.

Tossing her purse on the hall table, Candace trudged up the stairs to the bedroom. With a resigned sigh she stripped out of her clothes and pulled a silken nightgown over her head. Then she walked into the bathroom, surveying her reflection critically.

She was paler than usual, her cheekbones more defined, but there was a fierce light of determination in her eyes that even Con's rejection couldn't extinguish. She was going to have a baby, and come hell or high water, she was going to keep it. He wasn't going to take it from her.

Washing her face, she patted it dry with a fluffy gold towel, then brushed her silvery-blond hair until it crackled and fell in a luxuriant wave around her neck. She touched the smooth curve of her collarbone. Con had said she was beautiful. Well, she didn't feel beautiful right now.

Flipping off the lights, she climbed straight into bed, then grimaced as she recalled her promise to Dr. Evinrud. With a groan she threw back the covers and padded downstairs to the kitchen, catching a glimpse of herself in the mirror at the end of the hallway. The nightgown was split halfway up her thigh, and she saw long, sleek limbs. Candace stopped short, staring at herself. Con not only thought she was beautiful, she remembered with a start, he desired her; he'd made no secret about that.

Thoughtfully she went through the motions of preparing some soup and French bread—the pizza would have to wait until later. Could she make Con want her again? She loved him and she suspected he felt much the same way about her, regardless of his attitude. But could she make him realize that, maybe by stirring up his lust for her?

Could she play the part of a temptress?

Candace was still thinking that over when she crawled back into bed that evening. She crossed her hands behind her head, focusing her gaze at the ceiling through the soft darkness. Con had been distant, but he hadn't been indifferent. When she'd walked out of the office with Jeff that day she'd felt his eyes boring into her, and when she'd glanced back, the tormented expression on his face had warmed her heart.

So now how could she make Con want her again? How could she make him *desire* her? Candace considered. She had a closet full of expensive clothes, a dressertop covered with exotic perfumes, a jewelry box stuffed with diamonds and sapphires and every other color of gem under the rainbow. She had more feminine armor than any woman had a right to.

But did she have the nerve to pull it off?

What have you got to lose? she asked herself, and couldn't come up with an answer.

"... the Summerfields' corporate account will require a half a dozen attorneys working on it full-time. I've been trying to get all their business for years, and now it falls into our lap because of you."

Joshua Forsythe's piercing eyes glared into Con's cool, blue ones. "I don't mind telling you," he went on in the same flat voice, "that I've been wrestling with my conscience. I'd like to kick your ass out of this office, but I want this account too badly to make some rash, fool decision that'll lose it for me."

Con just stood quietly, his arms crossed on his chest, waiting, sure Joshua would slowly begin to wind down soon. "I'm not interested in corporate law," he said calmly.

"I know you're not. Damn it all to hell, it's that Brinkwood case that got them to come to Forsythe and Company! They've got some kind of family personal problem they think you can fix." He sat back hard in his chair. "But then we've got our own family crisis now, don't we?"

Con's temper started to sizzle, but he kept his outward expression unchanged. He'd had about all he would take of Joshua's grumbled threats and comments. He realized with uncharacteristic regret that he might have to leave the firm soon.

There was a soft rap on Joshua's door, and the older man barked out, "Who is it?"

The door cracked open. "It's just me," Candace said, slipping inside the room.

Immediately the sultry scent of jasmine floated past Con's nostrils. He stiffened, narrowing his eyes at the picture she made. She was dressed in a pale jade sweater dress with a scooped cowl neck, a chain of twisted gold delicately bouncing against her breasts as she moved. Her hair was plaited down her back, and he could see the lush curve of her nape. At her ears sparkling green stones—emeralds?— shivered under the light, and sleek, shimmery stockings whispered when she walked.

"I've got those letters you wanted done," she said, placing a neat stack on the edge of her father's desk. Flicking Con a glance, she murmured, "Hello, Con."

"Hello."

Seeing his daughter had made Joshua lose his train of thought. He blinked twice and said, "Thanks. I thought Pamela was typing my letters."

"She was, but I offered to help." She left in the same cloud of sweet perfume, and Con unconsciously filled his lungs with her scent.

"Where were we?" Joshua asked.

"You were about to tell me how I've ruined your daughter's life, I believe."

Glowering, he muttered, "Your impertinence isn't helping your case."

"What case?" Con tried to shake off the residual effect of Candace's brief appearance, but it was impossible. Over the past few weeks she'd acquired a tantalizing elusiveness that he couldn't get out of his mind. "My personal life is none of your concern."

"None of my concern?" He stabbed an angry finger toward the door. "That's my only daughter out there. Her happiness is all I care about. So help me God, I'd like to break you in half, but for some reason Candace doesn't want me to."

"You couldn't break me in half if you tried," Con said through his teeth. He slammed out of Joshua's office and strode to his own, breathing hard. If he stayed here one more minute he'd go crazy. He should hate Candace Forsythe McCall for being the scheming bitch she was, but all he wanted to do was drown himself in her.

His phone buzzed. Irritably he snatched it up. "Connor Holt."

"I wasn't through talking to you," Joshua said coldly. "I'm having members of the Summerfield corporation and family over to my house next Sunday evening. I want you to be there."

Con gritted his teeth. Joshua Forsythe might infuriate him, but Con had accepted a job with his company in good faith. In this case, he could hardly refuse. "I'll be there."

"Good," Joshua answered flatly, and hung up.

Swearing, Con jerked at his tie several times, finally snatching it from his neck with suppressed rage. Wadding it into a ball, he tossed it toward the clothes tree beside his door where it slithered over his jacket to land on the carpet—the moment before the door opened and Candace stood framed in the doorway.

Her face was carefully impassive. "I brought the documents you wanted typed, too," she said, picking up his tie and looping it over his jacket.

He eyed her warily. How could she be so cool? Whether she'd set out to use him or not, he knew she wasn't that contained. She had to be more emotional than she seemed. Good God, *he* certainly was!

"Pamela really must be slacking off," he observed tightly.

Candace leaned over his desk. The view down the front of her dress was remarkable—sleek skin and rounded, enticingly scented, voluptuous curves.

She glanced up at him, questions in her velvety eyes. "Is there anything else you need?

He gave her a short bark of laughter. "No."

She smiled demurely and drifted out. He stared after her for a long, long time. Now he knew why he couldn't make good his threat to bed Linda. As unpalatable as it was to admit, he still wanted Candace. Groaning, he ran a hand around the back of his neck. What sweet torture. So this—*this*—was what it was like to be in love.

With no plan in mind, he suddenly found himself at the reception desk. "Are you coming back today?" Terri asked when he pushed through the glass doors.

"God only knows," he muttered, and walked out.

Later, after two ice-cold beers at the Front Street Café & Bar, Con surfaced from the trance Candace had seemed to put him under. He had to make some decisions. All right, she was having his baby, and though he'd stated otherwise, he knew he was going to let her raise it. After his anger had subsided somewhat he'd thought about what she'd said. She was going to have her cervix removed. This was the only child she would have.

Tossing back the remains of his second beer, he tried to put himself in her shoes. How would he have reacted, knowing his biological clock for fatherhood was about to run out? Could he honestly say he would have done anything differently?

"Yes!" he muttered intensely.

The bartender looked up from the taps. "Would you like another beer?"

"No, thanks." Con tossed a few bills on the counter, thinking morosely that these decisions were going to have to be made very soon.

A familiar scent enveloped him, evoking an instant awareness throughout his body. Startled, he looked up to see Candace walking straight toward him.

"What are you doing here?" he demanded, watching the way she slid onto the stool next to him.

She licked her lips—nervously, he could have sworn—but then she regarded him through clear, ingenuous eyes. "Actually, I was looking for you."

"Really. And what may I do for you now?" he asked cuttingly.

"Would talking be out of the question? It's been a few weeks, and I'd really like to clear the air."

The way her dress hugged her flesh was enough to distract Con from remembering why he was furious with her. It caressed her breasts and smoothed over the swell of her hips. "There's nothing to talk about."

"We have a baby on the way, Con," she whispered unevenly. "I think we have a lot of things to discuss."

"The baby's yours." His tone was flat, irritated. He signaled to the bartender. "I'll have that beer after all."

Candace was frowning. "What do you mean by that?"

"I won't sue for custody. The child, whatever it is, is yours." There, he'd said it. Now she would go away and leave him alone.

She looked past him, staring straight at the lines of liquor bottles placed on the mirrored back wall. She said nothing. Her eyes were wide open. Slowly tears gathered in them.

"I see," she said, sliding off the stool.

Grabbing her arm, he demanded, "Well, what the hell do you want? You've got the baby. I won't fight you for it."

"I know." Her voice was a whisper.

"You *want* a fight?" he demanded frustratedly.

Shaking her head, she tried to extricate herself from his hand. For a moment Con tightened his grip. He wanted to shake some sense into her. But her bowed head got to him in a way her anger never had. He released her abruptly and she walked away without another word.

Fifteen minutes later he left the bar, turning up his collar at the soft autumn rain that had begun sometime in the course of the afternoon. His mood was black and dangerous. Pushing through the revolving doors of the Forsythe Building he nearly ran straight into Linda.

"Well, there you are," she said, obviously piqued. "I've been looking all over for you."

"What do you want?"

She lifted her brows. "What's the matter with you?"

For an answer he headed for the elevator to the subfloor underground parking levels. Linda, after a brief hesitation, dogged his heels. She stopped the door with her hand when he stabbed the down button, and he glared at her coldly.

"Get out of my way," he said in quiet determination.

"Don't you even want to know why I stopped by?" His silence was a clear answer and Linda sighed. "I'm going back to Los Angeles tomorrow. I've spent a long time here waiting for you to change your mind, but you're not going to." She gave him a sidelong look and added hopefully, "Are you?"

"No."

"You're staying on here, at Forsythe and Company, after what's happened?"

"Strains the credulity a bit, doesn't it?" Con replied with a return of his old humor.

"Why don't you come with me, Con?" she asked in a rush. "I've tried every way I know how to convince you. What reason have you got to stay?"

"None at all," he admitted, "but I'm staying nevertheless." Gently he took her hand off the elevator door, seeing the final admission of defeat in her eyes as the doors began to close.

"Goodbye, Con," she said.

"Goodbye, Linda," he answered. With a soft jerk and a whir the elevator bore him downward. Linda had finally given up, he realized. A chapter of his life closed, finished. But a new chapter had opened up—one filled with even more complexities.

The elevator doors opened on the first subfloor. Con reached in his pocket for his keys and began walking toward his car. He'd told Linda he was staying, but he'd meant that in the general sense. He didn't see how he could keep working at Forsythe and Company now, though he was curiously reluctant to leave.

It made no sense at all.

Candace's black Jaguar was in its usual spot, and Con frowned. She must have gone back upstairs to the office. The way she'd looked at the Front Street Café & Bar suddenly swam before his vision. He could have sworn she'd been upset when he'd promised not to fight for custody. What the hell did that mean?

Feeling uncomfortable about that interview for no reason he could put his finger on, Con passed the Jaguar and headed in the direction of his vintage T-Bird. He glanced back, however, in time to see a blond head slumped over the steering wheel of the car.

"Candace!" he called, shocked. He was at the driver's door in four long strides, jerking it open. Her head came up as if lifted by strings, and he saw the grip of her hands around the wheel. He also saw that she was crying. "What's wrong now?"

"Nothing's wrong *now*," she spat back angrily.

"Am I supposed to understand what you're getting at?"

To his amazement she practically pushed him out of the way, yanking on the door. "Everything's fine. Can't you see that? It's all perfect."

He held on to the door, fighting her. "I thought you'd left."

"I did leave. I'm still leaving." She flashed him a furious glance through tear-drenched eyes.

"Candace, I'm trying really hard to understand, but you're way beyond me. You do want this baby, don't you?"

"Yes." She was positive about that, staring at his hands as if the force of her gaze alone could break their hold on the car door. "After all, that's what I set out to do. Find the right man, seduce him and have his baby. I couldn't be happier."

She jerked viciously on the handle one more time, and Con stepped back. Given her mood, he half expected her to burn rubber out of the car park, but she drove with a decorum that perplexed him all the more. She's pregnant, he reminded himself as he walked to his car. That must explain it.

Candace slammed her front door with all her strength, ripping off her shoes and hurling them down the hall. She yanked the gold chain from around her neck and threw it, too, letting out a scream of frustration that echoed through the empty house. How could he be so dense?

"You are no damn good at seduction!" she berated herself as she ran up the stairs and pulled the sweater dress over her head. If Connor were around she'd murder him on the spot. Did he think she'd be happy that he was willing to cut her and his child out of his life? What kind of a cold-hearted monster did he think she was?

"I hope I never see him again. Never!" she screamed. She was breathing so hard she was gasping, and her stomach was trembling.

Then she collapsed onto the bed, digging her fingers into the covers, holding back the anguished tears that seemed to come so easily these days.

The day of Joshua Forsythe's party it rained. Purple clouds had crept in almost unnoticed, launching a sneak attack on all the guests who'd been expecting another bout of clear, warm weather. Joshua had been caught by surprise, too. His outdoor buffet tent was currently sagging under the weight of pooling rainwater, and the servants were darting around like angry bees, trying to collect everything and bring it inside.

Candace decided the weather fit her mood. She'd wanted to come to this party even less than the Christmas-in-July party. She felt tired and out of sorts, and her lower back ached persistently.

But Joshua was nothing if not persuasive.

"You don't want to come because Connor will be there," he'd said accusingly. "Where's your backbone, daughter?"

"My backbone is right where it should be. And Con isn't the only reason I don't want to go. You don't need me, and I don't feel like smiling at people I don't know and don't care about."

"You can do this for me. I don't ask for much, but I want you there."

"You ask for a lot," she retorted, "and you know it. You only want me there because the Summerfields are really strong on family ties."

"I want you there because I want you to face Connor Holt with your chin held high" had been his startlingly vengeful answer.

Her father's protective feelings were what had finally made Candace waver. She'd told him why Con was treating her like a pariah; she'd even confessed to not blaming him for his feelings. She understood that he believed she'd deliberately trapped him. She understood that he was rebelling.

Joshua, however, was not so generous. Once again he'd let Con know what a bastard he thought he was and what a fool he was for not seeing the worth of his only daughter. It would have been comical if Candace had been in any mood for humor. Her father, who'd never bothered to ask one word about her relationships with men, had suddenly appointed himself her watchdog. Only his immense respect for Con as a professional kept him from taking drastic action and firing Con outright—that and Candace's assurances that if he meddled she'd never speak to him again.

Now she gazed around the packed ballroom and wondered how in the world the Summerfields had managed to amass such a huge family. Some of the people were employees of the company, but the majority were sons and daughters and cousins and nephews and God knew what else. The Forsythes, Candace decided wryly, hadn't been keeping up their end of the population boom.

Except for her baby. Absently Candace ran her fingers over the slight rounding of her belly, feeling a moment of contentment. She glanced in the waved mirror to one side of the baby grand piano, seeing in the distorted reflection a ripple of royal-blue silk and yellow-white hair. The pain in her back intensified for a moment, and she shifted her weight to another foot. Then, behind her in the mirror, she saw a familiar dark presence. Her heart thudded. She recognized Con even through the distortion.

"I didn't think you'd come," he said to the back of her head, and she felt the hairs on her nape lift.

"I didn't think you would, either." She turned to look at him. His eyes were very blue in his dark face, his lashes long. The black suit made him seem somber yet highly charged, dangerous, and his forbidding expression only added to the impression. Drawing a breath, Candace added, "But then my father's hard to resist."

He glanced down thoughtfully at the glass of Scotch in his hand. "He hired me to work for him. This command performance is part of my job."

"I guess I'm doing my job, too." With difficulty she dragged her gaze away from the richness of his black hair. It had grown longer, she realized, and the thought made her heart wrench. Time was passing, and they were growing farther and farther apart.

She saw his gaze center on the telltale evidence of her pregnancy, but apart from a tensing of his jaw he made no comment. The baby meant nothing to him, she realized dully.

Rousing himself from his apparently dark thoughts, he asked politely, "Could I get you something? Maybe a soft drink of some kind?"

"No, thanks." Candace brushed back her hair. She felt so incredibly hot. "Well, maybe I could use a 7-Up," she said, contradicting herself.

Con twisted on his heel and a spasm of pain crossed his face. "Damn ankle," he muttered, limping slightly as he went in search of Candace's drink.

She took the opportunity to find a chair nearby, sinking into it as if her last bit of strength had deserted her. By the time Con returned she was feeling marginally better, and she accepted the crystal glass thankfully. "How did you reinjure your ankle?" she asked, taking a sip.

The ghost of a smile touched his lips. "By kicking in my front door."

"Were you locked out again?"

"No, it was open. I just . . . kicked it."

So he was frustrated, too. "I throw shoes and jewelry," she remarked.

"Probably a lot saner." His gaze swept the room, coming back to rest on the smooth contours of her face. "You look sort of tired. Are you all right?"

"I wish people would stop asking me that." Candace sighed. "I'm fine."

"Would you like to get some fresh air?"

She nodded, lifting her hand to him so he could help her out of the chair. He hesitated only a moment, enclosing her fingers in a warm clasp, pulling her upward. She teetered for a moment, trying to catch her balance. His arm settled easily around her waist, and the spicy scent of him had dramatic effects on her equilibrium. She actually felt faint!

"Candace..." From a distance she could hear the concern deepening his voice. Her feet were moving; Con was practically dragging her onto the balcony. Cool air fanned her face, but she saw pinpoints of lights flickering in front of her eyes.

"Con," she said, alarmed, reaching out an arm toward him.

"What the hell is going on?" he demanded, fear sharpening his tone.

She couldn't answer. Pain was traveling up her back in sickening waves, reaching around her abdomen, squeezing her. *My baby,* she thought fearfully. Then a floating, dark warmth enveloped her.

Chapter Thirteen

Candace went limp in Con's arms the second he tightened his grip, preventing her from slipping to the ground. Her face was white against the black sky, and total fear seized him. "My God," he whispered, his heart pounding. He had to get her to a doctor.

He swept her into his arms, and his hands encountered a terrifying dampness. Blood, he realized. The baby. She was losing the baby.

"Oh, God. God."

He didn't remember the next few minutes. Somehow he carried her to his car, Joshua calling after him to wait for an ambulance. But Con knew the route to Briar Park Hospital as well as anyone. Maggie and Tanner both worked there. He would take Candace himself. It was the quickest way.

She lay against the seat, so quiet that he was weak with fear. The road ribboned ahead of him and he concentrated on driving. Trees flashed by. The moon rode low in the sky to his left. The lake glimmered.

Then he was past Lake Oswego, and the highway straightened out. He didn't remember later how fast he drove; he didn't look at the speedometer.

The lights of Briar Park appeared over the last swell in the road and Con screeched to a halt at Emergency. Two attendants were ready with a gurney. Joshua had called ahead.

"Get out of the way," one of them said to Con when he tried to help Candace from the car.

"She's bleeding," Con said hoarsely.

"I know. Go inside. You'll be more help to us there."

But he couldn't leave. He tried to assist and was hustled away by one of the other attendants, forced into the emergency room.

The hospital was a stage of lights. Con blinked. His insides felt frozen. Candace could die. Because of him. Because of his baby.

Conversation was going on all around him, and only distantly did he realize questions were being directed at him. "Her name's Candace McCall," he said to a nurse with a clipboard. "She's pregnant."

"Doctor?" she asked.

Con shuddered, trying to remember. But all he could recall was the terrible way he'd treated her. "A Dr. Evinrud's her gynecologist. From Briar Park's medical offices."

Candace was wheeled into a small room, but when Con tried to follow the door was closed in his face.

Helpless, he thought about demanding to be with her. But he wasn't family. He wasn't related to her in any way.

Except for the baby.

"I need to use the phone," he rasped out to one of the nurses.

"There's a pay phone down the hall," she started to say, and he swore so pungently and furiously that she tightened her lips, glowered at him and turned away. He strode directly to the phone at the desk, sweeping up the receiver, his cold gaze daring anyone to stop him. Wisely, no one did.

"Hello?"

His sister's voice made his throat close, and he had trouble speaking. "Hello, Maggie. It's Con. I'm at Briar Park with Candace. I think she's miscarrying."

"Oh, Con."

The emotion in her voice drained him. He wished he could bury himself in Candace and beg her forgiveness. "Maggie, I don't know what to do."

"Hold on to yourself. Tanner and I'll be right there," she said crisply.

Con collapsed into a chair. He thought of all the horrible accusations he'd hurled at Candace and was filled with self-loathing.

Joshua arrived before Maggie and Tanner. His face was so gray that Con's anxiety increased a thousandfold. Joshua couldn't fall apart. Not Joshua.

"Sit down," Con ordered, but Joshua shook his head, drawing a trembling hand across his mouth.

"How is she?" he asked.

"They won't tell me anything. Maybe they don't know yet."

"She's my only daughter, Connor. She's all I have left." Con tried to guide him to a chair, but Joshua shook off his arm. "Damn it all to hell," he said, though without his usual punch. "It's the baby, isn't it?"

Con nodded grimly. "I think so."

"She never should have tried to have it." Joshua worried his hands together. "It was too dangerous."

Con was silent. He'd never thought of Candace's medical condition in this way. Had it been dangerous? A risk? She'd acted as if it were no problem, and he'd been so angry he'd never bothered to learn all the details.

Maggie and Tanner strode through the emergency room doors at that moment, and before Con could react Maggie had slipped her arms around his waist, squeezing him reassuringly. Tanner looked him over, saw the blood that stained his black tuxedo and dropped a hand on his shoulder. "Stop blaming yourself," he said. "It won't do Candace any good."

"Where's her doctor?" Joshua fretted, and when Tanner and Maggie glanced at him, questions in their eyes, Con introduced them to him.

"I'll check on Candace," said Tanner, pushing open the door to the room where Candace lay. Con took two steps after him, but Maggie clung tightly to his waist.

"Tanner will tell us the truth. Try to be patient."

"Patience isn't my strong suit," said Con dully, and he closed his eyes and fought back a rising panic.

Candace drifted upward toward a bright white light. Where am I? she wondered, confused.

"She's coming around," an unfamiliar male voice said.

She tried to speak, but her tongue felt woolly.

"Candace, it's Tanner," another voice said. "Don't try to talk. Just nod when I ask some questions."

"The baby," she whispered, ignoring him, seized by sudden fear.

"So far we believe you still have the baby. Dr. Evinrud's been called. Now don't talk. Just nod or shake your head."

Candace lay still. Her heart was beginning to race, and a tremor ran through her. She was at the hospital, she realized, and Tanner was with her. That meant Con must be nearby.

Con. She'd been with him on the balcony just before she'd blacked out. He must have called an ambulance.

"Candace, do you have pain?"

She nodded.

"Here?"

He was examining her abdomen and the small of her back. She nodded. Yes, there was pain. And it was intensifying.

"You've lost some blood," he told her calmly. "Try not to panic. Do you need a painkiller?"

She knew instinctively that it was better to feel what was happening, and she shook her head, numb with fear.

"Good. Okay. Hang in there. Con's outside and is pretty anxious to see you. Do you—"

"No," Candace spit out forcefully. "No, I don't want to see him."

She couldn't see him now. She was losing the baby. He'd never wanted this child, and though she knew he would hide his feelings, deep down he would be relieved. No, she couldn't see him. She couldn't bear it.

"Your father's also here," Tanner said quietly. "Would you like to see him?"

"Yes." Tears gathered in the corners of her eyes.

Tanner pushed through the door to the main waiting area. As soon as Con saw him he walked quickly up to him. Tanner drew a deep breath. Never had he seen his old friend look so close to breaking down.

"She wants to see her father," he said, and Joshua was on his feet in an instant.

For Con, however, it was the ultimate rejection. Needing to be alone, he walked out of the hospital into the dark night. He'd lost the only woman he'd ever loved.

"Dad," Candace choked, turning her tear-streaked face into his deeply veined hand.

"Shhh," he said, stroking her hair. "It's going to be all right. You're going to be all right."

"But the baby—"

"Don't think about it. Concentrate on yourself."

"I want this baby. I want this baby so much. It's the only one I'll ever have, and if I lose it I'll die."

"I know. I know." There was a catch in his voice, and he cleared his throat.

"Connor doesn't want it, though. He never did. He never wanted me, either." She cried bitterly, and Joshua continued helplessly stroking her hair.

"I don't think that's really true," he said.

"It's true. He never loved me. He told me that. He thinks I tricked him about this baby." She raised wounded jade-green eyes to his. "I didn't, Dad. I really didn't."

"I know, honey."

"I never want to see him again," she said painfully, closing her eyes, her face ravaged and swollen by tears of pure misery.

Dr. Evinrud's appearance lifted Con out of his self-destructive reverie. He didn't know who she was at first; he'd expected Candace's doctor to be a man. But the way she hurried up the steps to the hospital caught his attention, and he asked her as she passed, "Are you here to see Candace?"

She didn't stop, just threw him a glance. "Yes. Who are you?"

"The father."

"Since you're too young to be her father, I assume you're the baby's father." She held the door. "Come back inside. I'd like to talk to you."

Con rejoined his sister, Tanner and Joshua. After a brief conference with Tanner, Dr. Evinrud left to examine Candace. Joshua approached Con. "She's probably going to lose the baby," he said, and Con felt a quick spasm of pain cross his face.

"What about Candace?" he asked hoarsely.

"She said she loves you," said Joshua gravely, and Con saw Tanner's head turn sharply toward Candace's father, as if with surprise. "She didn't want me to tell you, but I thought you should know."

A glorious hope stirred somewhere deep within Con. He stared intently at Joshua, but the older man's face was unreadable.

"How long is it going to take?" Con growled. He paced in front of the doorway, checking his watch. "She's going to be all right, isn't she?" he asked Tanner anxiously.

"I think she'll be fine." He was staring at Joshua with a strange expression Con didn't understand.

"What happened to your ankle?" Maggie asked, noticing his limp for the first time.

"It got in the way of a door," Con said with irritation, his tone plainly indicating that this was no time to think of anything but Candace.

It seemed like hours before Dr. Evinrud came out of the room. When she did she was in too much of a hurry to say more than, "Candace will be fine. We're moving her to another room."

"A private suite," Joshua said in his most authoritative voice as relief swept over Con in a drowning wave.

"And the baby?" Con asked tensely, raising the question on everyone's mind.

"It's too early to know yet," Dr. Evinrud answered, but something about her tone made Con prepare for the worst.

Candace was wheeled by, her face white, her lips nearly colorless. She glanced at them as she passed, her eyes locking with Con's for just a moment before quickly shifting away. Had Joshua been wrong? Con worried fearfully. God, he loved her so much.

As soon as Candace was settled in her room, Con tried to see her, but Dr. Evinrud blocked his way at the door. "You can't upset her now. She's fighting to save her baby."

"I won't upset her," he promised solemnly.

"This baby is the most important thing in her life," Dr. Evinrud responded, just as solemnly. "I'm sorry. You'll have to wait."

Red mists of pain enveloped Candace, but she stubbornly refused any medication. She had a sense of Dr. Evinrud beside her, helping her, but a deep, instinctive part of her knew they were already too late.

Her body was rejecting Con's baby.

" . . . I'm going to give you Demerol," Dr. Evinrud said. "You need it."

"No." Her voice was a mere whisper.

"Candace, there's no sign of the baby. I doubt there's anything you can do now."

"No!" she screamed, clutching at the mattress. "I want this baby!" Tears streamed down her cheeks. "Please, don't let me lose it!"

"It's too late, honey," Dr. Evinrud said kindly. "I'm putting the Demerol in your IV." Candace felt the doctor grab hold of her now-slack fingers. "This may not be your only child, Candace. This miscarriage is just a statistic, nothing more."

"There'll be no baby now," she whispered brokenly.

Dr. Evinrud was insistent. "Candace, you still have some time, and there's a man out there who's very anxious to see you."

"I won't see him," she said, turning her face away. "I hate him."

She heard Dr. Evinrud confer with someone else, then a soft cloud seemed to dull the racking contractions as the medication took effect. "I'm going to talk to Mr. Holt," Dr. Evinrud said from a long way away. "I'll be back in a few minutes."

"My baby..." she whispered, aching inside from an un-happiness that seemed to grow larger by the second.

Con stood stock-still, a Styrofoam cup of vending-machine coffee forgotten in his hand. Dr. Evinrud was regarding him sympathetically, but her words were firm. "You cannot see her," she said again. "She doesn't want to see you. She's too overwrought."

"I need to talk to her," he said tonelessly. His eyes burned, but no tears formed. Candace had lost the baby, and she refused to see him. "It was my child, too."

"I know that." Dr. Evinrud was kind as she took his arm and tried to lead him back to where Tanner, Maggie and Joshua were sitting. But Con didn't move. He planted his feet and stood in passive confrontation.

Dr. Evinrud sighed, but her face showed her empathy. Con straightened his shoulders and tried to smooth his rumpled tuxedo jacket. He fingered one end of the bow tie that hung around the unbuttoned collar of his wilted white shirt. He knew he must look less than confidence-inspiring. Running a hand over his haggard face, Con drew in a deep breath, then stared steadfastly at the ceiling. "Dr. Evinrud, I appreciate that you think you're doing what's best, but I'm going to see Candace. I love her," he said simply. "I need to tell her that."

The doctor's face creased with worry. "Give her time," she advised. "She's emotionally unstable right now and she could hurt you."

He almost smiled. "I'd deserve it," he said. He moved toward Candace's room, watching Dr. Evinrud carefully. Shaking her head, Dr. Evinrud took the Styrofoam cup from his hands. Thanking her with his eyes, Con pushed open the door, his heart thudding with fear.

She was hooked up to an IV, her eyes open and set to some distant point. With a wrench he realized the fetal monitor was no longer hooked up to her—if it ever had been. The baby was gone. There was only Candace left, and she looked completely wrung out.

Her gaze swiveled to him, and he saw the swift flash of bitterness in her soft eyes. "Go away," she said in an odd voice. "I don't want to see you."

"Candace, Dr. Evinrud told me about the baby."

She turned her head away, fresh tears welling up in her eyes. Treading carefully, Con tried to clasp her hand, but she pulled back as if burned. Only Joshua's assurances that she'd said she still loved him kept Con forging onward. "Candace," he whispered hoarsely. "God, I'm sorry. I'm so sorry."

She stiffened but didn't look his way.

"The doctor also said you still could have another child," Con said. "She explained the nature of your condition to me, and it's not impossible—"

"Get out! Get out, get out, *get out!*" she screamed hysterically. "You didn't want this baby. You don't want another. I don't have time and I—I hate you!"

"You don't mean that," he said, shaken.

She fought the uncontrollable trembling of her lips. "Yes, I do."

"Well, I love you," he said raggedly. "I love you so much."

She squeezed her eyes closed. "It's just pity you feel."

"It's not pity. I've loved you a long time, Candace. I want to marry you, and I want to have a child. We still can."

"If you don't leave this room right now," she said, sobbing in fitful gasps, "I'm going to climb out of bed and throw you out myself."

"Candace," he said, his mouth quirking.

"I mean it, Con. I don't love you anymore. I don't want you around me. Now go away." She searched around blindly for the call button and pressed it down, staring at him, the feverish determination in her eyes making him realize with a deep, aching misery that she truly meant what she said.

Bowing his head, he took a breath, then silently left the room.

If Candace were to live her life over again, she knew she'd delete the last few weeks forever. The highs were too high, the lows too low, the joy too intense, the pain too deep. Just recalling all the hurtful moments still had the power to make her shudder, and she wound her bathrobe tightly around her as she walked onto her balcony and stared across the wind-ruffled waters of the lake.

She lifted her face to the breeze, feeling it fan her still-pale cheeks. Time, as they said, marched on, and just yesterday she'd actually placed an ad in the paper to sell the Jaguar. A small step, granted, but it was a symbol to her that the past was truly over, the future still ahead of her.

She didn't dare think about the loss of her child. The scars were still too raw. And she didn't allow herself to think about Con.

Instead, she'd spent the past few weeks recovering and making plans. To begin with, she would continue with her education. There had to be some career besides motherhood that would interest her. And then she would think about whether she was even interested in meeting other men; she'd been through two bad relationships, and she wasn't sure she could survive another.

And somewhere in there she was going to have to schedule surgery. Though Dr. Evinrud assured her she could still wait, she couldn't bear to harbor even the smallest hope that she could become pregnant again.

It would be better all the way around to have the surgery over and done with.

Chilled, Candace rubbed her arms briskly. A boat passed by on the lake, the driver's dark hair a wild tangle in the wind. Con, she thought with a jolt of her heart.

But it wasn't Con. It was just some teenager turning the boat in a tight circle in front of her small inlet.

Turning aside, Candace was appalled to find tears in her eyes. Would she ever get over this weepiness? With new determination she strode back through the house, intending to do something more constructive with the day than mope around and worry about what might have been.

Halfway up the stairs, she heard her doorbell chimes peal through the empty house. Candace gathered up her robe and slowly walked back down. Who would be calling on her at seven o'clock in the morning?

Peeking through the peephole, Candace was surprised and slightly alarmed to find Maggie on her front porch. Quickly she unlocked the door. "Well, hello there," she greeted her with a smile. "Come on in."

"This isn't really a social call," Maggie replied without preamble, following Candace inside. She wore her lab coat, and her normally mobile face was drawn into taut lines. "It's about Con."

Candace stared down at the floor. "Maggie, Con and I aren't—"

"I know you told him you hated him." At Candace's swift upward glance, Maggie shook her head. "How could you? He's taken it to heart. He believes you."

Candace had no response. She didn't hate Con. She loved him. But maybe it was better if he did believe she hated him.

"Look me in the eye and tell me you don't care about my brother," Maggie demanded.

Licking her lips, Candace said unevenly, "It's not that I don't care about Con, but we're not good for each other."

For the first time there were doubts in Maggie's eyes. "Then I could murder your father for ever giving Con false hope."

"False hope? What—what are you talking about?"

Maggie emitted a sound of impatience. "When you were in the hospital, Joshua told Con that you'd said you still loved him. So Con charged right into your room, against Dr. Evinrud's orders, ready to vow his undying love." Maggie drew a breath through her teeth. "And then you told him how you really felt, and it nearly killed him."

Candace stared at her in bafflement.

"I don't believe you hate my brother," Maggie went on. "I *know* you don't. But he doesn't know it. He's a wreck, Candace. I've never seen anyone lose weight so fast. He doesn't do anything. He doesn't go to work, he doesn't go out—"

"Doesn't go to work?" she repeated, horrified.

"Don't you realize he meant it when he told you he loved you?" Maggie asked softly.

Candace put a hand to her temple. She couldn't think straight. "How...how did you know...he told me he loved me?"

"Because when he came home from the hospital he drank himself into oblivion. The whole story came out in fits and starts. He was torn apart, Candace."

Candace felt a quiver of hope, but she refused to believe in it. She'd been hurt too many times. "He told me he loved me because he was sorry—"

Maggie swore distinctly. "Con has never told anyone he loves them, as far as I know. Not from the heart."

Candace couldn't listen to this. "My father never told me he wasn't at work."

"Would he?" Maggie demanded. "Would he tell you about Con?"

No, he wouldn't. Joshua had obviously made his pitch at the hospital, and when that had backfired he'd quit interfering. "Oh, my God," Candace whispered as she realized the truth of what Maggie was saying.

"Yes," Maggie said flatly. "Oh, my God." She checked her watch and sighed. "I've got to get to work. Please, go see Con and at least clear the air. If you ever loved him, please do that much."

"I will," Candace promised, and flew up the stairs to change her clothes.

No lights were on at Con's condominium as Candace pulled in the driveway behind his blue Thunderbird. She stepped outside and breathed deeply of the crisp morning air, drawing on her courage. If Maggie was wrong...

But she wouldn't think about that. She glanced at Mrs. Collingwood's windows and saw the spying spinster twitch the curtains. Candace waved, and the curtains closed.

A slow grin slid across her lips and then she laughed aloud, her heart uplifted, her voice ringing out across the lake, echoing softly. She realized it was the first time she'd laughed in a long, long time.

Candace knocked and knocked until her knuckles felt bruised, and Connor didn't answer. She pushed her finger against the bell and held it, wondering if he was truly home. Finally she heard his familiar swearing. The door was yanked open furiously.

"What the hell are you—" he began, only to cut himself off with a swift intake of breath. "Candace," he said stupidly.

Maggie hadn't overstated Con's current condition. He looked terrible, his black hair long and uncombed, his jaw covered with at least a week's growth of whiskers, his cheeks hollow, his eyes red-rimmed.

"Good God," said Candace. "Have you been on a week-long binge?"

Self-consciously he rubbed his jaw, staring at her as if she were an apparition. "Two weeks, I think."

She smiled and then couldn't come up with another thing to say. The force of the love rising within her stopped all other thoughts and misted her eyes.

At her expression, Con felt his heart lurch with hope, but he didn't trust his feelings to be able to discern the truth anymore. He swallowed and jerked his gaze away, saying distantly, "Was there something you wanted?"

"You," she choked, then tumbled into his arms, squeezing him with the pent-up need that had her crying into her pillow every night.

"Candace..." he murmured in a tortured voice.

"I love you. I love you, Con. I always have." She laughed, a bit hysterically. "I'm sorry. I love you."

"Oh, Candace," he muttered brokenly, his hands tangling in her gold-white hair. He pulled her head back to gaze searchingly into her eyes. "Do you mean it? By God, you'd better. I love you so much."

"Then marry me," she said breathlessly. "Right away. Don't make me wait."

Emotion raged in his blue eyes, and then he crushed her to him, his heartbeat fast and furious. "We'll apply for a license today. I love you, Candace," he said again, fiercely. "I won't let you change your mind about this."

"I won't," she promised, bubbling over with happiness. "I won't." And then she kissed him, molding her mouth to his, reveling in the feel of his virile body against hers again—the way it should be.

Epilogue

A gentle spring rain coalesced gently on Candace's hair as she hurried up the front porch steps, searching for her keys. Glancing over, she was surprised to find Mrs. Collingwood coming around the side of her condominium. The older lady stopped short.

"Hello, Mrs. Collingwood," Candace called cheerfully. It was a good day. She could afford to be generous with the suspicious old neighbor.

"Mornin'," she muttered, quickly opening her own front door and slamming it shut with a bang.

Candace raised her eyebrows in surprise. Mrs. Collingwood's disapproval of her marriage to Con had been made clear from the moment Con had carried her over the threshold. The fact that she'd actually spoken to Candace was worthy of mention in the *Lake Oswego Review*.

Stepping inside her own home, Candace called, "Mrs. Hoffman, I'm home."

A pile of mail lay on the table by the stairs, and she flipped through it quickly, anxious for the housekeeper to answer her. But when there was no immediate reply, Candace craned her neck to look up the stairway. "Mrs. Hoffman?"

From behind her strong masculine arms suddenly circled her waist, and she choked off a squeal of fright.

"Gotcha," Con whispered lecherously in her ear.

She pivoted in his arms, looping her hands around his neck. "And scared me half to death in the process. What are you doing home so early?"

"I came home to find out my wife's prognosis."

Candace smiled, loving the sensual curve of his lips, the concern in his blue eyes. She never tired of looking at him, admiring him. "Well, I checked out with flying colors. No problems. The operation took care of everything."

The tenderness that swept across his face made her love him all the more. "You're perfect," he told her, and she hugged him fiercely, needing to hear those exact words.

From upstairs came the sound of a baby's cry, and Candace cocked her head. "Queen Elizabeth awaits us," she said. "I assume you sent Mrs. Hoffman home."

They began mounting the stairs together, arm in arm. "I had the mistaken idea that with Mrs. Hoffman out of the picture, we'd have some time to ourselves," Con admitted, chagrined. "But Elizabeth must have other ideas."

"She's a little like her father," Candace remarked, shooting him a glance from beneath her lashes. "She likes things her way."

"She's a little like her mother, too." Con opened the door to the nursery with a flourish, his eyes glinting with amusement. "She likes things her way."

Candace wrinkled her nose at him, then walked quickly to the crib, snuggling the tiny blond-haired child to her breast. Con's arms wrapped around her waist once more, his lips warm and loving against her temple. Closing her eyes, Candace reveled in the feel of her family around her. There was nothing imaginary about them. They were real. And they were all hers.

* * * * *

ATTRACTIVE, SPACE SAVING BOOK RACK

Display your most prized novels on this handsome and sturdy book rack. The hand-rubbed walnut finish will blend into your library decor with quiet elegance, providing a practical organizer for your favorite hard-or soft-covered books.

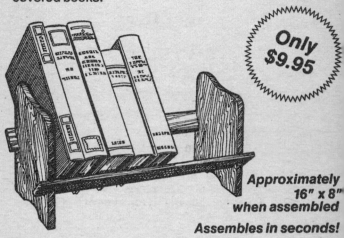

Only $9.95

Approximately 16" x 8" when assembled

Assembles in seconds!

To order, rush your name, address and zip code, along with a check or money order for $10.70* ($9.95 plus 75¢ postage and handling) payable to *Silhouette Books.*

Silhouette Books
Book Rack Offer
901 Fuhrmann Blvd.
P.O. Box 1396
Buffalo, NY 14269-1396

Offer not available in Canada.

*New York and Iowa residents add appropriate sales tax.

BKR-2A

Silhouette Special Edition

THE O'HURLEYS! CHANTEL'S STORY

from
Nora Roberts

Skin Deep

Available September 1988

The third in an exciting new series about the lives and
loves of triplet sisters—

In May's *The Last Honest Woman* (SE #451), Abby
finally met a man she could trust . . . then tried to
deceive him to protect her sons.

In July's *Dance to the Piper* (SE #463), it took some
very fancy footwork to get reserved recording mogul
Reed Valentine dancing to effervescent Maddy's
tune. . . .

In *Skin Deep* (SE #475), find out what kind of heat it
takes to melt the glamorous Chantel's icy heart.
Available in September.

THE O'HURLEYS!

**Join the excitement of
Silhouette Special Editions.**

Silhouette Special Edition

COMING NEXT MONTH

#475 SKIN DEEP—Nora Roberts
In book three of THE O'HURLEYS!, private eye Quinn Doran stakes out
Chantel O'Hurley's too-avid, threatening "fan." But his tougher case is
uncovering the warmth beneath Chantel's icy exterior.

#476 TENDER IS THE KNIGHT—Jennifer West
A spell had been cast that Juliet meet a man worthy of her tenderness.
And poof! armor-clad Rocco Marriani appeared. But could simple
conjuring conquer Juliet's private demons?

#477 SUMMER LIGHT—Jude O'Neill
A match between bohemian Wiley Ranahan and conservative Molly
Proctor couldn't possibly last forever. But after spending August basking
in his affection, Molly began wondering if summer love could linger....

#478 REMEMBER THE DAFFODILS—Jennifer Mikels
Knowing whimsical, unpredictable Ariel Hammond would eventually let
him down, sensible Pete Turner had left before she broke his heart. Now
he wanted her back, but had his practicality compromised their passion?

#479 IT MUST BE MAGIC—Maggi Charles
Upon meeting her volatile new client, Alex Grant, Josephine suspected her
rule about business and pleasure was about to be broken. But could the
magic of love make her deepest fears vanish?

#480 THE EVOLUTION OF ADAM—Pat Warren
For self-made Adam Kinkaid, to-the-manor-born Danielle Ames held the
key to high society. He thought he wanted in ... until rebellious Dani made
him long for so much more.